A PUBLIC LIBRARY FICTION

W9-AXD-758

Literature & Fiction Dept.
Los Angeles Public Library
630 W. Fifth Street
Los Angeles, CA 90071

· A PUBLIC LIBRARY - LITERATURE/FICTION

SKYLIGHT

Center Point
Large Print

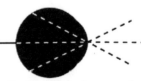

**This Large Print Book carries the
Seal of Approval of N.A.V.H.**

A PUBLIC LIBRARY - LITERATURE/FICTION

Literature & Fiction Dept.
Los Angeles Public Library
630 W. Fifth Street
Los Angeles, CA 90071

SKYLIGHT

José Saramago

*Translated from the Portuguese
by Margaret Jull Costa*

LT

CENTER POINT LARGE PRINT
THORNDIKE, MAINE

JUN 1 5 2015

2192 66963

This Center Point Large Print edition
is published in the year 2015 by arrangement with
Houghton Mifflin Harcourt Publishing Company.

First published with the title *Clarabóia* in 2011 by Editorial
Caminho, SA, Lisbon. First published in Great Britian in 2014
by Harvill Secker Random House.

Copyright © 2011 by the Estate of José Saramago, Lisbon,
by arrangement with Literarische Agentur Mertin, Inh.
Nicole Witt e.K., Frankfurt am Main, Germany.
Foreword copyright © 2014 by Pilar del Río.
English translation copyright © 2014 by Margaret Jull Costa.

All rights reserved.

The excerpt on pages 138–145 is from *Memoirs of a Nun*
(*La Religieuse*) by Denis Diderot, translated by Francis Birrell
(London: George Routledge and Sons, Ltd., and Kegan Paul,
Trench, Trubner and Co., Ltd., 1928).

The text of this Large Print edition is unabridged. In other
aspects, this book may vary from the original edition.
Printed in the United States of America on permanent paper.
Set in 16-point Times New Roman type.

ISBN: 978-1-62899-507-7

Library of Congress Cataloging-in-Publication Data

Saramago, José
  [Clarabóia. English]
  Skylight / José Saramago ; translated from the Portuguese by Margaret
Jull Costa. — Center Point Large Print edition.
    pages cm
  Summary: "A portrait of ordinary people, Skylight tells the intertwined
stories of the residents of a faded apartment building in 1940s
Lisbon"—Provided by publisher.
  ISBN 978-1-62899-507-7 (library bindng : alk. paper)
  1. Large type books. I. Costa, Margaret Jull, translator. II. Title.
  PQ9281.A66C5813 2015
  869.3′42—dc23
                                                    2014050343

In memory of Jerónimo Hilário,
my grandfather

In all souls, as in all houses, beyond the façade lies a hidden interior.

—RAUL BRANDÃO

Literature & Fiction Dept.
Los Angeles Public Library
630 W. Fifth Street
Los Angeles, CA 90071

The Book Lost and Found in Time

S aramago was shaving when the phone rang. He held the receiver to the unsoaped side of his face and said, "Really? How amazing. No, don't bother. I'll be there in about half an hour." And he hung up. I had never known him to take a shower so quickly. Then he told me that he was going to collect a novel he wrote in the 1940s or 1950s and which had been lost ever since. When he returned, he had under his arm *Clarabóia* (*Skylight*), or, rather, a bundle of typewritten pages, which had somehow not grown yellow or worn with time, as if time had proved more respectful of the original than the people to whom it was sent in 1953. "It would be a great honor for us to publish this manuscript, which we found when we moved offices," they said graciously in 1989, when José Saramago was working hard on finishing *The Gospel According to Jesus Christ.* "Thank you, but no," he said and left, taking with him the rediscovered novel and having finally received an answer that had been denied to him thirty-six years before, when he was thirty-one and still full of dreams. Being ignored by that publishing house had plunged him into a painful, indelible silence that lasted decades.

"The book lost and found in time" is how we

used to refer to *Skylight* at home. Those of us who read the novel tried to persuade its author to publish it, but Saramago stubbornly refused, saying that it would not be published during his lifetime. His sole explanation—his main principle of life, often spoken and often written—was this: no one has an obligation to love anyone else, but we are all under an obligation to respect each other. According to this logic, Saramago considered that while a publishing house is clearly under no obligation to publish every manuscript it receives, it does have a duty to respond to the person waiting impatiently and even anxiously day after day, month after month. After all, the book a writer submits in the form of a typescript is much more than just a collection of words; it carries within it a human being, with all his or her intelligence and sensibility. It occurred to us that perhaps each time Saramago saw a copy in print, it would be like reliving the humiliation of not receiving so much as a few short lines— even a brief, formal "we currently accept no submissions"—and so we, his friends and family, did not insist. We likewise attributed to that ancient grief the fact that he simply left the typescript on his desk to languish among all his other papers. José Saramago did not reread *Skylight* and did not miss it when I carried it off to have it bound in leather; when I presented him with the bound edition, he said I was being over the top, extravagant. And yet he knew—because he was the author—that the book was certainly not a bad one, that it contained themes that recurred in his later novels, and that in its pages one could already hear the narrative voice he would go on to develop more fully.

"But there is another way of speaking of all this," as Saramago would say when he had crossed deserts and navigated dark waters. If, after presenting all these facts and suppositions, we accept that statement, then we must interpret all the various signs and his apparent obstinacy in the light of a whole life marked by a pressing need to share and communicate. "Dying means that we were and no longer are," said Saramago. And it's true that he died and is no longer here, but suddenly, in the countries where *Skylight* has been published, in Portugal and Brazil, the countries that speak his language, people are talking excitedly about this *new* book. Yes, Saramago has actually brought out a new book, a fresh, illuminating work that touches our hearts and elicits cries of joy and astonishment, and then we realize that this is the gift the author wanted to leave to us so that he could continue to share his words with us now that he's no longer here. People keep saying: this book is a real gem; it contains all his later literary obsessions; it's like a map of the work to come; how could such a young man have written with such maturity, such confidence? Yes, that is the question his readers keep asking. Where did Saramago get his wisdom from, his ability to portray characters with such subtlety and economy, to reveal the profundity and universality of the most banal situations, to trample on convention in such a serenely violent way? This is a young man, remember, who had never been to university, the son and grandson of illiterates, a mechanic by trade and, at the time, an office worker, daring to take on the cosmos of an apartment building and its inhabitants, guided only by his own instincts and in the enjoyable company of Pessoa, Shakespeare, Eça de Queiroz, Diderot and Beethoven. This is our entry into Saramago's universe, which is already clearly delineated here.

In *Skylight* we find the prototypes of some of Saramago's male characters: the man known simply as H in *Manual of Painting and Calligraphy*, Ricardo Reis in *The Year of the Death of Ricardo Reis*, Raimundo Silva in *The History of the Siege of Lisbon*, Senhor José in *All the Names*, the cellist in *Death with Interruptions*, Cain, Jesus Christ, Cipriano Algor—that whole tribe of silent men, free, solitary beings who need to find love in order, however briefly, to break out of their focused, introverted way of being in the world.

In *Skylight* we also find some of Saramago's characteristically strong women. His treatment of them is even more unconventional: Lídia, for example, is a kept woman who gives lessons in dignity to her businessman lover; lesbian love is treated with remarkable frankness, as are the inherited submissiveness handed down within families, the fear of what others might say, rape, blind instinct, the struggle for power, narrow lives lived honestly despite straitened circumstances and sundry misfortunes.

Skylight is a novel of characters. It is set in the Lisbon of the early 1950s, when the Second World War has ended, but not the Salazar dictatorship, which hangs over everything like a shadow or a silence. It is not a political novel, and we should not, therefore, necessarily conclude that the reason it remained unpublished was because it fell victim to the censors. And yet, given the prudish times in which it was written, its content must have had some bearing on that decision not to publish. The novel rejects established values: the family is not a symbol of hearth and home, but of hell; appearances count for more than reality; apparently praiseworthy utopian dreams are revealed for the hollow things they really are. It is a novel that explicitly condemns the mistreatment of women, but treats love between two people of the same sex as natural, albeit, in the circumstances, anguishing. Coming from an unknown author, such a strong-minded book would have taken a lot of defending for very little reward.

That is probably why the book was relegated to a drawer, without a firm yes or no. Perhaps—and again we are conjecturing—they put it off until later on, when times would have changed, never imagining that it would take decades for any so-called liberalization to begin to make its mark, and meanwhile, in both the world and the publishing house, generations passed and any such good intentions were left to molder in a drawer along with the typescript. Saramago, by then, had a new profession, that of editor. Having made his journey through silence and solitude, he was preparing to write other books.

Life was not easy for Saramago. Not only was his book ignored by the publishers—a book written at night, after days spent engaged in unrewarding tasks—he was ignored too, because he was unknown, had no university education, and wasn't one of the intellectual elite, all of which were important factors in the small world of 1950s and '60s Lisbon society. Those who later became his colleagues made fun of him because he stammered, and his stammer, which he eventually managed to overcome, made him rather withdrawn; he let others do the talking while he watched, living very much in his own inner world, which is perhaps why he was able to write so much. After *Skylight*, he published nothing for another twenty years. He began again with poetry—*Os poemas possíveis* (*Possible Poems*) and *Provavelmente alegria* (*Joy Probably*)—then wrote *O ano de 1993* (*The Year of 1993*), which is already on its way to becoming a narrative, followed by two collections of his newspaper articles, which are also fictions in embryo. *Skylight* is there in his articles too—even though no one knew it existed—waiting for the moment when it would reach the reader as something more than just a lost book.

Skylight is the gift that Saramago readers deserved to receive. It is not the closing of a door; on the contrary, it flings the door wide open so that we can go back inside and read or reread his other novels in the light of what he was writing as a young man. *Skylight* is the gateway into Saramago's work and will be a real discovery for its readers. As if a perfect circle had closed. As if death did not exist.

Pilar del Río
President, José Saramago Foundation

1

Through the swaying veils filling his sleep came the clatter of crockery, and Silvestre could almost swear that light was beginning to filter through the loose weft of those veils. Just as he was starting to feel slightly irritated, he realized suddenly that he was waking up. He blinked several times, yawned, then lay quite still, as he felt sleep slowly moving off. Then he quickly sat up in bed and stretched, making the joints in his arms crack. Beneath his vest, the muscles in his back rolled and rippled. He had a powerful chest, solid, sturdy arms and sinewy shoulder blades. He needed those muscles for his work as a cobbler. His hands were as hard as stone and the skin on his palms so thick that he could pass a threaded needle through it without drawing blood.

Then, more slowly, he swung his legs out of bed. Silvestre was always deeply grieved and saddened by the sight of his scrawny thighs and his kneecaps worn white and hairless by constant friction with his trousers. He was proud of his chest, but hated his legs, so puny they looked as if they belonged to someone else.

Gazing glumly down at his bare feet on the rug, Silvestre scratched his graying head of hair. Then he ran one hand over his face, feeling his bones and his beard. Finally, reluctantly, he got up and took a few steps across the room. Standing there, in vest and underpants, perched on those long, stilt-like legs, he bore a faint resemblance to Don Quixote, with that tuft of salt-and-pepper hair crowning his head, his large, beaked nose and the powerful trunk that his legs seemed barely able to sustain.

He looked for his trousers and, failing to find them, peered around the door and shouted:

"Mariana! Where are my trousers?"

From another room, a voice called:

"Hang on!"

Given the slow pace of the approaching foot-steps, one sensed that Mariana was fairly plump and could not walk any faster. Silvestre had to wait some time, but he did so patiently. At last she appeared at the door.

"Here you are."

The trousers were folded over her right arm, which was considerably stouter than one of Silvestre's legs. She said:

"I don't know what you do with the buttons on your trousers to make them disappear every week. I'm going to have to start sewing them on with wire . . ."

Mariana's voice was as plump as its owner and as kindly and frank as her eyes. She certainly hadn't intended her remark as a joke, but her husband beamed at her, revealing every line on his face as well as his few remaining teeth. He took the trousers from her and, under his wife's benign gaze, put them on, pleased with the way his clothes restored proportion and regularity to his body. Silvestre was as vain about his body as Mariana was indifferent to the one Nature had given her. Neither of them had any illusions about the other, and both were more than aware that the fire of youth had long since burned out, but they loved each other dearly, as much today as they had thirty years ago, when they got married. Indeed, their love was perhaps even greater now, because it was no longer fueled by real or imagined perfections.

Silvestre followed his wife into the kitchen. Then he slipped into the bathroom and returned ten minutes later, having washed. He was still not particularly kempt, however, because it was impossible to tame the tuft of hair that dominated his head (and "dominate" is the right word)—his "cockscomb," as Mariana called it.

Two steaming bowls of coffee stood on the table, and the kitchen smelled fresh and newly cleaned. Mariana's round cheeks glowed, and her whole large body trembled and shook as she moved about the kitchen.

"You get fatter by the day, woman!"

And Silvestre laughed, and Mariana laughed with him. They were like two children. They sat down at the table and drank the hot coffee, making playful, slurping noises, each trying to outslurp the other.

"So, what's it to be, then?"

Silvestre was no longer laughing. Mariana had grown serious too. Even their faces seemed paler.

"I don't know. You decide."

"Like I said yesterday, the leather for soling is getting more and more expensive. My customers keep complaining about the price, but that's how it is. I can't perform miracles. Where are they going to find anyone to do the work more cheaply, that's what I'd like to know, but that doesn't stop them complaining."

Mariana interrupted him, saying that moaning would get them nowhere. What they had to do was decide whether or not to take in a lodger.

"It would certainly be useful. It would help us pay the rent, and if he's a man on his own and you don't mind doing his laundry for him, we could just about break even."

Mariana drained the last sugary drop of coffee from her bowl and said:

"That's fine by me. Every little bit helps."

"I know, but it does mean taking in lodgers again, when we've only just managed to rid ourselves of that so-called gentleman . . ."

"Oh well, maybe the next one will be a decent sort. I can get on with anyone, as long as they get on with me."

"Let's give it another go, then. A man on his own, who just needs a bed for the night, that's what we need. I'll put an ad in this afternoon." Still chewing his last piece of bread, Silvestre stood up and declared: "Right, I'm off to work."

He went back into the bedroom and walked over to the window. He drew aside the curtain that acted as a screen separating the window area from the rest of the room. Behind it was a high platform on which stood his workbench. Awls, lasts, lengths of thread, tins full of tacks, bits of sole and scraps of leather and, in one corner, a pouch containing French tobacco and matches.

Silvestre opened the window and looked out. Nothing new to be seen. A few people walking along the street. Not far off, a woman was crying her wares, selling a kind of bean soup that people used to eat for their breakfast. Silvestre could never understand how she could possibly make a living. No one he knew ate bean soup for breakfast anymore; he himself hadn't eaten it for more than twenty years. Different times, different customs, different food. Having thus neatly summed the matter up, he sat down. He opened his tobacco pouch, rummaged around for his cigarette papers among the hotchpotch of objects cluttering the bench and rolled himself a cigarette. He lit it, inhaled the smoke and set to work. He had some uppers to put on, a job requiring all his knowledge and skill.

Now and then he would glance out at the street. The morning was gradually brightening, although the sky was still cloudy and a slight mist blurred the edges of things and people alike.

From among the multitude of noises already filling the building, Silvestre could make out the sound of an immediately identifiable pair of heels clicking down the stairs. As soon as he heard the street door open, he leaned forward.

"Good morning, Adriana!"

"Good morning, Senhor Silvestre."

The girl stopped beneath the window. She was rather short and dumpy and wore thick glasses that made her eyes look like two small, restless beads. She was nearly thirty-four years old and her modest hairstyle was already streaked with the odd gray hair.

"Off to work, eh?"

"That's right. See you later, Senhor Silvestre."

It was the same every morning. By the time Adriana left the house, the cobbler was already seated at the ground-floor window. It was impossible to escape without seeing that unruly tuft of hair and without hearing and responding to those inevitable words of greeting. Silvestre followed her with his eyes. From a distance, she resembled, in Silvestre's colorful phrase, "a sack of potatoes tied up in the middle." When she reached the corner of the street, Adriana turned and waved to someone on the second floor. Then she disappeared.

Silvestre put down the shoe he was working on and craned his neck out of the window. He wasn't a busybody, he just happened to like his neighbors on the second floor; they were good customers and good people. In a voice constrained by his somewhat awkward position, he called out:

"Hello there, Isaura! What do you make of the weather today, eh?"

From the second floor came the answer, attenuated by distance:

"Not bad, not bad at all. The mist . . ."

But we never found out whether she thought the mist spoiled or embellished the beauty of the morning. Isaura let the conversation drop and slowly closed the window. It wasn't that she disliked the cobbler, with his simultaneously thoughtful and cheery air, she simply wasn't in a mood to chat. She had a pile of shirts to be finished by the weekend, by Saturday at the very latest. Given the choice, she would have carried on with the novel she was reading. She only had another fifty pages to go and had reached a particularly interesting part. She found them very gripping, these clandestine love affairs, buffeted by endless trials and tribulations. Besides, the novel was really well written. Isaura was an experienced enough reader to be a judge of this. She hesitated for a moment, but realized at once that she did not even have time to do that. The shirts were waiting. She could hear the murmur of voices inside: her mother and aunt talking. They talked a lot. Whatever did they find to talk about all day that they hadn't already said a hundred times before?

She crossed the bedroom she shared with her sister. The novel was there on her bedside table. She cast a greedy, longing glance at it, then paused in front of the wardrobe mirror, which reflected her from head to toe. She was wearing a housecoat that clung to her thin, yet still flexible, elegant body. She ran the tips of her fingers over her pale cheeks, where the first fine, barely visible lines were beginning to appear. She sighed at the image shown her by the mirror and fled.

In the kitchen the two old ladies were still talking. They were very similar in appearance— white hair, brown eyes, the same simple black clothes—and they spoke in shrill, rapid tones, without pauses or modulation.

"I've told you already. The coal is nothing but dust. We should complain to the coal merchant," one was saying.

"If you say so," said the other.

"What are you talking about?" asked Isaura, entering the room.

The more erect and brighter-eyed of the two old ladies said:

"This coal is just terrible. We should complain."

"If you say so, Auntie."

Aunt Amélia was, so to speak, the household

administrator. She was in charge of the cooking, the accounts and the catering generally. Cândida, the mother of Isaura and Adriana, was responsible for all the other domestic arrangements, for their clothes, for the profusion of embroidered doilies decorating the furniture and for the vases full of paper flowers, which were replaced by real flowers only on high days and holidays. Cândida was the elder of the sisters and, like Amélia, she was a widow, one whose grief had long since been assuaged by old age.

Isaura sat down at the sewing machine, but before starting work, she looked out at the broad river, its farther shore hidden beneath the mist. It looked more like the sea than a river. The rooftops and chimney pots rather spoiled the illusion, but even if you did your best to blot them out, the sea was right there in those few miles of water, the white sky somewhat sullied by the dark smoke belching forth from a tall factory chimney.

Isaura always enjoyed those few moments when, just before she bent her head over her sewing machine, she allowed her eyes and thoughts to wander over the scene before her. The landscape never varied, but she only ever found it monotonous on stubbornly bright, blue summer days when everything was too obvious somehow, too well defined. A misty morning like this—a thin mist that did not entirely conceal the view—endowed the city with a dream-like imprecision. Isaura savored all this and tried to prolong the pleasure. A frigate was traveling down the river as lightly as if it were floating on a cloud. In the gauze of mist, the red sail turned pink, then the boat plunged into the denser cloud licking the surface of the water, reappeared briefly, then vanished behind one of the buildings obscuring the view.

Isaura sighed, her second sigh of the morning. She shook her head like someone surfacing from a long dive, and the machine rattled furiously into action. The cloth ran along beneath the pressure foot, and her fingers mechanically guided it through as though they were just another part of the machine. Deafened by the noise, Isaura suddenly became aware that someone was speaking to her. She abruptly stopped the wheel, and silence flooded back in. She turned around.

"Sorry?"

Her mother said again:

"Don't you think it's a bit early?"

"Early? Why?"

"You know why. Our neighbor . . ."

"But what am I supposed to do? It's hardly my fault the man downstairs works at night and sleeps during the day, is it?"

"You could at least wait until a bit later. I just hate to annoy people."

Isaura shrugged, put her foot down on the pedal again and, raising her voice above the noise of the machine, added:

"Do you want me to go to the shop and tell them I'm going to be late delivering?"

Cândida slowly shook her head. She lived in a constant state of perplexity and indecision, under the thumb of her sister—three years her junior—and keenly aware that she was dependent financially on her daughters. She wanted, above all, not to inconvenience anyone, wanted to go unnoticed, to be as invisible as a shadow in the darkness. She was about to respond, but, hearing Amélia's footsteps, said nothing and went back to the kitchen.

Meanwhile, Isaura, hard at work, was filling the apartment with noise. The floor vibrated. Her pale cheeks gradually grew red and a bead of sweat appeared on her brow. She again became aware of someone standing beside her and slowed down.

"There's no need to work so fast. You'll wear yourself out."

Aunt Amélia never wasted a word. She said only what was absolutely necessary, but she said it in a way that made those listening appreciate the value of concision. The words seemed to be born in her mouth at the very moment they were spoken and to emerge replete with meaning, heavy with good sense, virginal. That's what made them so impressive and convincing. Isaura duly slowed her pace of work.

A few minutes later, the doorbell rang. Cândida went to answer it, was gone for a few seconds, then returned looking anxious and upset, muttering:

"Didn't I tell you, didn't I tell you?"

Amélia looked up:

"What is it?"

"It's the downstairs neighbor come to complain about the noise. You go, will you?"

Amélia stopped doing the washing, dried her hands on a cloth and went to the front door. Their downstairs neighbor was on the landing.

"Good morning, Dona Justina. What can I do for you?"

At all times and in all circumstances, Amélia was the very soul of politeness, but that politeness could easily turn to ice. Her tiny pupils would fix on the face they were looking at, arousing irrepressible feelings of unease and embarrassment in the other person.

The neighbor had been getting on fine with Cândida and had almost finished what she had come to say. Now there appeared before her a far less timid face and a far more direct gaze. She said:

"Good morning, Dona Amélia. I've come about my husband. As you know, he works nights at the newspaper, and so can only sleep in the morning. If he's woken up, he gets really angry and I'm the one who has to bear the brunt. If you could perhaps make a little less noise with the sewing machine, I'd be very grateful . . ."

"Yes, I understand, but my niece needs to work."

"Of course, and if it was up to me, I wouldn't mind, but you know what men are like . . ."

"Yes, I do, and I also know that your husband shows very little consideration for *his* neighbors' sleep when he comes home in the early hours."

"But what am I supposed to do about that? I've given up trying to persuade him to make less noise on the stairs."

Justina's long, gaunt face grew lively. A faint, malicious gleam appeared in her eyes. Amélia brought the conversation to a close.

"All right, we'll wait a while longer. You needn't worry."

"Thank you very much, Dona Amélia."

Amélia muttered a brusque "Now, if you'll excuse me" and shut the door. Justina went down the stairs. Dressed in heavy mourning, her dark hair parted in the middle, she cut a tall, funereal figure; she resembled a gangling doll, too large to be a woman and without the slightest hint of feminine grace. Only her dark, hollow eyes, the eyes of a diabetic, were, paradoxically, rather beautiful, but so grave and serious that they lacked all charm.

When she reached the landing, she stopped outside the door opposite hers and pressed her ear to it. Nothing. She pulled a sneering face and moved away. Then, just as she was about to enter her own apartment, she heard voices and the sound of a door opening on the landing above. She busied herself straightening the doormat so as to have an excuse not to go in.

From upstairs came the following lively dialogue:

"The only trouble with her is that she doesn't want to go to work!" said a female voice in harsh, angry tones.

"That may well be, but we have to treat her with care. She's at a dangerous age," said a man's voice. "You can never be sure how these things might develop."

"What do you mean 'a dangerous age'? You never change, do you? Is nineteen a dangerous age? If so, you're the only one who thinks so."

Justina thought it best to announce her presence by giving the doormat a good shake. The conversation upstairs stopped abruptly. The man started coming down the stairs, saying as he did so:

"Don't make her go to work. And if there's any change, call me at the office. See you later."

"Yes, see you later, Anselmo."

Justina greeted her neighbor with a cool smile. Anselmo walked past her on the stairs, solemnly tipped his hat and, in his warm, mellow voice, uttered a ceremonious "Good morning." There was, however, a great deal of venom in the way the street door slammed shut behind him. Justina called up the stairs:

"Good morning, Dona Rosália."

"Good morning, Dona Justina."

"What's wrong with Claudinha? Is she ill?"

"How did you know?"

"I was just shaking out the doormat here and I thought I heard your husband say . . ."

"Oh, she's putting it on as usual, but she only has to whimper and my Anselmo's convinced she's dying. She's the apple of his eye. She says she has a headache, but what she's really got is a bad case of lazyitis. Her headache's so bad she's gone straight back to sleep!"

"You can't be too sure, Dona Rosália. Remember, that's how I lost my little girl, God rest her soul. It was nothing, they told us, and then meningitis carried her off." She took out a handkerchief and blew her nose loudly before going on: "Poor little thing. And only eight years old. How could I forget . . . It's been two years, you know, Dona Rosália."

Rosália did know and wiped away a polite tear. Encouraged by her neighbor's apparent sympathy, Justina was about to recall more all-too-familiar details when a hoarse voice interrupted her:

"Justina!"

Justina's pale face turned to stone. She continued talking to Rosália until the hoarse voice grew still louder and more violent:

"Justina!!"

"What is it?" she asked.

"Come inside, will you? I don't want you standing out there on the landing, talking. If you worked as hard as I do, you wouldn't have the energy to gossip!"

Justina shrugged indifferently and went on with the conversation, but Rosália, finding the scene embarrassing, said it was time she went in. After Justina had gone back into her apartment, Rosália crept down a few stairs and listened hard. Through the door she heard a few angry exclamations, then silence.

It was always the same. You would hear the husband tearing into his wife, then the wife would utter some almost inaudible words and he would immediately shut up. Rosália found this very odd. Justina's husband had a reputation as a bit of a brute, with his big, bloated body and his crude manners. He wasn't quite forty and yet his flaccid face, puffy eyes and moist, drooping lower lip made him seem older. No one could understand why two such different people had ever married, and it was true that they had never been seen out in the street together. And, again, no one could understand how two such unpretty people (Justina's eyes were beautiful, not pretty) could have produced a delightful daughter like Matilde. It was as if Nature had made a mistake and, realizing its mistake later on, had corrected it by having the child disappear.

The fact is that, after he had made just two or

three aggressive comments, all it took to silence violent, rude Caetano Cunha—that obese, arrogant, ill-mannered Linotype operator on a daily newspaper—was a murmured comment from his wife, the diabetic Justina, so frail she could be blown away in a high wind.

It was a mystery Rosália could not unravel. She waited a little longer, but absolute silence continued to reign. She withdrew into her own apartment, carefully closing the door so as not to wake her sleeping daughter, always assuming she was asleep rather than merely pretending.

Rosália peered around the door. She thought she saw her daughter's eyelids flutter. She opened the door properly and advanced on the bed. Maria Cláudia had her eyes closed so tightly that tiny lines marked the spot where crow's-feet would one day appear. Her full lips still bore traces of yesterday's lipstick. Her short brown hair gave her the look of a young ruffian, which only made her beauty more piquant and provoking, almost equivocal.

Rosália glanced at her daughter, not quite trusting that deep but strangely unconvincing sleep. She gave a little sigh. Then, with a maternal gesture, she drew the bedclothes up around her daughter's neck. The reaction was immediate. Maria Cláudia opened her eyes and chuckled. She tried to suppress her laughter, but it was too late.

"You tickled me!"

Furious because she had been tricked and, even more, because she had been caught showing her daughter some motherly affection, Rosália said irritably:

"So you were sleeping, were you? The headache's gone, has it? Your trouble is you don't want to work, you lazy so-and-so!"

As if to prove her mother right, the girl stretched slowly and luxuriously, and, as she did so, her lace-trimmed nightdress gaped open to reveal two small, round breasts. Although Rosália did not know why that careless gesture offended her, she could not conceal her displeasure and muttered:

"Cover yourself up, will you? Young women nowadays aren't even embarrassed in the presence of their own mothers!"

Maria Cláudia opened her eyes wide. She had blue eyes, a very brilliant blue, but cold, like the distant stars whose light we see only because they are far, far away.

"What does it matter? Anyway, I'm decent now!"

"If I'd shown myself to my mother like that when I was your age, I'd have gotten a slap in the face."

"That seems a bit extreme."

"You think so, do you? Well, I reckon *you* could do with a good slap too."

Maria Cláudia raised her arms again, pretending to stretch. Then she yawned.

"Times have changed."

Rosália opened the window and said:

"They have indeed, and for the worse." Then she went back over to the bed. "So, are you going to work or not?"

"What time is it?"

"Nearly ten o'clock."

"It's too late now."

"It wasn't a little while ago."

"I had a headache then."

This short, sharp exchange indicated irritation on both sides. Rosália was seething with suppressed anger, and Maria Cláudia was annoyed by her mother's moralizing.

"A headache indeed! You're a malingerer, that's what you are!"

"Is it my fault I have a headache?"

Rosália exploded:

"Don't you talk to me like that, young lady. I'm your mother, remember."

The girl was unimpressed. She merely shrugged, as if to say that this last point was hardly worth discussing, then she jumped out of bed and stood there, barefoot, her silk night-dress draped about her soft, shapely body. Her daughter's youthful beauty cooled Rosália's irritation, which vanished like water into dry sand. Rosália felt proud of Maria Cláudia and her lovely body. Indeed, what she said next was tantamount to a surrender:

"You'd better tell the office."

Maria Cláudia, apparently oblivious to that subtle change of tone, replied dully:

"I'll ask Dona Lídia if I can use her phone."

Rosália grew irritated again, perhaps because her daughter had put on a housecoat, and her more discreetly clothed body had lost its power to enchant.

"You know I don't like you going to see Dona Lídia."

Maria Cláudia's eyes were even more innocent than usual.

"Why ever not?"

If the conversation was to continue, Rosália would have to say things she would prefer not to. She knew that her daughter understood perfectly well what she meant, but she nonetheless felt that there were subjects best not touched on in the presence of a young woman. She had been brought up with the idea that parents and children should respect each other, and she still clung to that. She therefore pretended not to have heard her daughter's question and left the room.

Once she was alone again, Maria Cláudia smiled. Standing in front of the mirror, she unbuttoned her housecoat and her nightdress and looked at her breasts. A shiver ran through her and she flushed slightly. Then she smiled again, feeling vaguely nervous, but pleased too, something like a frisson of pleasure tinged with guilt. Then she buttoned up her housecoat, took one last glance at herself in the mirror and left the room.

In the kitchen, she went over to her mother, who was making some toast, and kissed her on the cheek. Rosália could not deny that the kiss pleased her, and while she did not reciprocate, her heart beat faster with contentment.

"Go and have a wash, dear, the toast is nearly ready."

Maria Cláudia shut herself in the bathroom. She returned looking fresh and cool, her skin glossy and clean, her now unpainted lips slightly stiff from the cold water. Her mother's eyes shone when she saw her. Cláudia sat down at the table and began eagerly devouring the toast.

"It is nice to stay home sometimes, isn't it?" Rosália said.

The girl giggled:

"You see, I was right, wasn't I?"

Rosália felt she had gone too far and tried to backtrack a little:

"Yes, up to a point, but you mustn't make a habit of it."

"The people at work won't mind."

"They might, and you need to keep that job. Your father doesn't earn very much, you know."

"Don't worry, I can handle it."

Rosália would like to have asked her what she meant by this, but chose not to. They finished their breakfast in silence, then Maria Cláudia got up and said:

"I'm going to ask Dona Lídia if I can use her phone."

Her mother opened her mouth to object, but said nothing. Her daughter had already disappeared down the corridor.

"There's no need to close the door if you're not going to be gone very long."

Rosália heard the front door close, but preferred not to think that her daughter had done this on purpose in order to go against her wishes. She filled the sink and started washing the breakfast things.

Maria Cláudia did not share her mother's scruples about their downstairs neighbor; on the contrary, she really liked Dona Lídia. Before ringing the doorbell, she straightened the collar of her housecoat and smoothed her hair. She regretted not having applied a touch of color to her lips.

The bell rang out stridently and echoed down the stairwell. Maria Cláudia felt a slight noise behind her and was sure that Justina was peering through the spyhole in the door opposite. She was just about to turn and look when Dona Lídia's door opened.

"Good morning, Dona Lídia."

"Good morning, Claudinha. What brings you here? Won't you come in?"

"If I may . . ."

In the dark corridor, Maria Cláudia felt the warm, perfumed air wrap about her.

"So what can I do for you?"

"I'm sorry to bother you again, Dona Lídia."

"You're not bothering me at all. You know how much I enjoy your visits."

"Thank you. I wondered if I could phone the office to tell them I won't be coming in today."

"Of course, feel free, Claudinha."

She gently ushered her toward the bedroom, a room that Maria Cláudia could not enter without feeling slightly troubled, for the atmosphere made her positively dizzy. She had never seen such lovely furnishings; there were mirrors and curtains, a red sofa and a soft rug on the floor, bottles of perfume on the dressing table, the smell of expensive cigarettes, but none of those things alone could explain her disorderly feelings. Perhaps it was the whole situation, the presence of Lídia herself, something as vague and imponderable as a burning, corrosive gas that slips unnoticed through every filter. In that room, she always felt as if she somehow lost all self-control. She became as tipsy as if she had drunk champagne and felt an irresistible desire to do something silly.

"There's the phone," said Lídia. "I'll leave you in peace."

She made as if to go, but Maria Cláudia said urgently:

"No, no, really, Dona Lídia, there's no need. It's not a matter of any importance . . ."

The intonation she gave to these words and the smile that accompanied them seemed to suggest that there were other matters of importance and that Dona Lídia knew precisely what those were. Seeing Maria Cláudia still standing, Lídia exclaimed:

"Why don't you sit down on the bed, Cláudia?"

Legs trembling, Maria Cláudia did as she was told. She placed one hand on the blue satin eiderdown and, unaware of what she was doing, began to stroke the soft fabric almost voluptuously. Lídia appeared not to notice. She opened a pack of Camel cigarettes and lit one. She did not smoke out of habit or necessity, but because the cigarette formed part of a complicated web of attitudes, words and gestures, all of which had the same objective: to impress. This had become so much second nature to her that, regardless of whom she was with, she always tried to impress. The cigarette, the slow striking of the match, the first long, dreamy outbreath of smoke, were all part of the game.

With many gestures and exclamations, Maria Cláudia was explaining over the phone that she had the most *terrible* headache. She pouted tragically, as if she really were seriously ill. Lídia observed this performance out of the corner of her eye. Finally, Maria Cláudia put down the phone and got to her feet.

"Right. Thank you very much, Dona Lídia."

"There's no need to thank me. You know I'm always glad to help."

"May I give you the five tostões for the phone call?"

"Don't be silly. Keep your money. When are you going to stop trying to pay me for using the phone?"

They both smiled and looked at each other, and Maria Cláudia felt afraid, even though there was no reason to, certainly not such intense, physical fear, but she had suddenly become aware of a frightening presence in the room. Perhaps the atmosphere that had initially made her merely dizzy had all at once become suffocating.

"I'd better be going. Anyway, thank you again."

"Won't you stay a little?"

"No, I have things to do, and my mother's waiting for me."

"I won't keep you, then."

Lídia was wearing a stiff, red taffeta dressing gown, which had the iridescent gleam one sees on the wing cases of certain beetles, and she left behind her a trail of strong perfume. The rustle of taffeta and, above all, the warm, intoxicating smell given off by Lídia—an aroma that came not just from her perfume, but from her body—made Maria Cláudia feel as if she were about to lose control completely.

When Maria Cláudia left, having thanked Lídia yet again, Lídia went back into the bedroom. Her cigarette was slowly burning down in the ashtray. She stubbed it out, then lay full-length on the bed. She clasped her hands behind her neck and made herself comfortable on the same soft eiderdown that Maria Cláudia had been stroking. The telephone rang. With a lazy gesture she picked up the receiver.

"Hello . . . Yes, speaking . . . Oh, hello. (. . .) Yes, I do. What's on the menu today? (. . .) Yes, go on. (. . .) No, not that. (. . .) Hm, all right. (. . .) And what is the fruit today? (. . .) No, I don't like that. (. . .) It really doesn't matter. It's just that I don't like it. (. . .) All right. (. . .) Good. Don't be too late. (. . .) And don't forget to send the monthly bill. (. . .) Goodbye."

She put the phone down and again fell back onto the bed. She yawned widely, with the ease of someone who knows no one is watching, a yawn that revealed the absence of one of her back teeth.

Lídia was not pretty. Analyzed feature by feature, her face could not be categorized as either beautiful or ordinary. She was at a disadvantage just now because she had no makeup on. Her face was shiny with night cream and her eyebrows needed plucking at the ends. No, Lídia was not pretty, and there was, too, the important fact that she had already passed her thirty-second birthday and her thirty-third was not far off. And yet there was something irresistible about her. Her dark brown eyes, her dark hair. When she was tired, her face took on an almost masculine hardness, especially around the mouth and nostrils, but with just the slightest change of expression it became flattering and seductive. She was not the kind of woman who relies solely on her body to attract men; instead, she radiated sensuality from head to toe. She was skillful enough to be able to dredge up from within herself the kind of tremulous, shivering cry that could drive a lover quite mad with passion and render him incapable of defending himself against something he assumed to be perfectly natural and spontaneous, against that simulated wave into which he plunged in the belief that it was real. Yes, Lídia knew how to do that. These were the cards she had to play, her trump card being that sensual body of hers, slim as a reed and sensitive as a slender rod of steel.

She could not decide whether to go back to sleep or to get up. She was thinking about Maria Cláudia, about her fresh, adolescent beauty, and for a moment, though she knew it was foolish to compare herself to a mere child, she felt her heart contract and a frown of envy wrinkle her brow. She decided to get dressed, apply her makeup and put the greatest possible distance between Maria Cláudia's youthfulness and her own seductive powers as an experienced woman of the world. She sat up. She had turned on the boiler earlier, and the water for her bath was ready. She removed her dressing gown in a single movement, then

41

grasped the hem of her nightdress and pulled it up over her head. She stood there completely naked. She tested the water and allowed herself to slide into the tub. She washed herself slowly. Lídia knew the value of cleanliness for someone in her situation.

Clean and refreshed, she wrapped herself in a bathrobe and went into the kitchen. Before returning to the bedroom, she put the kettle on to boil for tea.

Back in her bedroom, she chose a simple but charming dress, which clung to her body and made her look younger, and quickly applied a little makeup, pleased with herself and the night cream she was currently using. Then she returned to the kitchen, where the kettle was already boiling. She took it off the gas. When she looked in the tea caddy, however, she found it was empty. She frowned, put down the tin and went back to her bedroom. She was about to phone the grocer's and had even picked up the receiver when she heard someone talking out in the street. She opened the window.

The mist had lifted and the sky was blue, the watery blue of early spring. The sun seemed to come from very far away, so far away that the air was refreshingly cool.

From the window of the ground-floor apartment a woman was issuing instructions, then repeating them to a fair-haired boy who was gazing up at her, wrinkling his little nose in concentration. The woman spoke voluminously and with a strong Spanish accent. The boy had already grasped that his mother wanted him to buy ten tostões' worth of pepper and was ready to set off, but she kept repeating what it was she wanted out of the sheer pleasure of talking to her son and hearing her own voice. When it seemed she had no further instructions to give, Lídia called out:

"Dona Carmen!"

"*¿Quién me llama?* Ah, *buenos días*, Dona Lídia!"

"Good morning. Would you mind asking Henriquinho to get me something from the grocer's too? I need some tea . . ."

She told him what sort of tea and sent a twenty-escudo note fluttering down to him. Henriquinho set off at a run down the street as if pursued by a pack of dogs. Lídia thanked Dona Carmen, who answered in her own strange idiolect, alternating Spanish and Portuguese words and murdering the latter in the process. Lídia, who preferred not to show herself for too long at her window, said goodbye. Henriquinho returned shortly afterward, red-faced from running, to bring her the packet of tea and her change. She thanked him with a ten-tostão tip and a kiss, and the boy left.

With her cup full and a plate of biscuits beside her, Lídia returned to bed. While she ate, she continued reading the book she had taken from a small cupboard in the dining room. This is how she filled the emptiness of her idle days: reading novels, some good, some bad. At the moment she was immersed in the foolish, inconsequential world of *The Maias*. She sipped her tea and nibbled on the biscuits while she read the passage in which Maria Eduarda is flattering Carlos with her declaration: "Not only my heart remained asleep, but my body too, it was always cold, cold as marble." Lídia liked that image. She looked for a pencil so that she could underline it, but, unable to find one, she got up and, still holding the book, went over to the dressing table, where she found a lipstick with which she made a mark in the margin, a red line highlighting that moment of drama or perhaps farce.

From the stairs came the sound of someone sweeping. Then she heard Dona Carmen begin a mournful song, accompanied, in the background, by the continuing clatter of the sewing machine and the sole of a shoe being hammered into place.

Taking another delicate bite of a biscuit, Lídia resumed her reading.

2

In the living room, the weary old clock—inherited by Justina after the death of her parents—gave a long, asthmatic wheeze followed by nine nasal chimes. The apartment was so quiet it seemed uninhabited. Justina wore felt-soled shoes and moved from room to room as subtly as a ghost. She and the apartment were so perfectly matched that, seeing them together, one could understand at once why they were as they were. Justina could exist only in that apartment, and the bare, silent apartment could not be as it was without Justina's presence. A smell of mold emanated from both furniture and floor, and a musty aroma hung in the air. The permanently closed windows contributed to the tomb-like atmosphere, and Justina was so slow and lackadaisical that the house was never entirely clean.

The vibrations from the chimes—which had temporarily driven out the silence—slowly died away, ever more tenuous and distant. Justina turned out all the lights, then went and sat by the window that gave onto the street. She liked sitting there, motionless, vacant, her hands lying limp in her lap, her eyes open to the darkness, waiting for what? Even she did not know. The cat, her sole companion in the evenings, came and curled up at her feet. He was a quiet creature with questioning eyes and a sinuous gait, and appeared to have lost the ability to meow. He had learned silence from his mistress and, like her, surrendered himself to it.

Time slipped slowly by. The tick-tock of the clock kept nudging the silence, trying to shoo it away, but the silence resisted with its dense, heavy mass, in which all sounds drowned. Both fought unremittingly on, the ticking clock with the obstinacy of despair and the certain knowledge of death, while the silence had on its side disdainful eternity.

Then another, louder noise interposed itself: people going down the stairs. Had it been day-light, Justina would immediately have rushed to see who it was, more out of habit or because she had nothing better to do than out of any real curiosity, but the night drained her of energy, leaving her tired and listless and filled with a foolish desire to weep and to die. However, she would unhesitatingly have said that it was Rosália, along with her husband and daughter, going off to see a film. She recognized the laugh: it belonged to Maria Cláudia, who was mad about the cinema.

The cinema . . . How long had it been since Justina went to the cinema? Yes, there had been the death of her daughter, but even before that, it had been a long time. Matilde used to go with her father, but she always stayed at home. Why? She had no idea, she just didn't go. She disliked walking down the street with her husband. She was very tall and thin, while he was short and stocky. On their wedding day, boys in the street had laughed when they saw them leave the church. She had never forgotten that laughter, just as she could never forget the photograph: the best man and maid of honor and the other guests lined up on the steps of the church like spectators in the stands at a soccer match; and she standing there stiffly, her bouquet drooping, her dark eyes dull and perplexed; and he, already fat, squeezed into a tailcoat and wearing a borrowed top hat. She had buried that ridiculous photograph in a drawer and never wanted to see it again.

The dialogue between the clock and the silence was again interrupted. From outside came the rumble of tires over the uneven surface of the street. The car stopped. There was a confusion of noises in the night: the creak of a hand brake being put on, the characteristic noise of a car door opening, the dull thud as it closed, a tinkling of keys. Justina did not need to get up to know who had arrived. Dona Lídia had a visitor, her usual visitor, the man who came to see her three times a week. He would leave at around two in the morning. He never spent the entire night there. He was methodical, punctual, correct. Justina did not like her neighbor. She hated her because she was pretty and, above all, because she was a kept woman and, more to the point, had a nicely furnished apartment, as well as enough money to pay for a cleaning lady, have meals from a restaurant sent up to her, and appear in public laden with jewelry and reeking of perfume. She was, however, grateful to Lídia because she had given her the excuse she needed to break off relations with her husband forever. Thanks to Lídia, she had added to her thousand other reasons the biggest reason of all.

Slowly, painfully, as if her body were refusing to move, she got up and turned on the light. The dining room, where she was sitting, was quite large, and the bulb that lit it was so feeble that it could only just manage to keep the darkness at bay, leaving shadows lurking in the corners. The bare walls, the hard, unwelcoming stiff-backed chairs, the table unpolished and unadorned by flowers, the stark, drab furniture—and alone in the midst of all that coldness sat tall, thin Justina, in her black dress and with her deep, dark, silent eyes.

The clock whirred twice and very timidly struck the quarter hour. A quarter past nine. Justina yawned slowly. Then she turned out the light and went into her bedroom. On the chest of drawers the photo of her daughter smiled cheerily out at her, the only brightness in that somber, musty room. With a sigh of resignation, Justina lay down.

She always slept badly. She spent the night jumping from dream to dream, confused dreams from which she awoke exhausted and perplexed. Try as she might, she could never reconstruct them. The only thing she could remember—and even then it was more like a presentiment or perhaps the memory of a presentiment—was the obsessive presence of someone behind a door that all the strength in the world could not open. Before falling asleep, she would try over and over to recall Matilde's face, her voice, her gestures, her laughter, yes, even her dead face, as if in her dreams she might succeed in breaking down that eternally locked door. All in vain. When Justina closed her eyes, Matilde would hide away so effectively that Justina would only find her again, beyond the mystery of dreams, when she woke the following morning. But finding her in that way meant losing her again; seeing her as if she were still alive meant not seeing her at all.

Her eyelids drooped beneath the weight of shadows and silence. The silence and the shadows entered Justina's mind. The slow saraband of dreams was about to begin, the strange, distressing presence was about to reappear, along with the locked door behind which lay the mystery. Suddenly, far off, dull, desperate moans could be heard. The night shuddered at these supernatural noises. Justina's already clouded eyes opened onto the darkness. Rolling down mountains and across plains, awakening echoes in shadowy caves and in the hollows of ancient trees, hurling out into the night a thousand tragic sounds, those moans came nearer and the moaning became weeping and each lament a tear as big as a fist that fell as hard as a fist.

Justina's eyes battled against the anxiety provoked by the noises filling her ears. She felt as if she were being dragged down into a deep, dark abyss and was struggling not to fall in. As she fell, though, Matilde's bright smile appeared to her and, clinging desperately to that smile, she plunged into sleep.

Penetrating the walls and rising to the stars, the music continued, the slow movement of the *Eroica* Symphony, crying out against pain, crying out against the injustice of man's mortality.

3

The final notes of the funeral march dropped like violets onto the tomb of the hero. Then came a pause. A tear that falls and dies, followed immediately by the dionysiac vitality of the scherzo, still heavy with the shades of Hades, but already savoring the joy of life and victory.

A tremor ran through the four women, who were sitting, heads bent. The enchanted circle of light falling from the ceiling held them fast in the grip of the same fascination. Their grave faces bore the intense expression of people witnessing the celebration of mysterious, impenetrable rites. The music, with its hypnotic power, opened doors in the minds of those women. They did not look at one another. Their eyes were focused on their work, but only their hands were present.

The music ran freely about in the silence, and the silence received it on its dumb lips. Time passed. The symphony, like a river that rushes down a mountain, floods the plain and flows into the sea, ended in the profundity of that silence.

Adriana reached out a hand and turned off the radio. A sharp click like a key turning in a lock. The mystery was over.

Aunt Amélia looked up. Her usually hard pupils had a moist gleam to them. Cândida murmured:

"It's so . . . so lovely!"

Timid, indecisive Cândida was not an eloquent speaker, but her pale lips were trembling, just as the lips of young girls tremble when they receive their first kiss. Aunt Amélia was dissatisfied with her choice of adjective:

"Lovely? Any silly song could be described as 'lovely,' but that music, well, it's . . ."

She hesitated. The word she wanted to say was there on her lips, but it seemed to her that she would profane it by speaking it. There are certain words that draw back, that refuse to be uttered, because they are too laden with significance for our word-weary ears. Amélia had suddenly lost some of her unerring confidence with words. It was Adriana who, in a tremulous voice, in the voice of someone betraying a secret, murmured:

"It's beautiful."

"Yes, Adriana. That's precisely what it is."

Adriana looked down at the stocking she was darning, a prosaic task, like that of Isaura, who was sewing buttonholes into a shirt, or like that of their mother, who was counting the stitches on the crochet work she was doing, or like that of Aunt Amélia, who was adding up the day's expenses. Tasks appropriate to plain, dispirited women, to narrow shriveled lives, lives lit by viewless windows. The music had ended, the music that kept them company each evening, their daily visitor, consoling and stimulating—and now they could speak about beauty.

"Why should the word 'beautiful' be so difficult to say?" asked Isaura, smiling.

"I don't know," said her sister. "But it is, and yet it should be just like any other word. It's easy enough to say, it only has three syllables. I don't understand the difficulty either."

Aunt Amélia, still shocked by her earlier inability to pronounce the word, attempted an explanation:

"I think I do. It's like the word 'God' for believers. It's a sacred word."

Yes, Aunt Amélia could always come up with

the right answer, but it stopped the flow of the debate. There was nothing more to be said. Silence, a silence bare now of music, weighed heavily on the air. Cândida asked:

"Isn't there anything else on?"

"No, nothing of any interest," said Isaura.

Adriana was daydreaming, the sock she had been darning lay forgotten in her lap. She was thinking about the mask of Beethoven she had seen in the window of a music shop many years before. She could still see that broad, powerful face, which, even in the form of an inexpressive plaster cast, bore all the marks of genius. She had cried for a whole day because she didn't have enough money to buy it. That had happened shortly before their father died. His death had meant a sudden diminution in their income and obliged them to leave their old home—and now, even more than it had been then, buying that mask of Beethoven was an impossible dream.

"What are you thinking about, Adriana?" asked her sister.

Adriana smiled and shrugged:

"Oh, silly things."

"Did you have a bad day?"

"Not particularly. It's always the same: invoices to receive, invoices to pay, debiting and crediting someone else's money."

They both laughed. Aunt Amélia finished her accounts and asked:

"Has there been any mention of a wage increase?"

Adriana shrugged again. She hated being asked this question. It seemed to her that the others thought she didn't earn enough, a suggestion she found offensive. She said sharply:

"Business is bad, apparently . . ."

"It's always the same old story. Some get a lot, some get a little, and others get nothing at all. When are they going to learn to pay people enough to live on?"

Adriana sighed. Aunt Amélia had a real bee in her bonnet about money matters, about employers and employees. It wasn't envy; she was simply outraged by how much waste there was in a world where millions of people were poor and starving. They weren't poor, and there was always food on the table, but they existed on a very tight budget, which excluded anything superfluous, even those superfluous things without which our lives are reduced almost to the level of animals. Aunt Amélia went on:

"You must speak up for yourself, Adriana. You've been working there for two years now, and what you earn barely pays for your tram fare."

"But what do you expect me to do, Auntie?"

"You know what to do! And don't look at me with those great, frightened eyes of yours!"

These words struck Adriana like a blow. Isaura shot her aunt a stern look:

"Auntie!"

Amélia turned first to her, then back to Adriana and said:

"Forgive me."

She got up and left the room. Adriana got up too, but her mother made her sit down again.

"Pay no attention, child. She's the one who has to do the shopping, and she really has to struggle to make ends meet, and very often they don't. You're both earning, you're both working, but she, poor thing, is the one who does all the worrying, and I'm the only one who knows just how much she worries."

Aunt Amélia appeared in the doorway. She seemed upset, but her voice was no less brusque, or perhaps she had to be brusque in order not to reveal how upset she was.

"Would anyone like a cup of coffee?"

(Just like in the good old days! A cup of coffee! Yes, why not, Aunt Amélia! Sit down here with us, that's right, with your face of stone and your heart of wax. Drink a cup of coffee and tomorrow you can redo your accounts, invent recipes, eliminate expenses, even eliminate this cup of coffee, this pointless cup of coffee!)

The evening resumed, slower and quieter now. Two old women and two who had already turned their backs on youth. They had their past to remember, the present to live in and the future to fear.

Around midnight, sleep slipped into the room.

There were a few yawns. Cândida suggested (she was always the first to make the suggestion):

"Shall we go to bed?"

They stood up, their chairs scraping the floor. As usual, Adriana hung back to give the others time to get ready for bed. Then she put away her sewing and went into the bedroom. Her sister was reading her novel. Adriana took a bunch of keys from her bag and opened a drawer. With another, smaller key she opened a box and took out a thick exercise book. Isaura peered up at her over the top of her book and smiled:

"Ah, the diary! One day I'll find out what it is you write in that book."

"Oh no, you won't!" answered her sister angrily.

"There's no need to get nasty with me."

"Sometimes I feel like showing it to you just to shut you up!"

"Do I annoy you?"

"No, but you could keep your thoughts to yourself. I simply don't see why you have to say those things. It's so rude. Don't I have a right to some privacy?"

Behind the thick lenses of her glasses, Adriana's eyes glinted with annoyance. Clutching the exercise book to her chest, she confronted her sister's ironic smile.

"Of course you do," said Isaura. "Go on, then, scribble away. But the day will come when you yourself will give me that notebook to read."

"Well, you're in for a long wait," retorted Adriana.

And with that she stormed out of the room. Isaura made herself more comfortable beneath the bedclothes, positioned the book at the best angle for reading and forgot all about her sister. Having walked through the now dark bedroom where her mother and aunt were sleeping, Adriana locked herself in the bathroom. Only there, away from her family's prying eyes, did she feel safe enough to write down her impressions of the day. She had started writing the diary shortly after she got her job. She had now written dozens of pages. She gave her pen a shake and began:

Wednesday, 3/19/52, five minutes to midnight. Aunt Amélia is very grumpy today. I hate it when they mention how little I earn. It's insulting. I almost answered back, saying that at least I earned more than she did, but, fortunately, I bit my tongue. Poor Aunt Amélia. Mama says she wears herself out trying to keep the books straight, and I can believe that. After all, that's how I spend my days. Tonight we listened to Beethoven's Third Symphony. Mama said it was pretty, and I said it was beautiful, and Aunt Amélia agreed. I love my aunt. I love my mother. I love Isaura. But what they don't know is that I wasn't thinking about the symphony or about Beethoven, I mean, I wasn't only thinking about that . . . I was thinking . . . and then I remembered that mask of Beethoven and how much I wanted it. But I was also thinking about "him." I'm feeling happy today. He spoke to me so nicely. When he gave me the invoices to check, he put his right hand on my shoulder. Oh, it was lovely! I trembled inside and went bright red. I had to pretend to be concentrating on my work so that no one would notice. Then came the bad bit. Thinking I couldn't hear, he started talking to Sarmento about some blond girl. The only reason I didn't burst into tears was because it would have looked bad and I wouldn't want him to know how I feel. He "toyed" with the girl, he said, for a few months, then dumped her. Good heavens, would it be the same with me? At least he doesn't know how I feel about him. He might make fun of me. If he did, I would kill myself!

She paused and chewed the end of her pen. She had begun by saying that she was happy, and now there she was talking about killing herself. This didn't seem right. She thought for a moment and closed with: *Still, it was so lovely when he touched me on the shoulder!*

That was better, as it should be, closing that day's entry with a hope, a small joy. Whenever the events of the day left her feeling discouraged or sad, she made a point in her diary of not being entirely honest. She reread what she had written and closed the exercise book.

She had brought her nightdress with her from the bedroom, a white nightdress, buttoned up to the neck and with long sleeves because the nights were still chilly. She quickly got undressed. Her inelegant body, freed from the constraints of her clothes, looked heavier, baggier, lumpier. Her bra cut into her back. When she took it off, a red weal encircled her body like the mark left by a beating. She put on her nightdress and, after performing her usual ablutions, went back to the bedroom.

Isaura was still reading. She had her free arm bent back behind her neck, a position that revealed one dark armpit and the curve of her breasts. Absorbed in her reading, she didn't look up when her sister got into bed.

"It's late, Isaura. Time to stop reading," Adriana murmured.

"OK, OK!" Isaura said impatiently. "It's not my fault you don't like reading."

Adriana shrugged, as she so often did. She turned her back on her sister, pulled the bed-clothes up so that the light wasn't in her eyes and, moments later, she was asleep.

Isaura continued to read. She had to finish the

book that night because it was due back at the library the next day. It was nearly one o'clock when she reached the final page. Her eyes were sore and her brain overexcited. She put the book down on the bedside table and turned out the light. Her sister was sleeping. She could hear her regular, rhythmic breathing and felt a twinge of irritation. In her view, Adriana was as cold as ice, and that diary of hers was merely a childish way of making people think she had some mysterious secret to hide. A faint glow from the streetlamp lit the room. In the darkness she could hear the gnawing of a woodworm. From the room next door came a muffled voice: Aunt Amélia talking in her sleep.

The whole building was sleeping. With eyes wide open to the dark, her hands folded behind her head, Isaura was thinking.

4

Don't make too much noise, you know I hate to disturb the neighbors," whispered Anselmo.

He was going up the stairs, with his wife and daughter behind him, using matches to light their way. However, distracted by his own words of advice, he burned his fingers. He let out an involuntary yelp and lit another match. Maria Cláudia had a fit of the giggles. Her mother muttered a reproof:

"Whatever's got into you, girl?"

They reached their apartment and entered furtively, like burglars. As soon as they went into the kitchen, Rosália sat down on a stool:

"Oh, I'm exhausted!"

She took off her shoes and stockings and showed them her swollen feet:

"Look at them!"

"Your albumin levels are too high, that's what it is!" declared her husband.

"Goodness," said Maria Cláudia, smiling. "He's quite the expert, isn't he?"

"If your father says my albumin levels are high, it's because they are," retorted her mother.

Anselmo nodded gravely. He studied his wife's feet, which only confirmed him in his diagnosis:

"Yep, that's what it is."

Maria Cláudia screwed up her small face in disgust. She found the sight of her mother's feet and the thought of some possible illness boring. Everything ugly bored her.

More in order to change the subject than out of any desire to be helpful, she took three cups out of the cupboard and filled them with tea. They always left the thermos full, ready for their return home. The five minutes devoted to that small late-night feast made them feel rather special, as if they had suddenly left the mediocrity of their lives behind them and risen a few rungs on the economic ladder. The kitchen disappeared and gave way to an intimate little drawing room with expensive furniture and paintings on the wall and a piano in one corner. Rosália no longer had high albumin levels, and Maria Cláudia was wearing a dress in the latest fashion. Only Anselmo did not change. He was always the same tall, distinguished, decorative gentleman, bald and slightly stooped and stroking his small mustache. His face was fixed and inexpressive, the product of years spent repressing all emotion as a way of guaranteeing respectability.

Alas, that illusion never lasted for more than five minutes. Rosália's bare feet once again dominated the scene, and Maria Cláudia was the first to go to bed.

In the kitchen, husband and wife began the dialogue-monologue of couples who have been married for more than twenty years. Banalities, things said merely in order to say something, a mere prelude to the tranquil sleep of middle age.

Gradually the noises died away, leaving the expectant silence that precedes sleep. Then the silence thickened. Only Maria Cláudia was still awake. She always had difficulty falling asleep. She had enjoyed the film. At the cinema during intermission, a boy had kept looking at her. On the way out, he had come right up to her, so close she had felt his breath on the back of her neck. What she didn't understand was why he hadn't followed her, otherwise what was the point of looking at her so insistently. She forgot about the cinema then and turned, instead, to her visit to Dona Lídia's apartment. She was so pretty. "Much prettier than me," she thought. She was sorry not to be more like Dona Lídia. Then she remembered the car she had seen parked outside. She was suddenly on tenterhooks, quite incapable now of going to sleep. She had no idea what time it was, but reckoned it couldn't be far off two o'clock. Like everyone else in the building, she knew that Dona Lídia's night visitor usually left at about two in the morning. Whether because of the film, the boy or that morning's visit to Dona Lídia, she felt brimful of curiosity, even though she found that curiosity wrong and inappropriate. She waited. Minutes later, coming from the floor below, she heard the sound of a bolt being drawn and a door opening, followed by the vague sound of voices and footsteps going down the stairs.

Gingerly, so as not to wake her parents, Maria Cláudia slipped out of bed and tiptoed over to the window, where she peered around the curtain. The car was still parked opposite. She saw a bulky male figure cross the street and get into the car.

The car set off and soon disappeared from view.

5

Dona Carmen had her own particular way of enjoying the morning. She was not one for staying in bed until lunchtime, which would have been impossible anyway because she had to prepare her husband's breakfast and get Henriquinho ready for school, but she made a point of never washing or brushing her hair until midday. She liked to wander about the house, still in her nightclothes, her hair loose and looking generally disheveled and slovenly. Her husband loathed this habit of hers, which went against what he considered the norm. He had tried over and over to persuade his wife to mend her ways, but time had taught him that he was wasting his breath. Although his job as a sales rep imposed no rigid timetable on him, he always escaped as early as he could so as not to begin the day in a bad mood. For her part, Carmen could not bear her husband to linger at home after breakfast. Not because this would oblige her to abandon her own beloved habits, but because her husband's presence made the morning so much less pleasurable. The result was that, whenever he did stay longer than usual, it ruined the whole day for both of them.

As Emílio Fonseca was preparing his case of samples that morning, he discovered that someone had tampered with both prices and samples. Not only were the necklaces out of their proper places, they were all mixed up with the bracelets and the brooches, which, in turn, had become jumbled together with the earrings and the dark glasses. The only possible culprit was his son. He considered confronting him, but decided against it. If his son denied all knowledge, Emílio would think he was lying, and that would be bad; if Henrique owned up, then Emílio would have to beat him or tell him off, and that would be even worse. And, of course, if his wife got angry and launched herself into the discussion, it would become an all-out row. And he was heartily sick of rows. He put his case on the dining table and, without a word, set about restoring order.

Emílio Fonseca was a small, wiry man, not thin, but wiry. He was about thirty years old and had sparse, pale hair, a rather wishy-washy blond color. He had a very high forehead, of which he had always been proud. Now, however, that it had grown still higher due to incipient baldness, he would have preferred a rather lower hairline. Meanwhile, he had learned to accept the inevitable, and the inevitable was not just his lack of hair, but the present need to sort out his sample case. In eight miserable years of marriage he had learned to remain calm. His firm mouth was marred by a few bitter lines, and when he smiled his mouth twisted slightly, lending his face a sarcastic look in keeping with the general tenor of his words.

With the awkward air of a criminal returning to the scene of the crime, Henriquinho came to see what his father was doing. He had the face of an angel and was fair-haired like his father, but his hair was of a warmer color. Emílio didn't even glance at him. There was no love lost between father and son; they merely saw each other every day.

The flip-flap of Carmen's slippers could be heard out in the corridor, an aggressive sound, more eloquent than any words. Emílio had almost finished restoring order to the contents of his case. Carmen peered around the dining room door in order to calculate how much longer her husband would be. He had, in her view, already taken quite long enough.

At that point, the doorbell rang. Carmen frowned. She wasn't expecting anyone at that hour. The baker and the milkman had already been by, and it was too early for the postman. The bell rang again. With an impatient "Coming!" she went to the door, her son dogging her heels. A small woman wearing a shawl was standing there clutching a newspaper. Dona Carmen eyed her distrustfully and asked:

"¿Qué desea?" (There were times when she would not speak Portuguese even if her life depended on it.)

The woman smiled humbly:

"Good morning, senhora. I understand you have a room to rent, is that right? Could I see it?"

Carmen was astonished.

"A room to rent, *aquí*? No, there's no room to rent here."

"But the advertisement in the newspaper—"

"What advertisement? Let me see."

Her voice trembled with ill-concealed irritation. She breathed deeply, trying to calm herself. The woman pointed at the advertisement with a finger that bore the scars of an old nail infection. There it was, in the section "Rooms to Let." No doubt about it. All the facts were there: the name of the street, the number of the building and, clear as day, ground floor, left. She handed the newspaper back and said curtly:

"Well, there are no rooms to let here!"

"But the newspaper says—"

"I've told you already. Besides, the advertisement specifies a gentleman, *un caballero*."

"There are so few rooms to let, and I—"

"If you'll excuse me."

And with that, Dona Carmen slammed the door in the woman's face and went to find her husband. From the doorway, she asked:

"Did you put an ad in the paper?"

Holding a necklace made of colored stones in each hand and raising one eyebrow, Emílio Fonseca looked at her and responded in a cool, ironic tone:

"An ad? Only if it was to drum up more customers."

"No, an ad offering a room to let."

"A room? No, my dear. When I married you, I agreed that we would share all our worldly goods, and I would never dream of renting out a room without consulting you first."

"*No seas gracioso.*"

"I'm not being funny. What man would dare to be funny with you?"

Carmen did not respond. Her imperfect knowledge of Portuguese meant that she was always at a disadvantage in these exchanges of barbed remarks. She chose instead to explain in a soft, insinuating voice:

"It was a woman, *una mujer.* She was carrying a newspaper and had come about the ad. It was definitely this apartment, *no había confusión.* And since she was a woman, I thought that perhaps you had put the ad in . . ."

Emílio Fonseca closed the case with a loud snap. It was not entirely clear what his wife meant, but he could see what she was getting at. He looked at her with his cold, pale eyes and said:

"And if it had been a man, should I then immediately have assumed that *you* had put the advertisement in?"

Carmen blushed, offended:

"You brute!"

Henriquinho, who was listening to the conversation unblinking, stared at his father to see how he would react. Emílio, however, merely shrugged and murmured:

"You're right. I'm sorry."

"I don't want your apologies," retorted Carmen, already getting agitated. "Whenever you apologize, what you're actually doing is making fun of me. I'd rather you hit me!"

"I've never hit you."

"And don't you dare, either."

"Don't worry. You're taller and stronger than me. Allow me at least to preserve the illusion that I belong to the stronger sex. It's the only illusion left to me. And, please, let's not argue."

"And what if I want to argue?"

"There would be no point. I always have the final word. I'm going to put on my hat now and leave, and I won't be back until tonight. Always assuming I do come back, of course."

Carmen went into the kitchen to fetch her purse. She gave some money to her son and sent him off to the grocer's to buy some sweets. Henriquinho tried to resist, but the pull of the sweets proved stronger than his curiosity and his courage, which was telling him to take his mother's side. As soon as the front door had closed, Carmen returned to the dining room. Her husband had sat down at one end of the table and was lighting a cigarette. His wife plunged straight into the argument:

"So you're not coming back, eh? I knew it.

You've got somewhere else to stay, haven't you? So the little god has clay feet, has he? *Y aquí estoy yo*, the skivvy, the slave, working away all day for whenever his majesty chooses to come home!"

Emílio smiled. His wife grew more furious still: "Don't you laugh at me!"

"Why shouldn't I laugh? What do you expect? This is all complete nonsense. There are plenty of boarding houses in the city. What's to prevent me staying in one of those?"

"¡*Yo*! Me!"

"You? Oh, don't be silly! Look, I have things to do. Just stop all this nonsense, will you?"

"Emílio!"

Carmen barred the way, trembling with rage. She was slightly taller than he; she had a square face and a strong jaw, and despite the two deep lines that ran from the sides of her nose down to the corners of her mouth, there was still the remnant of a now almost faded beauty, of warm, luminous skin, velvety, liquid eyes, youth. For a moment Emílio saw her as she had been eight years before. It was only a moment, a flash, then the memory flickered and burned out.

"You've been fooling around with someone else, Emílio!"

"Rubbish. Of course I haven't. I can swear on the Bible if you like. But even if I had been, what would you care? It's no good crying over spilled milk. We've been married for eight years and have we ever really been happy? There was the honeymoon, I suppose, but even then . . . We fooled ourselves, Carmen. We played with life and now we're paying for it. You really shouldn't play with life, don't you agree?"

His wife had sat down and was crying. Still sobbing, she exclaimed:

"¡*Soy una desgraciada*!"

Emílio picked up the sample case and with his free hand stroked his wife's head with a rare and now forgotten tenderness, murmuring:

"We're both of us unfortunate, each in our own way, but believe me, we both are, me possibly even more than you. At least you have Henrique . . ." The affectionate tone grew suddenly hard: "Anyway, enough of that. I might not be back for lunch, but I'll definitely be here for supper. See you later."

Out in the corridor, he turned and added, with a hint of irony in his voice:

"And as for the advertisement, it's obviously a mistake. Maybe it's meant for the neighbors."

He opened the front door and went out onto the landing, holding the case in his right hand, his right shoulder pulled slightly down by the weight. Without thinking, he adjusted his hat, a gray, broad-brimmed affair that cast a shadow over his pale, distant eyes and made his face and body look smaller.

6

Dona Carmen had sent two more would-be lodgers packing before she decided to test out her husband's idea. And when she did, still fuming from that earlier domestic dispute and from arguing with the various candidates for the room, she spoke very sharply to Silvestre. He, however—suddenly understanding the inexplicable absence of applicants—replied in the same vein, and Carmen was forced into retreat when she saw the plump, round figure of Mariana—sleeves rolled up and hands on her hips—hove into view behind Silvestre. To avoid any further confusion, Silvestre suggested that he put a notice on her door sending any more hopeful candidates to him. Carmen grumbled that she wasn't prepared to have bits of paper stuck on her front door, to which Silvestre replied that she would be the one to suffer then, because she would have to answer the door to anyone responding to the ad. Reluctantly she agreed, and Silvestre wrote an appropriate note on half a sheet of letter paper. Carmen, however, would not allow him to affix it to the door, and did the job herself with a dab of glue. Even so, she was faced by one more person asking the same question and brandishing the same newspaper as proof, for the simple reason that the interested party was unable to read. What she thought of Silvestre and his wife went far beyond what she said, but what she said also went far beyond what was right and just. Had Silvestre been of a bellicose nature, we could have had an international incident on our hands. Mariana, it's true, was spitting feathers, but her husband calmed her violent impulses and her desire to imitate that heroine of the Battle of Aljubarrota, who slew seven Castilians with her baker's shovel.

Silvestre returned to his place at the window, wondering how the mistake could possibly have arisen. He knew full well that his handwriting was not of the finest, but it was, he thought, pretty good for a cobbler, especially when compared with that of certain doctors. The only explanation seemed to be that the newspaper had got it wrong. He was sure it hadn't been his mistake; he could see in his mind's eye the form he had filled in, and he had definitely put ground floor, right. While engaged in these thoughts, he remained focused on his work, glancing out at the street now and then with the aim of spotting among the few passersby anyone who might be coming to see the room. The advantage of this tactic was that by the time he came to speak to the interested party, he would already have reached a decision, for he held himself to be a good judge of faces. As a youth, he had gotten used to studying other people, in order to know who they were and what they were thinking, at a time when knowing whom to trust was almost a matter of life or death. These thoughts, drawing him back along the path his life had taken, distracted him from his role as observer.

The morning was nearly over, the smell of lunch was already filling the apartment, and no one suitable had as yet turned up. Silvestre now regretted being so particular. He had spent good money on an advertisement, got into an argument with his neighbor (who, luckily, was not also a customer) and still they had no lodger.

He had just started nailing metal heel and toe taps onto a pair of boots when he saw a man walking slowly along on the pavement opposite, looking up at the buildings and at the faces of the other people passing by. He didn't have a newspaper in his hand or, it would seem, in his pocket. He stopped opposite Silvestre's window to study the building floor by floor. Pretending to be absorbed in his work, Silvestre continued to watch him out of the corner of his eye. The man was of medium height, dark-complexioned and probably not yet thirty. He was dressed in the unmistakable manner of someone caught midway between poverty and earning a modest income. His suit was well cut, but rather shabby. The creases in his trousers would have been the despair of Mariana. He was wearing a polo-neck sweater and no hat. Despite appearing quite satisfied with the results of his inspection, he still did not move.

Silvestre began to feel uneasy. Not that he had anything to fear; he hadn't had any trouble since . . . since leaving those things behind him, and besides, he was old now. Nevertheless, the man's immobility and ease of manner troubled him. His wife was singing to herself in the kitchen, in the out-of-tune way that so delighted Silvestre and provided him with a constant source of jokes. Unable to stand the suspense any longer, Silvestre raised his head and looked straight at the stranger, who, in turn, having finished his inspection of the building, met Silvestre's eyes through the window. They stared at each other, Silvestre with a slightly challenging air, the other man with an inquisitive look on his face. Separated by the street, the two men locked gazes. Silvestre glanced away so as not to appear too provoking, but the other man merely smiled and crossed the street with slow, firm steps. Silvestre felt a shiver run through him as he waited for the bell to ring. This did not happen as soon as he expected; the man must be reading the notice on the door opposite. Finally the bell rang. Mariana paused in the middle of a particularly painful dissonance. Silvestre's heart beat faster and, half joking to himself, he decided that it was mere presumption on his part to think that the man had come for

75

reasons unconnected with the room, reasons to do with remote events during the time when . . . The floor trembled beneath Mariana's approaching bulk. Silvestre drew back the curtain:

"What is it?"

"There's a man come about the room. Can you deal with him?"

What Silvestre felt was not relief exactly. His faint sigh was filled with sadness, as if an illusion, his very last, had just died, for it clearly *had* been presumption on his part, and as he made his way to the front door, the thought going around in his mind was that he was an old man now and over the hill. His wife had already told the potential lodger how much the rent would be, but when he'd asked to see the room, she had summoned Silvestre. When the young man saw Silvestre, he smiled, but only with his eyes. He had small, bright, very dark eyes beneath thick, clearly delineated eyebrows. He was, as Silvestre had already noted, dark-complexioned, with clear features, neither gentle nor severe, and a masculine face, slightly softened by a curved, somewhat feminine mouth. Silvestre liked the face.

"So you want to see the room, do you?"

"If that's all right. The price suits me fine, but I just need to know if the room does too."

"Come in."

The boy (or so he seemed to Silvestre) stepped

confidently into the apartment. He glanced around at the walls and floor, alarming the estimable Mariana, ever fearful that someone might find fault with her cleaning. The room looked out onto the small garden where Silvestre, in his scarce free time, grew a few equally scarce cabbages and kept a few chickens. The young man looked around him, then turned to Silvestre:

"I really like the room, but I can't take it!"

Slightly annoyed, Silvestre asked:

"Why not? Is it too expensive?"

"No, as I said, the price is fine, but it's not furnished."

"Oh, you want it furnished."

Silvestre glanced at his wife. She nodded and Silvestre added:

"That's easy enough to put right. We had a bed in here and a chest of drawers, but we took them out thinking we'd rent the room unfurnished, you see. You never know how other people are going to treat your things. But if you're interested . . ."

"And the price would be the same?"

Silvestre scratched his head.

"I wouldn't want to shortchange you," said the young man.

This remark immediately won Silvestre over. Anyone who knew him well would have used exactly those words in order to ensure that the rent for the room remained the same, furnished or unfurnished.

"Yes, furnished or unfurnished, what's the difference?" he said. "In fact, it suits us better that way. We don't have to be so cluttered up with furniture, then. Isn't that right, Mariana?"

If Mariana had given voice to her thoughts, she would have said "No, it's not," but instead she said nothing, shrugged in an offhand manner and wrinkled her nose disapprovingly. The young man noticed and added:

"No, no, I'll give you another fifty escudos. Would that be acceptable?"

Mariana was thrilled and decided that she liked the young man after all. Silvestre, for his part, was jumping for joy inside, not because they had reached a satisfactory agreement, but because he could see that he had been quite right about the young man. Their new guest was a thoroughly decent fellow. The young man went over to the window, studied the garden, smiled at the chicks scratching about in the earth and said:

"I'm so sorry, you don't know who I am. My name's Abel . . . Abel Nogueira. You can get references from my place of work and from the house I've been living in up until now. I'll give you the addresses."

Using the window ledge to rest on, he wrote the two addresses on a scrap of paper and handed it to Silvestre, who at first made as if to refuse, certain that he wouldn't bother to follow up those "references," but, in the end, he took it. Standing in the middle of the empty room, the young man was looking at the old man and the old woman and they were looking at the young man. All three of them were pleased, with that smile in their eyes that is worth more than any broad, toothy grin.

"I'll move in today, then. I'll bring my things over this evening. And I was hoping that perhaps I could come to some arrangement with the lady of the house as regards laundry."

Mariana said:

"I hope so too, then there'll be no need to have your laundry done elsewhere."

"And would you like some help moving the furniture back in?"

Silvestre hastened to reassure him:

"No, it's no bother. We'll sort that out."

"Are you sure?"

"Quite sure. It's not heavy."

"Good, then I'll see you later."

They accompanied him to the front door, all smiles. Out on the landing, the young man mentioned that he would need a key. Silvestre promised to have one made that very afternoon, and the young man left. Silvestre and Mariana went back into the room. Silvestre was still clutching the piece of paper on which their new lodger had written the addresses. He put it in his vest pocket and asked his wife:

"So, what do you think of him?"

"He seems nice enough. But honestly, when it comes to bargaining, you're such a pushover."

Silvestre smiled:

"It wouldn't have made that much difference to us . . ."

"No, but fifty escudos is still fifty escudos! I'm not sure how much I should charge him for his laundry, though . . ."

Silvestre wasn't listening. A look of irritation had suddenly appeared on his face, which made his nose look longer.

"What's up with you?" asked his wife.

"What's up? I mean, what were we thinking of? He told us his name and we didn't even tell him ours, he arrived at lunchtime and we didn't even ask him to join us. That's what's up!"

Mariana couldn't understand why he was so annoyed. There would be plenty of time to exchange names, and as for lunch, Silvestre should know that what would be enough for two might not be enough for three. Silvestre could tell from his wife's face that she judged the matter to be of little importance, and so he changed the subject:

"Shall we move the furniture back in?"

"All right. Lunch isn't ready yet anyway."

The move was quickly done. A bed, a bedside table, a chest of drawers and a chair. Mariana put clean sheets on the bed and gave the room a final tidying up. Husband and wife stood back to admire their work, but remained unsatisfied. The room still looked empty. Not that there was a lot of free space. On the contrary, you had to turn sideways to get in between the bed and the chest of drawers. But it lacked a certain something to cheer the place up and make it homey. Mariana went off and returned shortly afterward with a doily and a vase. Silvestre gave an approving nod. The furniture, so stiff and glum before, took on a more cheerful aspect. And with a rug to cover the bare floor and a few other such touches, the room took on an air of modest comfort. Mariana and Silvestre looked at each other and smiled, like people congratulating each other on the success of an enterprise.

And then they went and ate their lunch.

7

Lídia always took a nap after lunch. She had a tendency to lose weight, and her solution to this was to rest for two hours every afternoon. Lying on the soft, wide bed with her dressing gown undone, her arms by her sides, her eyes fixed on the ceiling, she would release any muscular, nervous tension and surrender herself to time. A kind of vacuum formed inside Lídia's mind and in the room. Time slipped by with the silky murmur of sand running through an hourglass.

Lídia's half-closed eyes followed her vague, hesitant thoughts. The thread grew thinner, shadows interposed themselves like clouds, then the thread would reappear with absolute clarity only to become veiled in shadows again and reemerge farther off. It was like a wounded bird dragging itself along, then fluttering into the air, appearing and disappearing, before falling down dead. Unable to keep her thoughts above the dimming clouds, Lídia fell asleep.

She was woken by the loud ringing of the doorbell. Confused, her eyes still heavy with sleep, she sat up on the bed. The bell rang again. Lídia got to her feet, put on her slippers and went out into the corridor. She peered cautiously through the spyhole, scowled, then opened the door:

"Come in, Mother."

"Hello, Lídia. May I come in?"

"Of course, isn't that what I just said?"

Her mother went in. Lídia led her into the kitchen.

"You look annoyed."

"Me? The very idea. Sit down."

Her mother perched on a stool. She was in her sixties, and her graying hair was covered by a black mantilla, as black as the dress she was wearing. She had a flabby, almost unlined face the color of grubby ivory. Beneath her near-lashless lids, her eyes were dull and fixed, and her sparse, thin eyebrows resembled circumflexes and gave her a look of permanent vacuous amazement.

"I wasn't expecting you today," said Lídia.

"No, it's not my usual day or my usual time," said her mother. "Are you well?"

"Pretty much. And you?"

"Mustn't grumble. If it wasn't for my rheumatism . . ."

Lídia tried to take an interest in her mother's rheumatism, but, failing utterly in the attempt, changed the subject:

"I was deep asleep when you rang. You woke me up."

"Hm, you don't look well," commented her mother.

"Really? It's probably because I've been asleep."

"Could be. They do say that sleeping too much is bad for you."

Neither of them was taken in by this exchange of banalities. Lídia knew perfectly well that her mother's visit had nothing to do with whether she was well or not; and for her part, her mother was only holding back before mentioning the real reason for her visit. Then Lídia realized that it was nearly four o'clock and she needed to go out.

"So what brings you here today?"

Her mother began smoothing a crease in her skirt, focusing all her attention on that task as if she had not heard the question. Then, finally, she murmured:

"I need some money."

Lídia was not surprised. This was what she had been expecting. However, she could not conceal her displeasure:

"Every month you come to me earlier and earlier . . ."

"You know how difficult things are for me . . ."

"I know, but you should try to put some money aside."

"I do, but it gets spent."

Her mother spoke in the serene voice of someone confident of getting what she wants. Lídia looked at her. Her mother was still sitting, eyes lowered, staring down at her skirt, watching the movement of her own hand. Lídia left the kitchen. Her mother immediately stopped smoothing her skirt and looked up. There was an expression of contentment on her face, that of someone who has sought and found. Hearing her daughter coming back, she resumed her modest pose.

"Here you are," said Lídia, holding out two one-hundred-escudo notes. "That's all I can afford right now."

Her mother took the money and put it in her purse, which she then buried in the depths of her handbag.

"Thank you. Are you going out, then?"

"Yes, I'm going down to the Baixa. I'm sick of being stuck at home. I'll probably have a cup of tea somewhere and do a bit of window-shopping."

Her mother's small, beady eyes, like those of a stuffed animal, remained fixed on her.

"Far be it from me to say," she said, "but do you think you should go out and about quite so much?"

"I don't. I just go out when I feel like it."

"Yes, but Senhor Morais might not like it."

Lídia's nostrils flared in anger. In a slow, sarcastic voice, she said:

"You seem to care more about what Senhor Morais might think than I do."

"It's for your own good. Now that you've got a . . . position . . ."

"Thank you for your concern, but I'm old enough not to need your advice. I go out when I want and I do what I want. Whether it's a good thing or a bad thing is my affair."

"I'm only saying it because I'm your mother and I want what's best for you."

Lídia gave a short, jeering laugh.

"What's *best* for me? It's only in the last few years that you've shown the slightest concern for my well-being. Before that, you didn't much care."

"That's not true," retorted her mother, once more turning her attention to the crease in her skirt. "I've always been concerned about you."

"Possibly, but you're much more concerned now. Don't worry. I haven't the slightest desire to return to my old life, to the days when you didn't care about me, or if you like, when you cared even less than you do now."

Her mother stood up. She had gotten what she wanted and the conversation was taking a disagreeable turn: best to leave. Lídia did nothing to stop her. She was furious at the minor exploitation of which she had been the victim, furious at her mother for daring to give her advice. She felt like sitting her down in a corner and keeping her there until she had told her exactly what she thought of her. All those concerns and suspicions, her fear of displeasing Senhor Morais, were nothing to do with love for her daughter; all she cared about was the small monthly allowance Lídia gave her.

Lips still quivering with rage, Lídia went back into the bedroom to get dressed and put on her makeup. She was going for a stroll in the Baixa, just as she had told her mother. What could be more innocent? And yet her mother's insinuating comments almost made her feel like going back to doing what she had done for years: meeting some man in a furnished room in the city, a room intended for brief assignations, with the inevitable bed, the inevitable screen, the inevitable bits of furniture with empty drawers. While she was applying cream to her face, she remembered what used to happen during those evenings and nights, and the thought depressed her. She didn't want to go back to that. Not because she loved Paulino

Morais; she would have no compunction about deceiving him, and the only reason she didn't was because she valued her security. She knew men too well to love any of them. Start over again? No! How often had she gone in search of a satisfaction she never received? She did it for the money, of course, and she got that because she deserved it. But how often had she emerged from one of those rooms feeling dissatisfied, offended, deceived! How often had the whole sequence been repeated—room, man, dissatisfaction! Later, it might be a different man, a different room, but the dissatisfaction never disappeared, never diminished.

On the marble top of the dressing table, among the bottles and jars, next to the photo of Paulino Morais, lay the second volume of *The Maias*. She leafed through it, looking for the passage she had marked with lipstick. She reread it, then slowly put the book down and, with her eyes fixed on her own reflection—where she saw a look of amazement reminiscent of her mother's—she rapidly reviewed her life: light and dark, farce and tragedy, dissatisfaction and deceit.

It was almost half past four by the time she had finished dressing. She looked very pretty. She had excellent taste in clothes and never wore anything outlandish. She had put on a gray tailored suit that gave her body a sinuous, supple shape, a body that obliged men in the street to stop and look. A combination of the miraculous skills of the dressmaker and the instincts of a woman who earns her living with her body.

She went down the stairs with a light step to avoid making too much noise with her heels. There were people outside Silvestre's apartment. The door stood wide open, and the cobbler was helping a young man carry in a large trunk. Out on the landing, Mariana was holding a smaller suitcase. Lídia greeted them:

"Good afternoon."

Mariana responded. Silvestre, in order to return her greeting, had to pause and look around. Lídia's gaze passed over his head and alighted with some curiosity on the face of the young man. Abel looked at her too. Seeing his new lodger's questioning expression, Silvestre smiled and winked at him. Abel understood.

8

When Adriana appeared around the corner, walking fast, the day was already growing dark and one could sense the night in the quiet onset of twilight, which all the noise of the city could not cancel out. She took the stairs two at a time, her heart protesting at the effort, then rang the bell frantically and waited with some impatience for her mother to open the door.

"Hello, Mama. Has it started yet?" she asked, kissing her mother on the cheek.

"Slow down, child, slow down. No, it hasn't started yet. Why all the rush?"

"I was afraid I might miss it. I was kept late at the office, typing some urgent letters."

They went into the kitchen. The lights were on. The radio was playing softly in the background. Isaura was still busy sewing, hunched over a pink shirt. Adriana kissed her sister and her aunt, then sat down to catch her breath.

"I'm absolutely exhausted! Good heavens, Isaura, what is that hideous thing you're making?"

Her sister looked up and smiled:

"The man who's going to wear this shirt must be a complete and utter idiot. I can see him now in the shop, gazing goggle-eyed at this 'thing of beauty,' ready to give the clothes off his back to pay for it!"

They both laughed. Cândida commented:

"You two don't have a good word to say about anyone!"

Amélia agreed with her nieces and, addressing Cândida, said:

"So, in your opinion, would it be a sign of good taste to wear a shirt like that?"

"People can dress as they like," said Cândida with unusual forthrightness.

"That's not an opinion!"

"Shh!" said Isaura. "Listen!"

The announcer was introducing a piece of music.

"No, that's not it," said Adriana.

There was a package next to the radio. Given the size and shape, it looked like a book. Adriana picked it up and asked:

"What's this? Another book?"

"Yes," said her sister.

"What's it called?"

"*The Nun.*"

"Who's the author?"

"Diderot. I've never read anything by him before."

Adriana put the book down and promptly forgot about it. She didn't care much for books. Like her sister, mother and aunt, she adored music, but she found books boring. They took pages and pages to tell a story that could have been told in just a few words. She couldn't understand how Isaura could spend so much time reading, sometimes into the small hours. With music, on the other hand, Adriana could happily sit up all night listening and never tire of it. And it was a pleasure they all enjoyed, which was just as well, because there would have been terrible arguments if they didn't.

"That's it," said Isaura. "Turn the volume up."

Adriana twiddled one of the knobs. The announcer's voice filled the apartment.

". . . *The Dance of the Dead* by Honegger.

Libretto by Paul Claudel. Performed by Jean-Louis Barrault."

In the kitchen, a coffeepot was whistling. Aunt Amélia removed it from the gas. They heard the sound of the needle being placed on the record, and then the stirring, dramatic voice of Jean-Louis Barrault made the four walls tremble. No one moved. They stared at the luminous eye on the front of the radio, as if the music were coming from there. In the interval between the first record and the second, they could hear, coming from the next room, the strident, grating, metallic sound of ragtime. Aunt Amélia frowned, Cândida sighed, Isaura stabbed her needle hard into the shirt, and Adriana shot a murderous glance at the wall.

"Turn it up," said Aunt Amélia.

Adriana did as asked. Jean-Louis's voice roared out *"J'existe!,"* the music swirled across the *"vaste plaine,"* and the jittery notes of ragtime mingled heretically with the dance *"sur le pont d'Avignon."*

"Louder!"

The chorus of the dead, in a thousand cries of despair and sorrow, declared their pain and remorse, and the Dies Irae smothered and overwhelmed the giggling of a lively clarinet. Blaring out of the loudspeaker, Honegger managed finally to vanquish that anonymous piece of ragtime. Perhaps Maria Cláudia had grown tired of her favorite program of dance tunes, or perhaps she had been frightened by the bellowing of divine fury made music. Once the last notes of *The Dance of the Dead* had dissolved in the air, Amélia, grumbling, set about making supper. Cândida moved away, fearing an approaching storm, even though she felt equally indignant. The two sisters, carried away by the music, were ablaze with holy anger.

"It just seems impossible," Amélia said at last. "I don't mean that we're better than other people, but it just seems impossible that anyone could possibly like that music of the mad!"

"But some people do, Aunt," said Adriana.

"I can see that!"

"Not everyone grows up listening to good music," added Isaura.

"I know that too, but surely everyone should be capable of separating the wheat from the chaff, putting the bad on one side and the good on the other."

Cândida, who was getting the dishes out of the cupboard, ventured to say:

"That's just not possible. The good and the bad, the bad and the good, are always intermingled. No one and nothing is ever completely good or completely bad. At least that's what I think," she added timidly.

Amélia turned to her sister, brandishing the spoon she was using to taste the soup.

"Now this soup is pretty good, and surely that's how you know if something is good, because you like it."

"Not necessarily."

"So why *do* you like it, then?"

"I like it because I *think* it's good, but I don't *know* it's good."

Amélia pursed her lips scornfully. Her sister's general inability to be sure of anything and to make fine distinctions grated on her practical common sense, her desire to divide the world into two clear halves. Cândida said nothing, regretting having spoken at all. Not that this subtle way of reasoning came naturally to her; she had learned it from her husband, simplifying its more problematic aspects.

"That's all very nice," Amélia went on, "but someone who knows what he wants, and what he has, runs the risk of losing what he has and not getting what he wants."

"How very confusing!" said Cândida, smiling.

Her sister was aware that she had been unnecessarily obscure, and this only irritated her all the more.

"It's not confusing, it's true. There is good music and bad music. There are good people and bad people. There is good and evil. And you can choose between them . . ."

"If only it were that easy. Often we don't know how to choose. We haven't learned how . . ."

"Some people can only choose evil, because they're naturally twisted!"

Cândida winced as if in pain, then said:

"You don't know what you're saying. That can only happen when people are mentally ill. We're talking about people who, according to you, are capable of making a choice. Someone as sick as that wouldn't be able to!"

"You're trying to trip me up, but you won't succeed. All right, let's talk about healthy people, then. I can choose between good and evil, between good music and bad!"

Cândida raised her hands as if about to launch into a long speech, but immediately lowered them again:

"Let's forget about music for the moment, because it's just getting in the way. Tell me, if you can, what is good and what is evil? Where does one end and the other begin?"

"I've no idea, there's no answer to that. What I do know is that I can recognize good and evil when I see them . . ."

"That depends on your particular point of view . . ."

"Of course it does. I can't make judgments using other people's ideas!"

"There's the sticking point! You're forgetting that other people have their own ideas about good and evil, ideas that might be better than yours . . ."

"If everyone thought like you, we would never

94

get anywhere. We need rules, we need laws!"

"But who makes them? And when? And why?"

Cândida paused for a moment before adding, with an innocently mischievous look:

"So when you think, are you using your own ideas or are you using rules and laws written by someone else?"

Having no answer to these questions, Amélia turned her back on her sister, saying:

"Oh, I should know by now that there's no talking to you!"

Isaura and Adriana smiled. This argument was merely the latest of many they had heard between those two poor old ladies, entirely restricted now to the domestic sphere, a long way from the days when they had broader, livelier interests, when their economic state allowed for such interests. There they were, lined and bent, gray and increasingly frail, their flickering fire throwing out its final sparks, resisting the accumulating ashes. Isaura and Adriana looked at each other and smiled again. In comparison to that crumbling old age, they felt young and vibrant, like a taut piano string.

Then they had supper. Four women sitting around the table. The steaming plates, the white tablecloth, the ceremonial of the meal. On this side—or perhaps on the other side too—of the inevitable noises lay a dense, painful silence, the inquisitorial silence of the past observing us and the ironic silence of the future that awaits us.

9

"Y ou don't look well, Anselmo!"
Anselmo tried to smile, an effort that really merited a better result. He was too caught up in his own thoughts to make proper use of the facial muscles involved in smiling. The face he made would have been comical had it not been for the evident pain in his eyes, which his mouth's muscular maneuvers failed to reach.

They were in the kitchen having lunch. On the table, Anselmo's watch showed him how much time remained of his lunch break. Its tiny tick-tock insinuated itself into the silence that followed Rosália's exclamation.

"Whatever's wrong?" she asked.

"Oh, nothing, a silly, piddling little problem."

Alone with his wife, Anselmo spoke somewhat more colloquially, and it never occurred to him that she might feel slighted by this. And, it must be said, Rosália did not.

"What 'piddling little problem' is that?"

"They've refused to give me an advance on my wages. And it's still ten days until the end of the month."

"I know, and I haven't got any money either. Today at the grocer's I had to pretend I'd forgotten my purse."

Anselmo slammed down his fork. His wife's words came like a slap in the face.

"Where on earth does the money go, that's what I'd like to know!" he said.

"I hope you don't think I waste it. My mother taught me to be frugal and I doubt there are many women more frugal than me."

"No one is saying you're not frugal, but we really ought to be able to manage better with two wages coming in."

"What Claudinha earns is barely enough for her to live on. And I'm not having a daughter of mine looking badly dressed."

"That's not what you say when she's around."

"Well, I don't want her getting ideas. I know what I'm doing."

Anselmo was finishing his last mouthful of food. He changed position, loosened his belt and stretched out his legs. The gray light of a rainy day sifted and sieved the shadows filling the covered balcony. Rosália, head bowed, continued to eat. At the other end of the table, Maria Cláudia's empty plate still waited.

Seeing Anselmo sitting there grave-faced, eyes fixed somewhere off in the distance, no one would have dared to suggest that he was not absorbed in thought. Beneath his shiny balding pate, slightly flushed from the digestive process, his brain was trying to squeeze out a few ideas, all of them with the same objective: how to get enough money to carry them through to the end of the month. However—possibly because the digestive process was getting in the way—Anselmo's brain signally failed to produce any useful ideas at all.

"Thinking will get you nowhere. We'll work something out," said Rosália encouragingly.

Her husband, who had been waiting for her to say those words in order to stop thinking about the whole discomfiting subject, eyed her angrily:

"Who's going to do the thinking if I don't?"

"But it's not good for you to go racking your brain just after lunch."

Anselmo made a grand despairing gesture and shook his head, like someone submitting to implacable Fate:

"You women have no idea what goes on inside a man's head!"

If Rosália had given him the necessary prompt, he would have plunged into a long soliloquy, setting out yet again his definitive ideas about the condition of men in general and office employees in particular. He did not have many ideas, but the few he had were "definitive." And his main idea, of which the others were mere satellites and consequences, was his avowed belief that money (to use his words) was the mainspring of life and that one could do whatever one had to in order to earn it, as long, that is, as one's dignity remained intact. This reservation was very important to Anselmo, who was a fervent believer in the importance of preserving one's dignity.

Rosália did not, however, give him the necessary prompt, not because she was fed up with hearing her husband's oft-repeated theories, but because she was entirely absorbed in studying his face, a face which, in profile, as it was now, resembled that of a Roman emperor. Anselmo's slight irritation at not being given the opportunity to hold forth was soothed by the respectful attention being bestowed on him. He considered his wife to be far beneath him, but feeling thus adored flattered him, so much so that when he saw the respect and awe in Rosália's eyes, he gladly renounced the pleasure of being able to demonstrate his superiority through words.

A sigh was heard: Rosália had achieved ecstasy, and the lyrical interlude was over. She descended from the lofty regions of adoration to more prosaic, earthly matters.

"Guess who's taken a lodger."

For Anselmo, the performance had not yet finished. He pretended surprise and asked:

"What?"

"I said, guess who's taken a lodger."

With the benevolent smile of an Olympian being who has agreed to descend to the plains, Anselmo asked:

"Who?"

"The cobbler. A young man this time, a very badly dressed one too."

"Oh well, birds of a feather . . ."

This was one of Anselmo's favorite sayings, indicating that one should hardly be surprised to find one ragamuffin living with another raga-muffin. However, what he said next was related to that other matter:

"We could do with a lodger here."

"If we had the room."

Since they didn't have the room, Anselmo was able to say:

"Oh, it was just an idea. I wouldn't really want to have an interloper living here . . ."

There were three short, sharp rings on the doorbell.

"That'll be Claudinha," said Anselmo. He glanced at the clock and added: "She's late."

When Maria Cláudia came in, the gloomy shadows in the kitchen got up and left. She was like the colorful cover of an American magazine, of the kind that prove to the world that in America no one and nothing is photographed without first being given a quick lick of paint. Maria Cláudia had unerring taste when it came to choosing the colors that best set off her youthful beauty. Presented with two similar tones, she would unhesitatingly, almost instinctively, choose the one that suited her best. The result was dazzling. Anselmo and Rosália—glum, dull-complexioned creatures dressed in somber out-fits—could never resist that influx of freshness.

And while they could not imitate her, they could admire her.

With the sixth sense of the incipient actress, she stood before her parents just long enough to seduce them with her elegance. She knew she was late, but didn't want to have to explain why. At just the right moment, she ran over to her father like a graceful bird and kissed him on the cheek. Then she spun around and fell into her mother's arms. As actors in the comedy of mistaken identities that was their life, all of this seemed so natural that neither of them even thought to express surprise.

"I am *so* hungry!" said Maria Cláudia, and without waiting, and still wearing her raincoat, she ran into her room.

"Take your coat off in here, Claudinha," said her mother. "You'll get everything wet."

No answer came, not that she had expected one. She made these observations and remarks without the faintest hope of her daughter paying any attention, but the mere fact of saying them gave her the illusion of maternal authority and chimed with her idea of how one should bring up one's children. And that authority remained undented despite the many defeats it suffered.

Anselmo's smug expression suddenly darkened. A flicker of distrust appeared in his eyes.

"Go and see what she's up to in there," he told his wife.

Rosália duly went and found her daughter peering down at the street from behind the curtains. Hearing her mother come in, Maria Cláudia turned, wearing a smile that was half impudent, half embarrassed.

"What are you doing? Why haven't you taken off your coat?"

Rosália went over to the window and opened it. Out in the street, immediately opposite, a boy was standing in the rain. She slammed the window shut and was about to tell her daughter off, but met with a pair of cold eyes, eyes that seemed to glitter with malice and rancor. She felt afraid. Maria Cláudia unhurriedly took off her raincoat. A few drops of water had made a wet patch on the rug.

"Didn't I tell you to take off your coat outside? Look at the state of this rug!"

Anselmo appeared at the door. Feeling safer in company, his wife burst out:

"The reason this young madam rushed in here was so she could stand at the window and see some foolish boy watching out there in the street. He probably walked her home, that's why she was late!"

Proceeding slowly across the room as if he were onstage and obeying the director's instructions, Anselmo went over to his daughter. Claudinha was standing with eyes downcast, but nothing about her indicated any shame or embarrassment.

102

Her calm demeanor seemed almost to repel. Her father, however, was too interested in what he was about to say to notice this.

"Now, Claudinha, you know perfectly well that this simply won't do. A young girl like you can't be seen walking the streets with a young man. What will the neighbors say? They have poisonous tongues, you know. Besides, such friendships never come to anything and can only compromise you. Who is the boy anyway?"

Silence from Maria Cláudia. Rosália, although seething with indignation, also said nothing. Confident of the dramatic effect his gesture would have, Anselmo placed one hand on his daughter's shoulder and went on in a slightly tremulous voice:

"You know we love you and only want what's best for you. You shouldn't be chasing after some insignificant young lad. There's no future in it. Do you understand?"

The girl looked up, made as if to free her shoulder from his hand and said:

"Yes, Papa."

Anselmo rejoiced; his pedagogical method never failed.

And so it was that, filled with this conviction, he left the house, protected from the increasingly heavy downpour and determined now to insist on being given an advance on his wages. The faltering domestic economy demanded it, and he, in his role as husband and father, deserved it.

10

Reclining on two pillows and still somewhat drugged with sleep, Caetano Cunha was waiting for his lunch. The light from the bedside lamp left half his face in darkness and emphasized the ruddy glow of his illuminated cheek. With a cigarette in one corner of his mouth, one eye half closed against the smoke, he looked like a villain from a gangster film whom the scriptwriter had abandoned in the inner room of some sinister house. To his right, on the dresser, the photograph of a little girl was smiling at him with unnerving concentration.

Caetano was not looking at the photo, therefore his smile had nothing to do with his daughter's. The smile in the photo bore no resemblance to his. The one in the photo was open and happy, and it was only its fixed quality that made one uneasy. Caetano's smile was lubricious, almost repellent. When grownups smile like that, they should not do so in the presence of children's smiles, even smiles in photographs.

After leaving work, Caetano had had a little "adventure," a sordid adventure—the kind he liked best. That's why he was smiling. He enjoyed the good things of life and enjoyed them twice over, once when he was experiencing them and again in retrospect.

Justina came in at that point and spoiled the second part of his pleasure. She entered carrying the lunch tray and placed it on her husband's lap. Caetano stared at her mockingly, his eyes bright. The lampshade was red and so the whites of his eyes glowed bloodily, reinforcing the malice in his gaze.

Justina was oblivious to his stare, just as she was to the fixity of her daughter's smile, having grown used to both. She returned to the kitchen, where a frugal, insipid, diabetic lunch awaited her. She ate alone. Her husband was never there for supper, except on Tuesdays, his day off; and at lunch they ate separately, he in bed and she in the kitchen.

The cat leapt up from his cushion beside the fireplace, where he had lain dreaming and drowsing. He arched his back and, tail aloft, rubbed against Justina's legs. Caetano called to him. The cat jumped onto the bed and stared at his owner, slowly twitching his tail. His green eyes, unaffected by the red light, were fixed on the plates of food on the tray. He was waiting for his friendliness to be rewarded. He knew perfectly well that the only thing he ever got from Caetano were beatings, but he nonetheless persisted. Perhaps in his cat brain he was curious to find out when, if ever, his owner would tire of hitting him. Caetano was not tired yet: he picked up a slipper and threw it. The cat was quicker than he and escaped in one bound. Caetano laughed.

The silence that filled the apartment from top to bottom, like a solid block, shattered at the sound of his laughter. Unaccustomed as it was to the noise, the furniture seemed to shrink in upon itself. The cat, forgetting that he was hungry, and still frightened by that loud guffaw, retreated once more into the oblivion of sleep. Justina remained unmoved, as if she had heard nothing. At home, she spoke only when necessary, and she did not consider it necessary to take the cat's part. She lived inside herself, as if she were dreaming a dream with no beginning or end, a dream about nothing and from which she did not wish to awaken, a dream composed of clouds that drifted silently past, covering a sky she had long since forgotten.

11

Her son's illness had completely disrupted Carmen's peaceful, lazy mornings. Henriquinho had been in bed for two days, suffering from mild tonsillitis. If she'd had her way, they would have called the doctor, but Emílio, thinking of the expense, said it wasn't worth it, that the illness wasn't that serious. A bit of gargling, a few applications of mercurochrome, lots of loving care, and their son would soon be up and about again. This provided Carmen with an opening to accuse Emílio of not caring about their child and, once in that accusatory mode, she seized the opportunity to give voice to her innumerable complaints. Emílio spent an entire evening listening to this litany of woes without saying a word. Finally, so that things did not become still more acrimonious and last long into the night, he agreed to do as his wife wanted. This unexpected agreement on his part had the effect of thwarting Carmen's permanent desire for contradiction. Accepting gracefully would mean that she then had nothing to complain about. She immediately went on the attack, with equal or greater vehemence, opposing the very position she had been defending. Weary and worn down, Emílio abandoned the fight, leaving it to his wife to make whatever decision she chose. This left her in something of a quandary: on the one hand, she wanted to call the doctor; on the other, she could not resist the desire to go against her husband's wishes, which would now mean *not* summoning the doctor. Unaware of this whole dispute, Henriquinho took the easiest way out and simply got better. Like any good mother, Carmen was pleased, but, deep down, she would not have minded some worsening of his condition (as long as Henriquinho was not in any real danger), just so her husband could see how reasonable and right she was.

Whatever the end result, however, she was

obliged to give up her lazy mornings for as long as Henriquinho lay ill in bed. She had to do the shopping before her husband went off to work and could not spend long about it either for fear of making him late. Had this not also involved some risk to the family budget, she would have leapt at the chance to play a nasty trick on her husband, but life was hard enough without making it worse purely for the sake of some mean-minded act of revenge. Even in this, Carmen felt that she was acting reasonably. Whenever she was alone and could give full vent to her despair, she would weep and feel sorry for herself because her husband did not recognize her many good qualities, while he, of course, had only faults: he was, in her view, either a frivolous spendthrift who took no interest in their home and child, or a self-centered bore with the permanently stricken air of someone who feels unloved and out of place. Early on in their marriage, Carmen had often asked herself what lay behind the constant friction between her and her husband. They had fallen in love like everyone else, they had loved each other, and then it had all ended, to be replaced by arguments, bickering and sarcastic remarks; but it was his air of victimhood that most enraged her. She was convinced now that her husband had a mistress, a girlfriend. That, in her view, was the source of all their marital disagreements. Men are like cockerels, who, even while they're treading one hen, already have their eye on the next.

That morning, very reluctantly because it was raining, Carmen went out to do the shopping. The apartment was suddenly peaceful, a small island surrounded by the silence emanating from their neighbors' apartments and by the soft murmur of rain. The building was enjoying one of those marvelous moments of quietness and tranquillity, as if it were inhabited not by flesh-and-blood creatures, but only by inanimate objects.

Emílio Fonseca, however, found nothing soothing about the quietness and peace surrounding him. Instead, he found it positively oppressive, as if the air had grown thick and suffocating. He was enjoying the pause, his wife's absence, his son's silence, but what weighed on him was the certainty that it was only a pause, a provisional calm, a postponement that resolved nothing. He was standing at the window that looked out onto the street, watching the gentle rain and smoking, although most of the time he merely played with the cigarette between his nervous fingers.

His son called to him from the next room. He put his cigarette down in an ashtray and went to see what he wanted.

"What is it?"

"I'm thirsty."

On the bedside table stood a glass of water. He

helped his son sit up and gave him a drink. Henrique swallowed carefully, grimacing with pain. He looked so weak and fragile from enforced fasting that Emílio felt his heart contract with fear. "What has he done to deserve this?" he thought. "Or indeed what have I done?" When Henrique had finished drinking, he lay down again and thanked his father with a smile. Emílio stayed where he was and sat on the edge of the bed, saying nothing and looking at his son. At first Henrique returned his gaze and seemed pleased to see him there. Moments later, though, Emílio realized that he was embarrassing the child. He glanced away and made as if to get up, but something stopped him. A new thought had entered his head. (Was it new? Or had he always brushed it aside because he found it too troubling?) Why did he feel so ill at ease with his son? Why was it that his son seemed so decidedly ill at ease with him? What was it that kept them apart? He took out his pack of cigarettes, then immediately put it away again, remembering that the smoke would be bad for Henrique's throat. He could have gone elsewhere to smoke, but he didn't. He again looked at his son, then blurted out the question:

"Do you love me, Henrique?"

This was such a strange question for his father to ask that the child responded lamely:

"Yes . . ."

"A lot?"

"Yes, a lot."

"Words," thought Emílio, "mere words. If I were to die now, he'd forget all about me within a year."

Emílio gave Henrique's toes an affectionate, absent-minded squeeze. Henrique found this funny and giggled—cautiously so as not to hurt his throat. Emílio squeezed harder, and Henrique, seeing that his father seemed happy, did not complain, although he was relieved when he slackened his grip.

"If I were to leave, would you be sad?"

"Yes . . ." murmured his son, perplexed.

"And would you then forget me?"

"I don't know."

What other answer could he expect? Of course the child didn't know if he would forget him. No one can know that he's forgetting someone until they're forgotten. If it were possible to know things beforehand, it would be so much easier to resolve all kinds of knotty problems. Again Emílio's hand reached for the pocket where he kept his cigarettes, but it stopped halfway and withdrew, as if it had forgotten what it was about to do. It wasn't only his hands that were confused. The expression on his face was that of someone who has reached a crossroads where there are no signposts, or only signs written in a strange, indecipherable language. All around lies the desert, and there's no one to tell us: "This is the way."

Henrique was looking at his father curiously. He had never seen him like this or known him to ask such questions.

Emílio's hands rose slowly, confidently this time. Palms uppermost, they were confirming what his mouth was saying:

"Of course you would forget me . . ."

He paused for a second, but an irrepressible desire to speak drove out all hesitancy. He wasn't sure if his son would understand him, but that didn't matter. He didn't even want him to understand. He would not necessarily choose words that were within his grasp. What he needed to do was talk and talk until he had said everything or had nothing more to say.

"Of course you would forget me, I'm sure of that. In a year from now, you would no longer remember me. Or perhaps it would take less time than that. After three hundred and sixty-five days of absence, my face would be a thing of the past. Later on, even if you saw a photo of me, you still wouldn't remember my face. And after still more time had passed, you wouldn't recognize me if I were standing right in front of you. Nothing about me would tell you that I am your father. For you I'm just a man you see every day, someone who gives you water when you're thirsty, a man your mother calls by his first name, a man your mother shares a bed with. You love me because you see me every day. You don't love me for who I am, you love me because of what I do or don't do. You don't know who I am. If I had been swapped for another man when you were born, you wouldn't even notice and you would love him just as you love me. And if I were to come back one day, it would take a very long time for you to get used to me. Indeed, despite the fact that I am your real father, you might still prefer the other one. You would see him every day too, and he'd take you to the movies like I do . . ."

Emílio had spoken almost without stopping, not looking at his son's face. Then, unable to resist the desire to smoke any longer, he lit a cigarette. He glanced at his son. He saw the look of astonishment on his face and felt sorry for him. But he still hadn't finished:

"You don't know who I am and you never will. No one knows . . . I don't know who you are either. We don't know each other. I could leave, and all you would lose are my wages . . ."

No, that wasn't what he really wanted to say. He breathed in the smoke and continued talking. As he spoke, the smoke emerged along with the words in short, articulated bursts. Henrique was watching the smoke intently, oblivious to what his father was saying:

"When you grow up, you'll want to be happy. You don't give a thought to that now, which is why you are happy. The moment you think about it, the moment you want to be happy, you will cease to be happy. Forever. Possibly forever. Do you hear? Forever. The stronger your desire to be happy, the unhappier you will be. Happiness isn't something you can conquer. People will tell you that it is. Don't believe them. Happiness either is or isn't."

This, too, led him far away from his objective. He again looked at his son and saw that his eyes were closed, his face calm, his breathing easy and regular. He had fallen asleep. Then, very softly, his eyes fixed on his son's face, Emílio murmured:

"I'm unhappy, Henrique, very unhappy. One day I will leave. I don't know when, but I know that I will. Happiness isn't something you conquer, but I want to try to conquer it anyway. I can't do that here. Everything has died. My life is a failure. I live in this house as if I were a stranger. I love you and possibly even your mother, but there's something missing. It's like living in a prison. Then there are all these rows, all this . . . Yes, one day I'll leave."

Henrique was sleeping deeply. A lock of fair hair lay across his forehead. His half-open mouth revealed small, bright teeth. His whole face was lit by a faint smile.

Suddenly Emílio felt his eyes fill with tears, quite why he didn't know. Then, distracted by the cigarette burning his fingers, he went back to the window. It was still raining, quietly, monotonously. When he thought about what he had said, he felt ridiculous. And imprudent too. His son would doubtless have understood something. He might tell his mother. He wasn't afraid of that, of course, but he didn't want any more scenes, more scoldings, more tears, more protests. He was tired, so tired. Yes, Carmen, I'm tired.

In the street, outside the window, he saw his wife pass by, barely protected from the rain by her umbrella. Emílio said again, out loud this time:

"Do you hear that, Carmen? I'm tired."

He went into the dining room to fetch his sample case. Carmen came in. They bade each other a cold goodbye. It seemed to her that her husband was leaving with suspicious haste, and she feared that something might have happened. Finding nothing untoward in her son's bedroom, she went into their bedroom and immediately spotted what it was. On the dressing table, next to the ashtray, lay the stub of a cigarette. When she brushed away the ash, she saw the burn mark on the wood. Her anger burst forth in the form of violent words. She overflowed with misery. She bemoaned the fate of the dressing table, her own fate, her own sad life. She mumbled these complaints in between sobs and sniffs. She looked around her, afraid she might find further signs of damage. Then, casting one fond, despairing look at the dressing table, she went back into the kitchen.

While she was preparing lunch, she was imagining what she would say to her husband. He needn't think it would stop there. Oh, she would tell him a thing or two, all right. If he wanted to spoil things, then he should spoil something that belonged to him, not the bedroom furniture bought with money given to them by her parents. So this was his way of saying thank you, was it, the ungrateful wretch!

"He always has to spoil everything," she was muttering as she walked back and forth between stove and table. "That's the only thing he knows how to do!" Senhor Emílio Fonseca, always so full of fine words! Her father had been quite right; he had never approved of the marriage. Why hadn't she married her cousin Manolo, who owned a brush factory in Vigo? She would be a lady now, the owner of a factory, with maids to do her bidding! Silly fool! She cursed the hour she had decided to come to Portugal to spend some time with her aunt Micaela! She had caused quite a sensation there. All the men had wanted to court her, and that had been her downfall. She had gloried in being so much more sought-after than she had been at home, and this was where her blindness had led her. Her father had told her: "*Carmen, eso no es hombre bueno!*" He's not a good man, Carmen. But she had refused to listen to his advice, had dug in her heels and rejected cousin Manolo and his brush factory.

She stood in the middle of the kitchen and wiped away a tear. She hadn't seen cousin Manolo for nearly six years and suddenly she missed him. She wept for all the good things she had lost. She would be the owner of a factory now, and Manolo had always been so smitten with her. *Ay, desgraciada, desgraciada*!

Henrique called out from his room. He had woken up. Carmen ran to his side.

"*¿Qué tienes? ¿Qué tienes?*"

"Has Papa gone?"

"Yes."

Henrique's lips began to tremble and, to his mother's astonishment—half resentful, half concerned—he began to weep slow, silent tears.

12

On the bench a pair of eviscerated shoes were crying out to be mended, but Silvestre pretended not to notice them and went and read the newspaper instead. He always read it from first page to last, from the editorial to the crime reports. He liked to keep up with international affairs and follow their development, and he had his own particular views on things. Whenever he turned out to be wrong, when what he had said was white turned out to be black, he would lay the blame squarely on the newspaper, which never published the most important items and altered or neglected others, with who knows what intentions! Today the newspaper was neither better nor worse than usual, but Silvestre could hardly bear to read it. He kept glancing impatiently at the clock. Then he would laugh at himself and go back to the paper. He tried to take an interest in the political situation in France and the war in Indochina, but his eyes slid over the lines and his brain refused to take in the meaning of the words. In the end, he flung down the paper and called to his wife.

Mariana appeared at the door, almost filling it with her vast bulk. She was drying her hands, having just finished the washing.

"Is that clock right?" he asked.

With infuriating slowness, Mariana studied the position of the hands.

"Yes, I think so . . ."

"Hm."

She waited for him to expand on that apparently meaningless grunt, but Silvestre merely snatched up the newspaper again. He felt himself observed and had to admit that there was something ridiculous or even childish about his impatience.

"Don't worry, he'll be here," Mariana said and smiled.

Silvestre looked up.

"Who do you mean? Oh, him. He's the least of it."

"So what are you so edgy about?"

"Me? Edgy? Honestly!"

Mariana's amused smile grew broader. Then Silvestre smiled too, realizing that he really was getting steamed up about nothing.

"That lad has me bewitched!"

"Bewitched, my eye! He's just found your weak spot—playing checkers. You're a hopeless case!" And she went back into the kitchen to starch some clothes.

Silvestre shrugged good-humoredly, again glanced at the clock, then rolled himself a cigarette to kill time. Half an hour went by. It was nearly ten o'clock. Silvestre was just thinking that he would have no alternative but to start work on those shoes when the doorbell rang. The door to the dining room, where he was sitting, opened onto the corridor. He picked up the newspaper, adopted a studious pose and pretended to be immersed in his reading. Inside, though, he was beaming with pleasure. Abel walked down the corridor, said "Evening, Senhor Silvestre" and continued on to his room.

"Good evening, Senhor Abel," answered Silvestre, then immediately abandoned the poor, weary newspaper and ran to set up the checkerboard.

Abel went into his room and made himself comfortable. He pulled on some old trousers, replaced his shoes with slippers and took off his jacket. He opened the suitcase where he kept his books, chose one, which he placed on the bed, and prepared to get down to work. No one else would call it work, but that's how Abel thought of it. He had before him the second volume of a French translation of *The Brothers Karamazov*, which he was rereading in order to clarify his thoughts after having read it for the first time. Before sitting down, he looked in vain for his cigarettes. He had smoked them all and forgotten to buy more. He left the room, quite prepared to get wet again rather than be left with nothing to smoke. As he passed the dining room door, he heard Silvestre ask:

"Going out again, Senhor Abel?"

Abel smiled and said:

"Yes, I've run out of cigarettes, so I'm just going down to the local bar to see if they have any."

"I've got some here. I don't know if it's to your taste, though, it's shag tobacco."

"Oh, that's fine by me. I'll smoke anything."

"Help yourself!" said Silvestre, offering him the tobacco pouch and the packet of cigarette papers.

In doing so, he revealed the checkerboard he had kept hidden until then. Abel glanced at Silvestre and caught a look of anguished embarrassment in his eyes. Beneath Silvestre's critical gaze, he quickly rolled himself a cigarette and lit it. Out of pride now, Silvestre was trying to conceal the checkerboard with his body. Abel noticed that the glass fruit bowl, which usually stood in the center of the table, had been pushed to one side and that opposite Silvestre stood an empty chair. The chair, he realized, was intended for him. He murmured:

"Do you know, I fancy a game of checkers. What about you, Senhor Silvestre?"

Silvestre felt a slight tingling in the tip of his nose, a sure sign of excitement. Without quite knowing why, he felt that he and Abel had, at that moment, become very good friends. He said:

"I was just about to say the same thing."

Abel went back to his room, put away his book and returned to the dining room.

Silvestre had already set out the pieces, placed the ashtray where Abel could reach it and had moved the table slightly so that the ceiling light wouldn't cast any shadows on the board.

They started playing. Silvestre was radiant. Abel, although less demonstrative, reflected Silvestre's contentment and continued to observe him intently.

Mariana finished her work and went to bed. The two men stayed on. At around midnight, after a particularly disastrous game for Abel, he declared:

"That's enough for tonight! You play much better than I do, I've learned that much!"

Silvestre looked slightly disappointed, but no more than that. They had been playing for quite a while and it would, he agreed, be best to stop.

Abel picked up the tobacco, rolled another cigarette and, looking around the room, asked:

"Have you lived here long, Senhor Silvestre?"

"A good twenty years. I'm the oldest tenant."

"And you obviously know the other tenants."

"Oh, yes."

"Decent people?"

"Some good, some bad. Well, it's the same the world over, isn't it?"

"Yes, it is."

Abel began absent-mindedly piling up the checkers, alternating white and black pieces. Then he knocked the pile over and asked:

"And the man next door, I assume, isn't one of the better ones."

"Oh, he's all right, just rather silent, and I don't usually like silent men, but he's not a bad sort. She's a real viper, though, and Spanish to boot."

"What's that got to do with it?"

Silvestre regretted the sneering way in which he had said the word "Spanish":

"I didn't mean it like that, but you know what they say: 'From Spain expect only cold winds and cold wives.'"

"Ah, so you don't think they get on, then?"

"I know they don't. You hardly hear a peep out of him, but she's got a voice on her like a foghorn—I mean, she talks really loudly."

Abel smiled at Silvestre's embarrassment and at his careful choice of vocabulary.

"What about the others?"

"Well, I don't understand the couple who live on the first floor left at all. He works for the local newspaper and is a real bastard. I'm sorry, but he is. She, poor thing, has looked as if she was at death's door for as long as I've known her. She gets thinner by the day."

"Is she ill?"

"She's diabetic, at least that's what she told Mariana. But unless I'm very much mistaken, I reckon she's got TB. Their daughter died of meningitis, and after that, the mother aged about thirty years. As far as I can see, they're a very unhappy pair. She certainly is . . . And as for him, like I said, he's a real brute of a man. I mend his shoes because I have a living to make, but if I had my way . . ."

"And next door to them?"

Silvestre smiled mischievously: he thought that his lodger's interest in the other neighbors was really an excuse to find out more about their upstairs neighbor, and so he was quite put out when he heard Abel add:

"Well, I know about her, of course. What about the top floor?"

This, Silvestre thought, was taking curiosity too far, and yet, although Abel kept asking questions, he didn't really seem that interested.

"On the top floor right lives a man I really can't abide. You could turn him upside down and shake him and you wouldn't get a penny out of him, but anyone looking at him would take him for a . . . for a capitalist."

"You don't seem to like capitalists," said Abel, smiling.

Distrust suddenly made Silvestre take a mental step back. He said very slowly:

"I don't like or dislike them really. It was just a manner of speaking."

Abel appeared not to hear.

"And the rest of the family?"

"The wife's a fool, it's always 'my Anselmo this' and 'my Anselmo that' . . . And the daughter, well, it's as clear as day that she's going to give her parents a fair few headaches later on. Especially since they absolutely dote on her."

"How old is she?"

"She must be about twenty now. We know her as Claudinha. And let's hope I'm wrong."

"And on the other side?"

"On the other side live four very respectable ladies. I think they had money once, but have fallen on hard times. They're educated folk. They don't stand on the landing gossiping, and that's quite something here. They keep themselves to themselves."

Abel was now amusing himself arranging the pieces into a square. When Silvestre fell silent, Abel looked up expectantly, but Silvestre didn't feel like saying anything more. It seemed to him there was some other motive behind his lodger's questions and, although he had said nothing compromising, he regretted having talked so much. He remembered his initial suspicions and cursed his own gullibility. Abel's remark about him not liking capitalists bristled with potential booby traps.

The silence between them made Silvestre feel uncomfortable, which bothered him, especially since Abel seemed perfectly at ease. He had lined up the pieces along the length of the table now, like steppingstones in a river. This childish game irritated Silvestre. When the silence became unbearable, Abel gathered the pieces together with exasperating care and then, out of the blue, asked:

"Why didn't you follow up my references, Senhor Silvestre?"

The question dovetailed so well with Silvestre's own thoughts that he sat stunned for a few seconds, not knowing what to say. The only way he could think of to gain time was to take two glasses and a bottle from a cupboard and say:

"Do you like cherry brandy?"

"I do."

"With a cherry or without?"

"With."

He filled their glasses while he was pondering what to say, but became so absorbed in getting the cherries out of the jar that, by the time he'd done so, he still hadn't come up with an answer. Abel sniffed his drink and said innocently:

"You haven't answered my question."

"Ah, yes, your question!" Silvestre's discomfort was obvious. "I didn't follow them up because . . . because at the time I didn't think it was necessary."

He said this in such a way that any attentive listener would understand that he now had his doubts. Abel understood.

"And do you still think that?"

Feeling cornered, Silvestre tried to go on the attack:

"You're a bit of a mind reader, aren't you, Senhor Abel?"

"No, I'm simply in the habit of listening to what people say and how they say it. It's not hard. Anyway, do you or do you not distrust me?"

"Why would I distrust you?"

"That's what I'm hoping to find out. I gave you the chance to check up on me, and you chose not to . . ." He took a sip of his drink, smacked his lips and, with his smiling eyes fixed on Silvestre, asked: "Or would you prefer me to tell you?"

Silvestre, his curiosity aroused, could not help leaning slightly forward in interested anticipation. Abel added:

"Although, of course, who's to say I'm not pulling the wool over your eyes?"

Silvestre suddenly understood how a mouse must feel when caught between the paws of a cat.

He had a strong desire to put the young man firmly in his place, but that desire quickly melted away and he didn't know what to say. Abel, however, as if he hadn't really expected an answer to either of his questions, went on:

"I like you, Senhor Silvestre. I like your home and your wife and I feel very comfortable here. I may not stay long, but when I leave, I will take some very good memories with me. I noticed from the very first day that you, whom I already, if I may, consider to be my friend . . . Am I right to do that?"

Silvestre, busy biting into his cherry, nodded.

"Thank you," said Abel. "I noticed a certain initial distrust, mainly in the way you looked at me. Whatever the reason for that distrust, I feel it's only fair that I should tell you about myself. It's true that, alongside that distrust, there was a touching warmth. I can still see that combination of warmth and distrust in your face . . ."

Silvestre's expression shifted from warmth to unalloyed distrust and back again, and Abel watched this putting on and taking off of masks with an amused smile.

"And there they both are. When I've finished telling you my tale, I hope to see only warmth. So let's get straight on with the story. May I take a little more of your tobacco?"

Silvestre had now eaten his cherry, but did not feel it necessary to respond. He was slightly put out by the young man's lack of ceremony and was afraid that, had he responded, he might have done so somewhat brusquely.

"It's rather a long story," said Abel, having lit his cigarette, "but I'll try and keep it short. It's getting late and I don't want to exhaust your patience. I'm twenty-eight now and have still not done my military service. I have no fixed profession, and you'll soon see why. I'm single and unattached and know the dangers and advantages of freedom and solitude and am equally at home with both. I've been living like this for twelve years, since I was sixteen. My memories of childhood are of no interest here, partly because I'm not yet old enough to enjoy recounting them, but also because they would do nothing to contribute to either your distrust or your warmth. I was a good student at junior and senior school. I was well liked by both classmates and teachers, which is quite rare. There was, I can assure you, nothing calculated about this; I neither flattered my teachers nor kowtowed to my classmates. Anyway, I reached the age of sixteen, at which point I . . . Ah, but I haven't yet told you that I was an only child and lived with my parents. You're free to imagine what you like now: that they both died in some disaster or that they separated because they could no longer bear to live with each other. You choose. It comes down to the same thing anyway: I was left alone. If you choose the second option, you'll say that I could have continued living with one of them. Imagine, then, that I didn't want to live with either of them. Perhaps because I didn't love them. Perhaps because I loved them both equally and couldn't choose between them. Think what you like, because, as I say, it comes to the same thing: I was left alone. At sixteen—can you remember being sixteen?—life is a wonderful thing, at least for some people. I can see from your face that, for you, life at that age wasn't wonderful at all. It was for me, unfortunately, and I say 'unfortunately' because it didn't help me at all. I left school and looked for work. Some relatives in the country asked me to go and live with them. I refused. I had taken a bite out of the fruit of freedom and solitude and wasn't prepared to let them take it away from me. I didn't know at the time how very bitter that fruit can be sometimes. Am I boring you?"

Silvestre folded his strong arms and said:

"You know very well you're not."

Abel smiled.

"You're right. Onward. For a sixteen-year-old boy who wants to set up on his own, but who knows nothing—and what I knew was as good as nothing—finding work isn't easy, even if you're not that choosy. And I wasn't choosy. I just grabbed the first thing that came my way, which was an ad for an assistant in a cake shop. There were a lot of applicants, I found out later, but the owner chose me. I was lucky. Perhaps my clean suit and my good manners helped. I tested this theory out later on, when I tried to find another job. I turned up looking like a scruffy, badly brought-up kid, and as people say nowadays, enough said. They hardly looked at me. Anyway, my wages at the cake shop just about kept me from starving, and I had accumulated enough reserves from sixteen years of being well fed to survive. When those reserves were exhausted, the only thing I could do was fill up on my boss's cakes. I can't so much as look at a cake now without wanting to throw up. Could I have another cherry brandy?"

Silvestre filled his glass. Abel took a sip and went on:

"If I keep going into so much detail, we'll be here all night. It's past one o'clock already, and I'm only on my first job. I've had loads, which is what I meant when I said that I have no fixed profession. At the moment, I'm clerk of works on a building site over in Areeiro. Tomorrow, I don't know what I'll be. Unemployed possibly. It wouldn't be the first time. I don't know if you've ever been without work, without money or a place to live. I have. Once, it coincided with a medical inspection to see if I was fit enough to do my military service. I was in such a debilitated state that they rejected me outright. I was one of those men the nation did not want. I didn't care, to be honest, although a couple of years of guaranteed bed and board does have its attractions. I managed to get a job shortly afterward, though. You'll laugh when I tell you what it was. I was employed as a salesman, selling a marvelous tea that could cure all ills. Funny, don't you think? You certainly would've found it funny if you'd heard me talking about it. I have never lied so much in my life, and I hadn't realized how many people are prepared to believe lies. I traveled all over the country, selling my miraculous tea to whoever would believe me. I never felt guilty about it. The tea didn't do any harm, I can assure you, and my words gave such hope to those who bought it that I reckon they might still owe me money, because hope is beyond price . . ."

Silvestre nodded in agreement.

"You agree, don't you? Well, there you have it, there hardly seems any point in telling you much more about my life. I've been cold and starving. I've known excess and privation. I've eaten like a wolf who can't be sure he'll catch anything tomorrow and I've fasted as if determined to starve myself to death. And here I am. I've lived in every part of this city. I've slept in dormitories where you can count the fleas and the bedbugs in their millions. I've even set up 'home' with certain good ladies of whom there are hundreds in Lisbon. Apart from the cakes I stole from my first employer, I've only ever stolen once, and that was in the Jardim da Estrela. I was hungry, and as someone who knows what hunger is, I can safely say that I had never been that hungry before. A pretty little girl came over to me. No, it's not what you're thinking. She was only about four years old at most. And if I describe her as pretty, that's perhaps to make up for having robbed her. She was carrying a slice of bread and butter, almost uneaten. Her parents or her nursemaid must have been around somewhere, but I didn't even think about that. She didn't scream or cry, and a few moments later I was standing behind the church eating my bread and butter . . ."

There was a glimmer of tears in Silvestre's eyes.

"And I've always paid my rent, so you don't need to worry about that."

Silvestre shrugged. He wanted Abel to go on talking, because he liked listening to him and, more than that, he still didn't know how to answer his question. There was something he wanted to ask, but he feared it might be too soon to do so. Abel preempted him:

"This is only the second time I've told anyone this story. The first time was to a woman. I thought she would understand, but women never understand anything. I was wrong to tell her. She wanted to settle down and thought she could hold on to me. She was wrong about that. I don't even know why I've told my story to you now. Perhaps because I like your face, perhaps because I haven't spoken about it for some years and needed to get it off my chest. Or perhaps for some other reason. I don't know . . ."

"You told me so that I would stop distrusting you," said Silvestre.

"No, it wasn't that. Plenty of people have distrusted me, but never heard my story. It was possibly the lateness of the hour, the game of checkers, the book I would be reading if I hadn't joined you in here. Who can say? Whatever the reason, you now know all about my life."

Silvestre scratched his unruly head of hair with both hands. Then he filled his glass and drank it down all at once. He wiped his mouth with the back of his hand and asked:

"Why do you live like this? And forgive me if I'm being indiscreet . . ."

"No, not at all. I live like this because I want to. I live like this because I don't want to live any other way. Life as other people understand it has no value for me. I don't want to be trapped, and life is an octopus with many tentacles. It just takes one to trap a man. Whenever I start to feel trapped, I cut off the tentacle. Sometimes that's painful, but there's no other way. Do you understand?"

"I understand perfectly, but that doesn't lead anywhere useful."

"I'm not interested in usefulness."

"You must have hurt a few people along the way."

"I've done my best not to, but when there's no alternative, I don't hesitate."

"You're a hard man!"

"Hard? No, I'm really fragile. And it's probably my fragility that makes me avoid any ties that bind. If I give myself, if I allow myself to be trapped, I'll be lost."

"But one day . . . Look, I'm an old man, and I have experience of life . . ."

"So do I."

"Mine is the experience of many years . . ."

"And what does it tell you?"

"It tells me that life, as you said, does indeed have many tentacles, but however often you cut them off, there's always one that resists, and that's the one that ends up getting a hold of you."

"I didn't think you were so . . . how can I put it?"

"Philosophical? As someone once said, all cobblers have a little of the philosopher in them . . ."

They both smiled. Abel looked at the clock:

"It's two in the morning, Senhor Silvestre. It's long past our bedtime. But first I wanted to say something else. I started living like this on a whim, I continued out of conviction, and I continue still out of curiosity."

"I don't understand."

"You will. I have a sense that life, real life, is

hidden behind a curtain, roaring with laughter at our efforts to get to know it. And I want to know life."

Silvestre gave a gentle, slightly weary smile:

"But there's so much to do on this side of the curtain, my friend. Even if you lived for a thousand years and experienced everything that everyone had experienced, you would never know life!"

"You may be right, but it's still too early to give up the struggle."

He got to his feet and held out his hand to Silvestre:

"See you tomorrow!"

"Yes, see you tomorrow . . . my friend."

Left alone, Silvestre slowly rolled a cigarette. The same gentle, weary smile was on his lips. He was staring down at the tabletop, as if figures from a distant past were moving across it.

13

From Adriana's diary:

Sunday, 3/23/52, half past ten at night. It's been raining all day. You would never know it was spring. I remember lovely spring days when we were children and they started being lovely from March 21st onward. It's the 23rd now and it's done nothing but rain. Maybe it's the weather, but I don't feel at all well. I haven't even been out. My mother and aunt went to visit some cousins in Campolide after lunch. They arrived home soaked to the skin. My aunt was in a bad mood because of something that was said, I've no idea what. They brought some cakes back for us, but I didn't eat any. Isaura didn't want them either. It's been a really boring day. Isaura has barely put down the book she's reading. She carries it around with her everywhere, as if she didn't want anyone else to look at it. I've been embroidering a sheet for my trousseau. Sewing the lace onto the sheet takes ages, but there's no hurry. I might never use it. I feel sad. If I'd known I was going to feel like this, I would have gone with them to Campolide. It would have been better than spending the day here. I feel like crying. It can't be because of the rain. It rained yesterday too. It's not because of him either. At first I found it hard to spend Sundays without seeing him. Not anymore. I'm pretty sure now that he doesn't care for me. If he did, he wouldn't make those phone calls in the office. Unless he wants to make me jealous. Oh, I'm so stupid. Why would he want to make me jealous when he doesn't even know I like him? And why would he like me anyway, when I'm so ugly? Yes, I know I'm ugly, I don't need anyone to tell me. When people look at me, I know what they're thinking. I'm better than the other girls, though. Beethoven was ugly too, and no woman ever loved him, and he was Beethoven! He didn't need to be loved in order to do what he did. He just needed to love and he did. If I'd been alive in his day, I would have kissed his feet, and I bet none of those pretty women would have done that. In my view, pretty women don't want to love, they just want to be loved. Isaura says I don't understand these things. Perhaps it's because I don't read novels. The fact is, though, she seems to under-stand about as much as I do, despite all the novels she's read. I think she reads too much. Take today, for example. Her eyes were red, as if she'd been crying. And she was so edgy. I've never seen her like that before. At one point, I touched her on the arm, just to say something or other, and she almost screamed. It quite frightened me. Later on, I came in from the bedroom and there she was, reading. (I think she had finished the book and started again from the beginning.) She had such a strange

137

look on her face, a look I've never seen before on anyone's face. It was as if she were in pain, but happy too. No, not happy. How can I put it? It was as if the pain gave her pleasure, or as if the pleasure caused her pain. Oh, I'm not making any sense today. My brain isn't working. Everyone else has gone to bed now. I'm going too. What a miserable day! Roll on tomorrow!

The extract from *The Nun* by Diderot that Isaura had read that night:

My Superior began to fall victim to nerves. She lost her gaiety, and her plumpness, and slept badly. The following night, when everybody was asleep and the House was silent, she got up. After having wandered for some time about the corridors, she came to my cell. I was sleeping lightly and thought I recognized her step. She stopped. Apparently she rested her head against the door, and in so doing made enough noise to wake me up if I were asleep. I remained quiet, and I thought I heard a voice which wailed, somebody who sighed. I shivered slightly and determined to say *Ave*. Instead of answering, whoever it was withdrew. But she came back some time afterward: the wails and sighs began again. I again said *Ave*, and the steps again withdrew. I reassured myself and fell asleep. While I slept, someone came in and sat down beside my bed. The curtains were partly withdrawn. She had a little candle, the light of which fell on my face, and she who carried it watched me sleeping: so I judged at least from her attitude when I opened my eyes. And this person was the Superior.

I sat up suddenly. She saw that I was frightened and said: "You need not be alarmed, Suzanne, it is I." I put my head back on my pillow and said: "Mother, what are you doing here at this hour? What can have brought you? Why are you not asleep?"

"I cannot sleep," she answered. "I shall not sleep for a long time yet. I am tortured by horrid dreams. No sooner are my eyes closed than I live in imagination through all the agonies you have experienced. When I picture you in the hands of those inhuman monsters I see your hair falling over your face, your feet bleeding, the torch in your hand, the rope round your neck: I feel they are going to take away your life: I shiver and tremble: my whole body breaks into a cold sweat: I want to run and help you: I wake up screaming and wait in vain for the return of sleep. This is what has happened to me tonight. I feared Heaven was announcing that some misfortune had come to my friend: I got up and came to your door and listened. You did not seem to be sleeping: you spoke and I withdrew: I came back, you spoke again, and I withdrew again. I came back a third time, and when I thought you were asleep, I came in. I have been at your side some time and have been afraid to wake you. I hesitated at first to draw aside your curtains. I wanted to go away for fear of disturbing you. But I could not resist the desire to see if my dear Suzanne was well. I looked at you. How lovely you are even when you are asleep . . ."

"How good you are, Mother."

"I am quite cold. But now I know that I need not worry about my child. I think I shall get to sleep. Give me your hand." I gave it to her.

"How calm your pulse is! How regular! Nothing disturbs it!"

"I sleep quietly."

"How lucky you are!"

"You will get colder than ever."

"You are quite right; goodbye, my darling, goodbye. I am going away."

Still she did not go at all, but continued

looking at me. Two tears rolled down her cheeks. "Mother," I said, "what is the matter? What has happened? You are crying. I am so sorry I told you of my misfortunes." At that moment, she shut the door, blew out the candle, threw herself upon me. She held me in her arms. She was lying on the coverlet beside me. Her face was pressed to mine, her tears damped my cheeks. She sighed and said to me in a disturbed, choking voice: "Pity me, my darling."

"Mother," I said, "what is the matter? Are you ill? What can I do?"

"I am shivering and trembling," she said. "I have turned mortally cold."

"Would you like me to get up and give you my bed?"

"No," she said, "you need not get up. Just pull the coverlet aside a little that I may get near you. Then I shall get warm and be well."

"But that is forbidden, Mother dear! What would people say if they knew? I have seen nuns given penance for much less serious things than that. At St. Mary's a nun happened to pass the night in another's cell; she was her particular friend, and I cannot tell how badly it was thought of. The Director asked me sometimes if nobody had ever suggested coming and sleeping by my side, and warned me gravely never to tolerate it. I even spoke to him of your caresses. I thought them quite innocent, but he did not think so at all. I do not know how I came to forget his advice. I had meant to speak to you of it."

"Everything round us is asleep, darling," she said. "Nobody will know anything about it. It is I who distribute rewards and penalties, and, whatever the Director may say, I cannot see what harm there can be in one friend taking in beside her another friend who has felt upset, woken up, and has come during the night, despite the rigor of the season, to see if her darling was in any danger. Suzanne, at your parents' have you never shared a bed with your sisters?"

"No, never."

"If the occasion had arisen you would not have scrupled to do so? If your sister had come frightened and stiff with cold to ask for a place by your side, would you have refused her?"

"I think not."

"But am I not your Mother?"

"Yes, you are, but it is forbidden."

"Darling, it is for me to forbid it to

others, to allow it to you and to ask it of you. Let me warm myself a moment and I will go away. Give me your hand . . ."

I gave it to her.

"Come," she said, "touch me and see. I am trembling, shivering, and like marble."

It was quite true.

"My poor Mother will be ill," I said. "See, I will go to the edge of the bed, and you can put yourself in the warm place."

I went to the edge, lifted up the coverlet, and she got into my place. How ill she was! She was trembling in every limb. She wanted to talk to me and come nearer. She could not articulate or move. She said in a low voice: "Suzanne, dear, come a bit nearer . . ."

She stretched out her arms: I turned my back on her; she took me quietly and pulled me towards her. She passed her right arm under my body and the left over it, and said: "I am frozen; I am so cold that I am frightened to touch you, for fear of doing you some harm."

"Don't be afraid, Mother."

She immediately put one of her hands on my breast and another round my waist. Her feet were under mine and I pressed them to warm them, and she said: "See how quickly my feet have got warm, darling, now that nothing separates them from yours."

"But what prevents you warming yourself elsewhere in the same way?"

"Nothing, if you are willing . . ."

Suddenly there were two violent knocks on the door. In terror I immediately threw myself out of the bed on one side and the Superior threw herself out on the other. We listened and heard someone gaining the neighboring cell on tiptoe. "Oh," I said, "it is Sister Theresa. She must have seen you passing in the corridor and coming in to me. She must have listened to us and overheard our conversation. What will she say?"

I was more dead than alive.

"Yes, it is she," said the Superior in an exasperated voice. "It is she: I have no doubt of it. But I hope she will not easily forget her rashness."

"Mother," I said, "do not do her any harm."

"Suzanne, goodbye, goodnight. Get into bed again and sleep well. I dispense you from prayers. I am now going to see this young fool. Give me your hand."

I stretched it to her from one side of the bed to the other. She pulled back the sleeve which covered my arms, and with a sigh kissed it along from the end of my fingers to my shoulder; then she went out protesting that the rash girl who had dared disturb her should not forget it. Immediately, I went to the other end of my bed near the door and listened. She went into Sister Theresa's cell. I was tempted to get up and go and interpose between them, supposing a violent scene occurred. But I was so upset, so ill at ease, that I preferred to remain in bed: I said nothing however. I thought that I should become the talk of the House, and that this adventure in which there was nothing that could not be easily explained would be recounted in all its most unfavorable aspects: that it would be worse here than at Longchamps, where I was accused of I know not what: that our fault would come to the knowledge of our superiors: that our Mother would be deposed and both of us severely punished. Meanwhile, I was all ears, and waited impatiently for the Mother to leave Sister Theresa's cell.

Apparently the matter was difficult to arrange, as she remained there nearly all night.

14

Despite his long years of training to become a respectable gentleman of few words and measured gestures, Anselmo had one weakness: sport, or to be exact, sports statistics, or to be even more precise, soccer statistics. Entire seasons came and went without him going to a single match, although he never missed an international game, and only a grave illness or a recent bereavement would prevent him seeing a match between Portugal and Spain. He would subject himself to the worst indignities in order to buy a ticket on the black market, and if he ever had any spares, he could not resist doing a little speculation, buying them for twenty escudos and selling them for fifty. He was careful, however, not to do such deals at the office. As far as his colleagues were concerned, he was a serious fellow who listened with a wry smile to their post-match Monday-morning debates, a man who only had eyes for the serious side of life, who considered sport to be suitable entertainment for apprentices and waiters. There was no point asking him for facts and figures or about trades or famous dates in the annals of Portuguese soccer or to name the various national squads who had played between 1920 and 1930. But, he said, he had a cousin who, poor thing, was mad about the game. If they wanted, he could ask his cousin when they next met up and he would be sure to know the answer. Anselmo delighted in his colleagues' eager anticipation. He would leave them waiting for days and days, saying that he hadn't seen his cousin for a while or that things were a bit tense between them or that his cousin had finally agreed to consult his records, but all these lies were merely delaying tactics designed to strain his colleagues' patience further. There were often bets at stake. Excited Benfica fans and excited Sporting fans were waiting to hear Anselmo give his ruling. At home in the evening, Anselmo would search for the desired fact among his meticulously kept statistics, his precious newspaper cuttings, and then, the following day, having first carefully positioned his glasses on his nose—for he now needed reading glasses—he would proffer, as if *ex cathedra*, the disputed fact or result. This admirable cousin of his did as much for Anselmo's reputation as did his professional competence, his circumspect air and his exemplary punctuality. Had such a cousin existed, Anselmo, although always in firm control of his emotions, would have embraced him, because it was thanks to him (or so everyone thought) that he was able to give the manager a detailed report of the second Portugal–Spain match in 1922, from the number of spectators to the makeup of the teams, their respective team colors and the names of the referee and the line judges. It was thanks to that information that he had finally managed to get an advance on his wages and had in his jacket pocket the three one-hundred-escudo notes that would cover expenses until the end of the month.

Sitting between his wife and daughter, both of whom were busily sewing, Anselmo, his fact sheets spread out on the dining room table, was savoring this victory. Finding that he did not have the names of the substitutes selected for the third Portugal–Italy match, he decided that he would write the next day to the information desk of a sports newspaper and find out.

He could not, alas, forget that the three hundred escudos would be deducted from that month's wages, and this rather soured his joy. He could, at most, hope to be allowed to pay back the debt in installments. The worst thing was that any deduction from his wages, however small, threw a large monkey wrench in the works of the household budget.

While Anselmo was pondering these thoughts, the radio was blaring out the most blatantly plangent, painful, piercing *fado* ever to emerge from a Portuguese throat. As everyone knew, Anselmo was no sentimentalist, but even he was profoundly moved by this lament. His feelings had much to do with the terrible prospect of that deduction from his wages at the end of the month.

Rosália paused, needle in the air, and suppressed a sigh. Maria Cláudia, although apparently unmoved, was following the words of that unhappy love spilling forth from the loudspeaker and softly repeating them to herself.

What remained after the singer's final "Ay!" resembled the atmosphere at the end of a Greek tragedy or, in more modern terms, the air of suspense to be found in certain American films. Another song like that and those three normally healthy people would be transformed into hopeless neurotics. Fortunately, the broadcast was coming to an end. There were a few bits of news from abroad, a summary of the schedule for the following day, and then Rosália turned up the volume slightly to hear the twelve chimes at midnight.

Anselmo stroked his bald head and declared, as he was putting away his papers in the china cabinet:

"Midnight. Time for bed. Tomorrow we have to work."

At these words, everyone stood up. And this flattered Anselmo, who saw in these small things the excellent results of his methods of domestic education. He prided himself on having a model family and believed, moreover, that this was entirely his doing.

Maria Cláudia planted two smacking kisses on her parents' cheeks. With the evening newspaper dangling from his fingertips—a little bedtime reading before lights-out—Anselmo set off down the corridor. Rosália stayed on, tidying away her and her daughter's sewing. She straightened the chairs around the table, put a few other objects back in their proper places and, once she was certain everything was in order, followed her husband.

When she went into the bedroom, he peered at her over the top of his glasses, then continued reading. Like every good Portuguese citizen, he had his favorite soccer clubs, but was happy to read reports of all the matches, albeit only as a source of more statistical material. Whether they played well or badly was their business. What mattered was knowing who scored the goals and when. What mattered was what history would record.

According to a tacit agreement between them both, Anselmo did not lower his newspaper when Rosália was getting undressed for bed. To do so would, in his view, be undignified. She, on the other hand, might have seen nothing wrong with it. Once undressed, she lay down without her husband having glimpsed so much as her toes. That was the dignified, decent way to do things.

He turned off the bedside lamp. A fringe of light was still visible underneath the door opposite. Anselmo saw it and called:

"Lights out, Claudinha!"

Seconds later, the light went off. Anselmo smiled in the darkness. It was so good to be respected and obeyed! Darkness, however, is the enemy of smiles and always suggests grave thoughts. Troubled, Anselmo tossed and turned. Beside him, pressed against him, his wife's body snuggled into the soft mattress.

"Whatever's wrong?" asked Rosália.

"It's that advance they gave me," muttered Anselmo. "They'll take it off my wages at the end of the month and then we'll be back to square one."

"Can't you pay it off in installments?"

"The boss doesn't like that."

The sigh that had been trapped inside Rosália's breast ever since the *fado* had ended finally burst forth and filled the apartment. Anselmo could not repress a sigh either, albeit a less exuberant, more manly one.

"But what if they were to give you a raise," suggested Rosália.

"Oh, they're not going to do that. They're even talking about getting rid of people."

"Goodness! I hope they don't get rid of you!"

"Me?" said Anselmo, as if this were the first time he had considered such an eventuality. "No, it won't happen to me. I'm one of the oldest employees there . . ."

"Things are so bad at the moment, though. All you hear now are complaints."

"It's the international situation . . . ," began Anselmo.

But he stopped. What was the point of getting on his soapbox and giving a speech about the international situation in the dark and with the problem of that advance still unresolved?

"I'm worried they might sack Claudinha. I know the five hundred escudos she earns isn't much, but every little bit helps."

"Five hundred escudos! A pittance!" muttered Anselmo.

"Maybe, but I just hope we don't have to do without it."

Then she fell silent, seized by an idea. She was about to tell her husband, but decided to approach the subject obliquely:

"Couldn't you find her another job with one of your acquaintances?"

Something in his wife's voice alerted Anselmo to the possibility of a trap.

"What do you mean?" he asked.

"What else would I mean?" she said casually. "It's a perfectly simple question."

Anselmo could see that it was a simple question, but he could see, too, that his wife had something else in mind. He decided not to make things too easy for her.

"And who was it who got her the job she has now? It was you, wasn't it?"

"But couldn't we find her something better?"

Anselmo did not reply. He would get his wife to tell him her idea by dint of force or guile. Silence was the best tactic. Rosália shifted in bed. She turned toward her husband, her slightly plump belly pressed against his hip. She tried to drive away the idea, certain that Anselmo would vehemently reject it, but the idea kept coming back, stubborn and seductive. Rosália knew she wouldn't be able to sleep until she had told him her idea. She cleared her throat so as to make the murmur that followed more audible:

"I just thought . . . and I know you'll be angry with me, but I just thought I could perhaps have a word with Dona Lídia downstairs."

Anselmo saw immediately what his wife was leading up to, but preferred to pretend otherwise:

"Why? I don't understand."

As if physical contact might reduce the expected indignant reaction, Rosália moved closer. Years before, that movement would have had a very different meaning.

"I just thought . . . given that we get on well with her, that she might consider . . ."

"I still have no idea what you mean."

Rosália was sweating now. She moved away again and, without pausing to choose her words, blurted out:

"She could ask the man who visits her. He's a director or something of an insurance company and he might have some suitable post for Claudinha."

Had Anselmo's indignation been genuine, it

would have burst forth at that very first sentence. Instead, he waited until she had finished, and then he reacted only very quietly, because the night obliges us to speak softly:

"I can't believe you could suggest such a thing! You want us to go and ask a favor from that . . . that woman? Have you no dignity? I would never have expected you, of all people, to come up with such an idea!"

Anselmo was going too far, which would have been fine if, deep down, he did not agree with her suggestion. He didn't seem to realize that, by speaking in those terms, he was making his eventual acquiescence even more illogical and his wife's further promotion of the idea near impossible.

Offended, Rosália moved farther off. Between them lay a small space that could have been leagues. Anselmo saw that he had overstepped the mark. The ensuing silence made them both feel awkward. They knew the matter had to be resolved, but said nothing: she was thinking about how best to broach the subject again, and he was struggling to find a way to make surrender easier, despite what he had just said. Meanwhile, they both knew that they would not be able to sleep until some solution had been found. Anselmo made the first move:

"All right, we'll think about it . . . I don't like the idea at all, but . . ."

15

As comfortably installed as if he were in his own house, Paulino Morais crossed his legs and lit a cigarillo. When Lídia moved the ashtray closer to him, he smiled his thanks and leaned back again in the maroon armchair, which was "his" armchair on the nights when he visited. He sat there in his shirtsleeves. He was plump and red-faced. His small eyes bulged slightly as if under pressure from his fleshy eyelids. His thick, straight eyebrows met over his nose, whose sharpness was softened by a layer of fat. He had large, prominent, bristle-filled ears. He allowed the hair on the side of his head to grow long enough to be combed carefully over his otherwise bald pate. He had the prosperous air of a fifty-year-old in possession of old money and a young wife. Through the cloud of perfumed smoke surrounding him, his whole face oozed smug contentment; he wore the look of someone who has eaten well and is quietly, easily digesting his food.

He had just recounted a particularly amusing anecdote and was enjoying Lídia's laughter, and not just her laughter. He was in an excellent mood, and this led him mentally to congratulate himself on the idea he'd had, sometime before, about what clothes Lídia should wear when he visited her. Feeling slightly spent and worn down by excess and age, he had decided that he needed some new stimuli and that what his mistress wore could be one such stimulus. No male fantasies, nothing pornographic, as he had known some of his friends to indulge in, just something simple and natural. Lídia was to receive him wearing a low-cut negligee, with her arms bare and her hair loose. The negligee had to be made of silk, not so transparent as to reveal everything, but transparent enough not to hide everything either. The result was a kind of chiaroscuro effect that inflamed his brain on those nights when he was in the mood or merely pleased his eye when he was tired.

Lídia resisted at first, then decided it was best to submit. All men have their eccentricities, and this was certainly not the worst she had known. So she gave in, especially when he bought her an electric heater. In a warm room, she was less likely to catch cold in those skimpy outfits.

She was sitting on a low stool, leaning toward her lover, showing him her braless breasts, which was how he liked them. She knew that the only thing that bound him to her was her body, and so she took every opportunity to show it off, especially now, when her body was still young and shapely. After all, there wasn't much difference between exhibiting it here or on the beach, apart from the arousing nature of the clothes she was wearing and her provocative position.

When the evening went no further than having to exhibit herself in that flimsy attire, she thought the sacrifice well worth the bother and Paulino Morais's tastes perfectly reasonable. And if things did go further, as she always hoped they would not, she simply resigned herself to it.

She had been living at his expense for three years now. She knew all his tics and idiosyncrasies and gestures. The gesture she feared most was when he, still seated, unbuttoned both his braces at the same time. Lídia knew what this meant. She was quite relaxed at the moment, though: Paulino Morais was smoking, and for as long as his cigarillo lasted, his braces would remain safely buttoned.

In a graceful gesture that emphasized the beauty of her neck and shoulders, Lídia turned to look at the small faience clock. Then she got up, saying:

"It's time for your coffee."

Paulino Morais nodded. On the marble-topped dressing table, the coffeepot stood ready and waiting. Lídia lit the little burner and placed it underneath the pot, then prepared the cup and the sugar bowl. While she was walking to and fro in the room, Paulino Morais followed her with his eyes, ogling her long legs, which were visible beneath the light fabric that clung voluptuously to her hips. He mentally yawned and stretched. He had nearly finished his cigarillo.

"Guess who asked me for a favor today," Lídia said.

"A favor?"

"Yes, my upstairs neighbors."

"What did they want you to do?"

Lídia was waiting for the water to rise up the funnel into the coffee grounds.

"Not me, you."

"Oh, please! What do they want, Lili?"

Lídia shuddered. Lili was the pet name he used when he was feeling amorous. The water began to boil, and as if being sucked up from above, it rose into the upper chamber of the pot. Lídia filled his cup, added just the right amount of sugar and gave it to him. Then she sat down again on the stool and said:

"You may not know it, but they have a nineteen-year-old daughter. She has a job, but according to her mother, she doesn't earn very much. They asked me to ask you if you could find her something better."

Paulino put his cup down on the arm of his chair and lit another cigarillo.

"And you'd like me to grant this favor, would you?"

"I wouldn't be talking to you about it if I didn't."

"It's just that I have all the staff I need . . . too

many, in fact. Besides, I'm not the only one who makes these decisions."

"But if you wanted to . . ."

"There's the board of directors . . ."

"But if you really wanted to . . ."

Paulino picked up his cup again and took a sip. It seemed to Lídia that he wasn't very keen to help. She felt rather hurt. This was the first time she had ever asked him for such a favor and she could see no reason why he should refuse. Besides, given her irregular situation and the fact that everyone in the building looked down their noses at her, she would like to find a job for Maria Cláudia, because Rosália would be so pleased she'd be sure to tell everyone, and that would give Lídia a certain prestige among the other neighbors. The near isolation in which she lived weighed on her, and although, to be honest, she hadn't shown much interest when Rosália first came to her with the request, now, given her lover's resistance, she became determined to get his agreement. She leaned further forward, as if to stroke the pink leather of her slippers, and in doing so revealed her bare breasts.

"I've never asked you for anything like this before. If you can find her a job, then you should. It would please me immensely, plus you'd be helping a family in need."

Lídia was exaggerating her interest and, as far as she could judge, she was exaggerating the neediness of her neighbors too, but once launched along the path of exaggeration, she made a gesture that, by its very rarity, surprised Paulino Morais: she placed one hand on her lover's round, plump knee. Paulino's nostrils quivered as he said:

"No need to get sulky about it. I haven't definitely said no yet . . ."

From the look on his face, Lídia knew the price she would have to pay for this near acquiescence. She felt disinclined to pull back the bedcovers, and yet she could see that he desired her. She tried to undo the effect she'd had on him, even pretending to have lost all interest in the subject, but Paulino, roused by that caress, was saying:

"I'll see what I can arrange. What kind of work does she do?"

"She's a typist, I think."

Every drop of Lídia's irritation was distilled in those words "I think." When she stood up and removed her hand from her lover's knee, it was as if she had covered herself with the heaviest, thickest clothes she owned. He noticed this transformation and was puzzled, but had no inkling of what was going on in her head. He finished his coffee and stubbed out his cigarillo in the ashtray. Lídia rubbed her arms as if she were cold. She glanced at her dressing gown abandoned on the bed. She knew that if she put it on, Paulino would get annoyed. She felt tempted to put it on anyway, but fear got the better of her. She valued her financial security too much to risk it all with a fit of the sulks. Paulino folded his hands over his belly and said:

"Tell the young woman to come here on Wednesday and I'll talk to her."

Lídia shrugged and said in a brusque, cold voice:

"All right."

Out of the corner of her eye she saw Paulino frown. She scolded herself for creating a scene. She was behaving like a child and decided the moment had come to pour oil on troubled waters. She smiled at him, but her smile froze: Paulino was still frowning. She began to feel afraid. She had to find a way to cheer him up. She tried to speak, but could think of nothing to say. If she ran over to him and kissed him on the mouth, everything would be fine, but she felt incapable of doing that. She didn't want simply to hand herself over. She wanted to surrender, but not to take the first step.

Without thinking, and acting entirely on instinct, she turned out the bedroom light. Then, in the darkness, she went over to the dressing table and turned on the standard lamp next to it. She stood quite still for a moment, bathed in that light. She knew that her lover could clearly see the outline of her naked body beneath her negligee. Then, very slowly, she turned. Paulino Morais was unbuttoning his braces.

16

A bel paused on the landing to light a cigarette. At that moment, the stairwell lit up. He heard a door open on the floor above and the muffled sound of voices, followed immediately by heavy footsteps that made the stairs creak. He took his key out of his pocket and pretended to be fumbling with the lock. He only "found" it when he felt the person coming down the stairs walk right past him. He turned and saw Paulino Morais, who murmured a polite "Good evening," to which Abel—who had now opened the front door—responded in the same manner.

As he walked along the corridor inside the apartment, he heard light footsteps above heading in the same direction. When he went into his room, the footsteps sounded farther off. He turned on the light and looked at his wristwatch: five past two.

The room was stuffy. He opened the window. The night was overcast. Slow, heavy clouds drifted across the sky, lit by the lights of the city. It had grown hotter, and the atmosphere was warm and humid. The sleeping buildings surrounding the back yards were like the wall around a deep, dark well. The only light was the glow emanating from his room. It flooded out of his open window and spilled into the yard below, revealing the stalks of the shrunken, useless cabbages that, plunged in darkness up until then, now had the startled look of people torn abruptly from sleep.

Another light went on, illuminating the backs of the buildings opposite. Abel could see clothes hung out to dry, flowerpots, and windows glinting. He decided to finish his cigarette sitting on the garden wall, and so as not to have to go through the kitchen, he jumped down from the window. He could hear the chicks piping in the chicken run. He walked through the cabbages bathed in light. Then he turned and looked up. Through the panes of the glazed balcony, he could see Lídia making her way to the bathroom. He smiled a sad, disenchanted smile. At that hour, hundreds of women would be doing the same as Lídia. He was tired, he had walked many streets, seen many faces, followed many nameless shapes. And now there he was in Silvestre's back yard, smoking a cigarette and shrugging his shoulders at life. "I'm like Romeo in the Capulets' garden," he thought. "All that's missing is the moon. Instead of innocent Juliet, we have the highly experienced Lídia. Instead of a delicate balcony, a bathroom window. A fire escape instead of a 'tackled stair.'" He lit another cigarette. "Any moment now, she'll say: 'What man art thou that, thus bescreen'd in night, so stumblest on my counsel?'"

He smiled smugly, rather pleased with his ability to quote Shakespeare. Carefully avoiding the abandoned cabbages, he went and sat on the wall. He felt strangely sad. Doubtless the influence of the weather. It was very close and there was a hint of thunder in the air. He looked up again: Lídia was coming out of the bathroom. Perhaps because she, too, felt hot, she opened the window and leaned on the sill.

"Juliet saw Romeo," thought Abel. "What will happen next?" He jumped down from the wall and walked into the middle of the yard. Lídia was still at the window. "Now it's my turn to say: 'But, soft! what light through yonder window breaks? It is the east, and Juliet is the sun.'"

"Good evening," said Abel, smiling.

There was a pause, then he heard Lídia's voice say "Good evening" and she promptly vanished. Abel threw down his cigarette and, much amused, mumbled to himself as he returned to his room:

"There's an ending Shakespeare didn't think of."

17

Henrique's condition took an unexpected turn for the worse. The doctor, summoned urgently, ordered tests to be made for diphtheria bacilli. The boy was running a very high fever and was delirious. Carmen, desperate with anxiety, blamed her husband for allowing the illness to get this far. She made a terrible scene. Emílio merely listened and, as usual, said nothing. He knew his wife was right, because she had been the first to think of calling a doctor. He was filled with remorse. He spent the whole of Sunday at his son's bedside and, on Monday, at the appointed time, rushed off to get the results of the analysis. He breathed a sigh of relief when he saw that it was negative, but the comment on the report that one such test was often not enough plunged him back into despair.

The doctor, however, declared himself satisfied and predicted a rapid recovery—once they had got through the next twenty-four hours. Emílio did not leave his son's side all that day. Carmen, who had been cold and silent since supper, found her husband's presence hard to bear. She found it exasperating enough on normal days, but now that her husband refused to leave the room, she felt she was being robbed of the one thing that was most precious to her: her son's love.

In order to get rid of Emílio, she reminded him that he wasn't going to earn any money stuck at home, and that they needed the money more than ever, what with the additional expense of Henrique's illness. Once again Emílio responded only with silence. She was right about that too; he would do more good leaving her to take care of

Henrique, but still he did not go. He was convinced now that he was responsible for that relapse, because his son's condition had only worsened after the night he had spoken to him. His presence there was like a penance, as futile as all penances are, and which only made sense because it was entirely self-imposed.

Despite his wife's insistence, he did not go to bed at the usual hour. Carmen also stayed up, anxious to demonstrate that she did not love her child any less than he did.

There was little they could do. Once the crisis was over, the illness followed its natural course. The medicines had been administered, and now it was a matter of waiting for them to take effect. But neither of them wanted to give in. It was a kind of standoff, a mute battle. Carmen was struggling to hang on to Henrique's affection, which she felt she risked losing because of her husband's caring presence there. Emílio was struggling to quell his feelings of remorse and to make up for his earlier indifference with his present concern. He was aware that his wife's battle was the worthier one and that in his own battle there was a substratum of egotism. Of course he loved his son: he had engendered him, how could he not love him? Not to do so would be unnatural. However, he knew full well that he was a stranger in that house, that nothing there really belonged to him, even though it had been bought with his money. Having is not the same as owning. You can have even those things you don't want. Owning means having and enjoying the things you have. He had a home, a wife and a son, but none of them was truly his. He only had himself, but even then not entirely.

Sometimes Emílio wondered if perhaps he was mad, if this life of conflicts, storms and constant misunderstandings was a consequence of some nervous imbalance in him. Away from home, he was, or thought he was, a normal creature capable of laughing and smiling like everyone else, but he only had to cross the threshold of their apartment for an unbearable weight to fall on him. He felt like a drowning man who fills his lungs not with the air that would allow him to live, but with the water that is killing him. He felt he had a duty to declare himself satisfied with what life had given him, to acknowledge that other, far less fortunate men managed to live contentedly. This comparison, however, brought him no peace. He didn't know what would give him peace or where he would find it, or if it even existed. What he did know, after all these years, was that he did not have it. And he knew that he wanted to find it, the way a shipwrecked man desperately wants to find a plank of wood to cling to, the way a seed needs the sun.

These thoughts, repeated over and over, always brought him back to the same point. He compared himself to a mule harnessed to a waterwheel and walking miles and miles, round and round in the same circle, eyes blinkered, not realizing that he is treading the same ground he has trodden a thousand times before. He wasn't a mule, he wasn't wearing blinkers, but he had to agree that his thoughts were leading him round and round a well-trodden path. Knowing this only made matters worse, because there he was, a human being behaving like an irrational animal. You can't blame the mule for submitting to the yoke, but should he be blamed? What was it that kept him tied to the yoke? Habit, cowardice, fear of hurting other people? Habits can be changed, cowardice can be overcome, and other people's suffering is almost always less than we think. Had he not already proved—or at least tried to prove— that his absence would quickly be forgotten? So why did he stay? What force was it that bound him to that house, that woman, that child? Who had tied those knots?

The only answer he came up with was "I'm tired." So tired that, even though he knew full well that all the doors of his prison could be opened and that he had the key, he still did not take a single step toward freedom. He had grown so accustomed to feeling tired that he took a certain pleasure in it, the pleasure of someone who has given up, the pleasure of someone who, when the moment of truth arrives, turns back the clock and says: "It's too early." The pleasure of self-sacrifice. But sacrifice is only complete when it is kept hidden from view; making it visible is tantamount to saying, "Look at me, look how self-sacrificing I am," and making sure that other people don't forget it. Therefore he had not yet given up entirely, and behind his resignation hope still lingered, just as the blue sky is always there behind the clouds.

Carmen was looking at her husband sitting there absorbed in thought. The ashtray was full, and Emílio continued to smoke. One day she had worked out how much money he spent on cigarettes and had criticized him harshly for it. She had told her parents, and they, of course, had sympathized with her. It was like burning money, like throwing it away, money they badly needed. Vices are for the rich, so if you want to have vices, you have to get rich first. Emílio, though, was a commercial traveler for want of any better employment, out of necessity, not out of vocation, and had never shown any desire to get rich. He contented himself with the bare minimum and went no further than that. What a useless man! What a useless life! Carmen belonged to a different race, a race for whom life is not a matter of standing and staring, but of struggling. She was active, he was apathetic. She was all nerves, bones and muscles, all the necessary ingredients for generating power and energy; he was all those things too, but he wrapped his bones, muscles and nerves in a mist of apathy, trammeling them with dissatisfaction and doubt.

Emílio got up and went to his son's room. The boy had fallen into a restless sleep, which he kept waking from and then sliding back into. Incoherent words emerged from his dry lips. In the corners of his mouth, small translucent bubbles of saliva marked the passing of the fever. Very gently, Emílio slipped the thermometer under his son's arm. He left it there for the required amount of time, then went back to the dining room. Carmen looked up from her sewing, but asked no questions. He checked the thermometer: 102.5. Henrique's temperature appeared to be going down. He placed the thermometer on the table where his wife could reach it, but despite her longing to know the result, she made no attempt to get up and read it. She waited for her husband to speak.

Emílio took a few hesitant steps. The clock in the apartment upstairs struck three. Carmen was waiting, her head pounding, her teeth gritted to keep from heaping insults on her husband. Emílio went to bed without saying a word. He was worn out by that prolonged vigil and weary both of his wife and of himself. His throat was tight with anxiety: it was her fault he could not speak; she was the one obliging him to withdraw like someone creeping away in order to die or to weep.

For Carmen this was the final proof that her husband lacked all human feeling. Only a monster would behave like that: leaving her in ignorance and going to bed as if there were nothing wrong, as if their son's illness were of no importance.

She got up and went over to the table. She looked at the thermometer, then went back to her chair. She did not go to bed that night. Like the victors in medieval battles, she remained on the field after the fight was over. She had won. Besides, she would have found the slightest contact with her husband that night unbearable.

18

Given the nature of the job he did, Caetano Cunha led a rather bat-like existence. He worked while others slept, and while he rested, with windows and eyes closed, those others went about their business in the daylight. This fact gave him the measure of his own importance, for he firmly believed that he was better than most people and for various reasons, not the least of which was that nocturnal life of his, spent hunched over a Linotype machine while the city slept.

It was still dark when he left work, and the sight of the deserted streets, damp and shining from the dank river air, made him happy. Rather than going straight home, he would wander those silent streets haunted by the dark shapes of women. However tired he was, he would stop and talk to them. If he fancied something more, he would go a little further than mere talk, but even if he didn't, talking to them was enough.

Caetano liked women, all women. He could be aroused by the merest twitch of a skirt. He felt an irresistible attraction for women of easy virtue. Vice, dissolution, love for sale, all fascinated him. He knew most of the city's brothels, knew the price list by heart, could tell you off the top of his head (or so he boasted to himself) the names of a good few dozen women he had slept with.

Only one woman despised him: his own wife. As far as he was concerned, Justina was a totally asexual creature, with no needs and no desires. If he happened to touch her while they were in bed together, he would recoil in disgust, repelled by her hard, thin body, her dry, almost parchment-like skin. "She's not a woman, she's a bag of bones," he would think.

Justina saw the disgust in his eyes and said nothing. The flame of desire had long since burned out in her. She reciprocated her husband's contempt with her own still more boundless contempt. She knew he was unfaithful to her and frankly didn't care, but what she would not tolerate was having him boast about his conquests at home. Not because she was jealous, but

172

because, aware of how far she had fallen in marrying a man like him, she preferred not to descend to his level. And when Caetano, carried away by his naturally loud, irascible temperament, abused her verbally or compared her with other women, she could silence him with just a few words. To someone of Caetano's Don Juanesque character, those words constituted a humiliation, a reminder of a failure that still burned in his flesh and in his mind. Whenever he heard them, he was tempted to attack his wife physically, but at such moments, Justina's eyes blazed with a fierce fire, her mouth curled into a sneer, and he shrank back.

That's why, when they were together, silence was the rule and words the exception. That's why only icy sentiments and indifference filled the vacuum of the hours they spent together. The mustiness that permeated the apartment, its whole subterranean atmosphere, was redolent of an abandoned tomb.

Tuesday was Caetano's day off. This meant he didn't need to arrive home until late morning; he would sleep until the afternoon and only then have lunch. Maybe it was that late lunch, or possibly the prospect of spending the night in bed beside his wife, but Tuesdays were the days when Caetano's ill humor was most likely to surface, however hard he tried to suppress it. On those days, Justina's reserve became still more marked and seemed to double in thickness. Accustomed to the insuperable distance between them, Caetano could never understand why it should become even greater. In revenge, he would exaggerate the crudeness of his words and gestures, the brusqueness of his movements. What particularly annoyed him was the fact that his wife always chose Tuesday as the day on which to air their dead daughter's clothes and carefully polish the glass on her eternally smiling photo. He felt this ceremony was intended as a criticism of him, and though he was sure that, in this respect at least, he did not deserve any criticism, he nevertheless found that weekly parading of memories deeply troubling.

Tuesdays were unhappy days in the Caetano Cunha household, nervous, edgy days when Justina, if pried out of her usual state of abstraction, would turn violent and aggressive. Days when Caetano was afraid to open his mouth because every word seemed charged with electricity. Days on which some evil little devil seemed to take pleasure in making the atmosphere in their apartment unbreathable.

The clouds that had covered the sky the previous night had cleared away. The sun poured in through the glass canopy over the enclosed balcony at the back, its iron struts casting a shadow on the floor like prison bars. Caetano had just had his lunch. He looked at the clock and saw that it was nearly four. He lumbered to his feet. He was in the habit of sleeping without his pajama bottoms on. His large abdomen strained at the buttons of his loose pajama jacket, giving him a striking resemblance to one of those plump, doll-like figures created by Rafael Bordalo. While his swollen belly might be laughable, his flushed, scowling face could not have been more unpleasant. Oblivious to both these things, he left the bedroom, walked through the kitchen, without saying a word to his wife, and went into the bathroom. He opened the window and looked up at the sky. The intense light made him blink like an owl. He gazed indifferently out at the neighboring back yards, at three cats playing on one of the roofs, and didn't even notice the pure, supple flight of a passing swallow.

Then his eyes fixed on a point much closer to home. In the neighboring window, that of Lídia's bathroom, he could see the sleeve of a pink dressing gown moving about. Now and then, the sleeve fell back to reveal a bare forearm. Leaning on the windowsill, with the lower part of his body hidden, Caetano could not take his eyes off her window. He could see very little, but what he saw was still enough to excite him. He leaned farther out and met the ironic gaze of his wife, watching him from the balcony. His face hardened. Then suddenly she was there before him, handing him a coffeepot.

"Here's your hot water."

He didn't thank her, he merely closed the

bathroom door again. While he was shaving, he kept peering across at Lídia's window. The sleeve had disappeared. In its place, Caetano found his wife's eyes staring at him. He knew that the best way to avoid the imminent storm was to stop looking, which would be easy enough given that Lídia was no longer there. However, temptation won out over prudence. At one point, exasperated by his wife's spying, he opened the door and said:

"Haven't you got anything better to do?"

They never addressed each other by their first names. She looked at him without answering and, still without answering, turned her back on him. Caetano slammed the door and did not look out of the window again. When he emerged, washed and shaved, he noticed that his wife had taken from a suitcase that she kept in the kitchen the diminutive items of clothing that had once belonged to Matilde. Were it not for the adoring look she bestowed on the clothes, Caetano might have passed by without a word, but yet again, he felt she was criticizing him.

"When are you going to stop spying on me?"

Justina took her time before replying. She seemed to be returning very slowly from somewhere far away, from a distant land with only one inhabitant.

"I was admiring your persistence," she said coldly.

"What do you mean 'persistence'?" he asked, taking a step forward.

He looked utterly ridiculous in his underpants, his legs bare. Justina eyed him sarcastically. She knew that she was ugly and unattractive, but seeing her husband like that, she felt like laughing in his face:

"Do you really want me to tell you?"

"Yes."

From that moment on, Caetano was lost. Before he said that word, there had still been time to avoid receiving the inevitable slap in the face, but he had said yes and was already regretting it. Too late.

"You still haven't lost hope, then? You still think she'll fall into your arms one day, do you? Aren't you embarrassed by what happened?"

Caetano's chin was trembling with rage. Saliva appeared at the corners of his thick lips.

"Do you want her lover to come and rip you to shreds again for overstepping the mark?"

And in a tone of ironic concern, as if she were giving him a piece of advice, she said:

"Have a little self-respect. She's far too classy a piece for you to lay hands on. Make do with the other women, the ones whose photos you carry around in your wallet. I can't say I care for your taste. I suppose when they have their mug shots taken they give you a copy, is that right? You're a sort of branch office of the police, aren't you?"

Caetano turned deathly pale. His wife had never gone so far before. He clenched his fists and took a step toward her:

"One day I'll break every bone in your body! One day I'll beat you to a pulp, do you hear? Just don't push me!"

"You wouldn't dare."

"You . . ." and a particularly filthy word emerged from his lips.

Justina said only:

"You're not insulting me but yourself, because that's how you see all women."

Caetano's heavy body swayed stiffly like that of a robot. Fury and impotent rage sent words up into his mouth, but there they stumbled and died. He raised his clenched fist as if to bring it down on his wife's head. She didn't flinch. His fist, defeated, slowly descended. Justina's eyes resembled two burning coals. A humiliated Caetano vanished from the room, slamming the door.

The cat, who had been observing his owners with glaucous eyes, slipped away along the dark corridor and lay down on the doormat, silent and indifferent.

19

Isaura, unable to sleep, had been tossing and turning in bed for two hours now. The whole building was quiet. Occasionally, from outside in the street, she heard the footsteps of some night owl returning home late. The pale, distant light of the stars came in through the window. In the darkness of the bedroom she could just make out the still-darker shapes of the furniture. The wardrobe mirror vaguely reflected the light from the window. Every quarter of an hour, as inflexible as time itself, the clock in the downstairs apartment reminded her of her insomniac state. Everything was silent and asleep, except for Isaura. She did all she could to get to sleep. She counted to a thousand, then counted again, she relaxed her muscles one by one, she closed her eyes, tried to forget about her insomnia and slip past it into sleep. In vain. Every single one of her nerves was awake. Despite the effort required to make her brain concentrate on the need to sleep, her thoughts were leading her along vertiginous paths into deep valleys from which arose the dim murmur of voices calling to her. She was hovering high up on the powerful back of a bird with wide wings, which, after soaring above the clouds, where it was hard to catch her breath, fell like a stone into the misty valleys in which she could make out white figures so pale they appeared to be naked or covered only by transparent veils. She was tormented by an objectless desire, by a desire for desire and by an equal fear of it too.

At her side, her sister was sleeping peacefully. Isaura found her quiet breathing and her stillness exasperating. She twice got up and went over to the window. Random words, half-finished sentences, vague gestures were going round and round in her head. It was like a scratched record that repeats over and over the same lovely musical phrase, which becomes odious with endless repetition. Ten times, a hundred times, the notes recur and mesh and meld until all that remains is a single, obsessive sound, terrible and implacable. You feel that just one minute of that obsession will bring madness in its wake, but the minute passes and madness does not come. Instead you grow still more lucid. Your spirit embraces far horizons, travels here, there, everywhere, with no frontiers to contain it, and with each step you take you become more and more painfully lucid. To forget about it, to stop the sound, to crush it with silence would mean peace and sleep, but the words, the phrases, the gestures rise up from beneath the silence in a dumb, endless spiral.

Isaura told herself that she was mad. Her head was burning, her forehead too, and her brain seemed to have grown so large it was about to burst out of her skull. It was her insomnia that was to blame, and it would not leave her until those thoughts left her as well. And what thoughts, Isaura! What monstrous thoughts! What repellent aberrations! What subterranean furies were pushing at the trapdoors of her will!

What diabolical, malicious hand had guided her toward that book? And it was supposed to serve a moral purpose too! Of course, said cold reason, almost lost in the whirlwind of sensations. Why, then, this turmoil of unchained instincts erupting in her flesh? Why had she not read it coolly, dispassionately? Weakness, said reason. Desire, screamed her long-buried instincts, for years shunned and ignored as being shameful in the extreme. And now those instincts had risen to the surface, and her will was drowning in a pool darker than night and deeper than death.

Isaura gnawed at her wrists. Her face was drenched in sweat, her hair clung to her scalp, her mouth was twisted into a violent grimace. Close to madness, she sat on the edge of the bed, ran her hands through her hair and looked around her. Night and silence. The sound from that scratched record was rising from the abyss of silence. Exhausted, she fell back on the bed. Adriana shifted slightly, but continued to sleep. Her indifference felt like a recrimination. Despite the suffocating heat, Isaura pulled the sheet up over her head. She covered her eyes with her hands, as if the night were not dark enough to hide her shame, but the darkness behind her eyelids filled up with red and yellow lights, like the sparks from a bonfire. (If only dawn would break, if only the sun would miraculously leave the other side of the world and burst into the room!)

Slowly, Isaura's hands moved toward her sister. Her fingertips could feel the heat of Adriana's body from a centimeter away. They stayed there for several long minutes, neither advancing nor retreating. The sweat had dried on Isaura's forehead, but her face was scalding hot as if a fire were burning inside her. Her fingers advanced until they touched Adriana's bare arm, then withdrew as if they had received an electric shock. Isaura's heart was beating dully. Her wide, dilated eyes could see nothing but blackness. Again her hands advanced. Again they stopped. Again they moved forward. Now they were resting on Adriana's arm. With a slithering, sinuous movement, Isaura moved closer to her sister. She could feel the heat emanating from her body. Slowly, one of her hands ran along Adriana's arm from wrist to shoulder, where it slipped in beneath her hot, damp armpit and insinuated itself beneath one breast. Isaura's breathing became rapid and irregular. The hand slid beneath the light fabric of Adriana's nightdress as far as her stomach. Adriana turned abruptly onto her back. Her bare shoulder was on the same level as Isaura's mouth, which sensed the proximity of flesh. Like iron filings drawn to a magnet, Isaura's mouth fixed itself on Adriana's shoulder. It was a long, fierce, hungry kiss. At the same time, her hand grabbed Adriana's waist and drew her closer. Adriana woke with a start. Isaura did not release her grip. Her mouth was still planted on her shoulder like a sucker and her fingers fastened on her thigh like claws. With a cry of terror, Adriana pulled away and leapt out of bed. She ran to the bedroom door, then, remembering that her mother and aunt were sleeping on the other side, turned back, taking refuge by the window.

Isaura had not moved. She tried to pretend she was asleep, but Adriana still did not come back to bed. She could hear her sibilant breathing. Through half-closed lids, she could see her sister's body silhouetted against the opalescent backdrop of the window. Then, abandoning all pretense at sleep, she said softly:

"Adriana."

Her sister's tremulous voice answered:

"What do you want?"

"Come here."

Adriana did not move.

"You'll get cold," insisted Isaura.

"It doesn't matter."

"You can't stay there. If you don't come over here, I'll come to you."

Adriana approached, sat down on the edge of the bed and reached out to turn on the light.

"Don't," said Isaura.

"Why not?"

"I don't want you to see me."

"Why ever not?"

"I'm ashamed . . ."

These words were spoken in a murmur. Adriana's voice was becoming firmer, but Isaura's trembled as if she were about to break into sobs:

"Please, I beg you, lie down . . ."

"No, I won't."

"Why? Are you afraid of me?"

Adriana took a while to answer:

"Yes, I am . . ."

"I won't do anything, I promise. I don't know what came over me. I swear . . ."

Isaura began to cry softly. Adriana opened the wardrobe door and, by touch alone, found a woolen jacket. She put it on and sat down again at the foot of the bed.

"Are you going to stay there?" asked her sister.

"Yes."

"All night?"

"Yes."

Isaura let out a louder sob. Almost immediately, the light in the room next door came on and they heard Amélia say:

"Is something wrong?"

Adriana quickly stuffed her jacket behind the

bed and slipped beneath the sheets. Amélia appeared in the doorway, a shawl wrapped about her shoulders.

"What is it?"

"Isaura had a bad dream," said Adriana, sitting up in order to hide her sister.

Amélia came closer:

"Are you ill?"

"It's nothing, Aunt. It was just a nightmare. Go back to bed," said Adriana, pushing her away.

"All right, but if you need anything, just call."

The bedroom door closed again, the light went out, and silence gradually returned, broken only by a few muffled sobs. Then the sobs became fewer and farther between, and only the shaking of Isaura's shoulders betrayed her agitation. Adriana kept her distance, waiting. Slowly the sheets grew warm again. The warmth from their two bodies mingled. Isaura said:

"Do you forgive me?"

Adriana did not respond at once. She knew that she should say yes, in order to reassure Isaura, but the word she wanted to say was an abrupt no.

"Do you forgive me?" Isaura asked again.

"Yes, I forgive you."

Isaura felt an impulse to embrace her sister and weep, but she controlled herself, fearing that Adriana might misinterpret the gesture. She felt that, from then on, everything she did or said would be poisoned by the memory of those few minutes, that her love for her sister had been distorted and soiled by that terrible bout of insomnia and by what had followed. Breathlessly, she murmured:

"Thank you."

The minutes and hours passed very slowly. The clock downstairs chimed at regular intervals, measuring out the time as if it were an endless skein of wool. Isaura finally fell asleep, exhausted. Adriana did not. She remained awake until the bluish light of night filling the window had become the gray light of dawn, which, in slow gradations, was replaced by the white light of morning. Motionless, staring up at the ceiling, her head pounding, she was obstinately struggling with the awakening of her own hunger for love, which was equally repressed, hidden and frustrated.

20

That evening, in Anselmo's apartment, they dined earlier than usual. Maria Cláudia had to get dressed up in order to be introduced to Paulino Morais, and it was best not to keep a person waiting when you were planning to ask him a favor. Mother and daughter had eaten quickly, then disappeared into the latter's bedroom. There were various problems to resolve as how best to present Claudinha, and the most difficult of all was what to wear. None of her dresses set off her beauty and her youth better than a yellow sleeveless number in a light, airy fabric. When she turned, its full, gathered skirt resembled an inverted flowerhead and fell languidly from her waist like a lazy wave. This won Rosália's vote; however, Claudinha, with her natural good sense and good taste, realized that while the dress would be ideal for the summer months, it looked out of place in a still-rainy spring. Besides, Senhor Morais might disapprove of its not having sleeves. Rosália agreed, but made no further suggestions. She had chosen that dress and that alone, and had no other preferences.

The choice was not easy, but in the end Claudinha plumped for a gray-green dress, which was discreet and appropriate for the season. It was a woolen dress, with long sleeves that fastened at the cuffs with buttons of the same gray-green color. It had a modest neckline that barely revealed her throat. For a future employee it was perfect. Rosália disagreed, but as soon as her daughter put the dress on, she saw that she was right.

Maria Cláudia was always right. She studied herself in the wardrobe mirror and liked what she saw. The yellow dress made her look younger, but what she wanted now was to look older. No frills, no bare arms. The dress she had chosen fitted her like a glove, seemed to cling to her body and respond to her slightest movement. It had no belt, but the cut of the dress gave it a natural waist, and Maria Cláudia's waist was so slender anyway that a belt would spoil the effect. Seeing herself in the mirror, Claudinha realized which direction she should take in future as regards what she wore. No frills and fripperies to hide her figure. And at that moment, turning this way and that in front of the mirror, it occurred to her that she would look good in a lamé dress, the kind that resembles a second skin, as flexible and supple as her own.

"What do you think, Mama?" she asked.

Rosália was left speechless. She was hovering around her daughter like a dresser preparing the star for her big moment. Maria Cláudia sat down, took lipstick and rouge from her handbag and began to apply her makeup. Her hair could wait; it required only a quick brush. She didn't overdo the makeup, though; it was even more discreet than her dress. She was relying on her understandably nervous state to give her a good color—a little nervousness always suited her. When she had finished, she stood before her mother and said again:

"What do you think?"

"You look lovely, sweetheart."

Claudinha smiled at her own reflection, gave herself one last probing look and declared that she was ready. Rosália summoned her husband, and Anselmo duly appeared. He had adopted the noble expression of a father about to decide his daughter's future, and he seemed genuinely moved.

"Do you like it, Papa?"

"You look charming, my dear."

Anselmo had learned that, at key moments such as this, "my dear" was the best form of address to use. It conferred seriousness on the occasion, suggested fatherly affection and pride tinged with respect.

"I'm so nervous," said Claudinha.

"You must keep calm," said her father, smoothing his neat mustache with one firm hand. Nothing could trouble the firmness of that hand.

When Claudinha walked past him, Anselmo slightly adjusted the string of pearls she was wearing: the final touch, and made, as was only right, by the firm, loving hand of her father.

"Off you go, my dear," he said solemnly.

Her heart fluttering inside her like a caged bird, Maria Cláudia went down the stairs to the first floor. She was far more nervous than she seemed. She had been to Lídia's apartment on innumerable occasions, but never when her lover was there. This visit, then, had about it an air of complicity and secrecy, of something forbidden. She was being admitted into the presence of Paulino Morais, into direct knowledge of Lídia's "irregular situation." This excited and dizzied her.

Lídia opened the door, smiling broadly.

"We were expecting you."

These words reinforced Maria Cláudia's feeling of intimacy. She entered, trembling all over. Lídia was wearing her taffeta dressing gown and a pair of dance shoes that were attached to her ankles by two silvery straps. They looked more like sandals than shoes, and yet Maria Cláudia would have given anything to own such a pair.

Accustomed as she was to being shown straight into the bedroom, she took a step in that direction. Lídia smiled:

"No, not that way."

Claudinha blushed scarlet. And so it was, blushing and confused, that she appeared before Paulino Morais, who was waiting for her in the dining room; he was wearing a jacket and smoking his usual cigarillo.

Lídia introduced them. Paulino got up. With the hand holding the cigarillo, he gestured to Maria Cláudia to take a seat, and they all sat down. Paulino was looking fixedly at Claudinha. She averted her gaze and stared down at the geometric figures in the carpet.

"Please, Paulino," said Lídia, still smiling, "can't you see you're embarrassing Maria Cláudia?"

Paulino started slightly, then he smiled too and said:

"That certainly wasn't my intention." And turning to Maria Cláudia: "I didn't think you were so . . . so young!"

"I'm nineteen, Senhor Morais," she said, looking up.

"As you see, she's still a child," said Lídia.

Claudinha glanced across at her. The look they exchanged was suspicious and suddenly hostile. Maria Cláudia saw in a flash what Lídia was thinking, and what she saw sent a shiver of fear and pleasure through her. She sensed that Lídia was now her enemy, and she understood why. She saw herself and Lídia as if from another person's perspective, from Paulino Morais's perspective, for example, and the comparison clearly favored her.

"I'm not that much of a child, Dona Lídia, although I am, as Senhor Morais said, very young."

Lídia bit her lip: she could see what Claudinha was hinting at. She immediately regained her composure, however, and laughed:

"Oh, I was just the same when I was your age. It used to drive me mad when anyone called me a child, but of course now I see they were right. So why can't you see that too?"

"Perhaps because I'm not yet as old as Dona Lídia?"

Maria Cláudia was quick on the uptake when it came to these female skirmishes. This was her very first bout and, although she had already scored two hits and was herself as yet untouched, she was a little frightened: she feared she might

191

not have breath enough or the right weapons to survive the rest of the duel. Fortunately for her, Paulino intervened. He took out a gold cigarette case and offered both women a cigarette. Lídia accepted.

"Don't you smoke?" Paulino asked Maria Cláudia.

She blushed. She had smoked on several occasions in secret, but felt she should not accept. It might look bad and, besides, she was sure she would never be able to compete with Lídia when it came to holding the cigarette and raising it to her lips in a sufficiently elegant manner. She said:

"No, I don't, Senhor Morais."

"Very sensible." He paused to inhale the smoke from his cigarillo, then went on: "Anyway, I don't think it's very nice of you two to talk about age when I'm old enough to be the father of you both."

This remark had a soothing effect and established a truce. However, Claudinha immediately took the initiative, and with what Anselmo would have termed a charming smile, she remarked:

"You're making yourself out to be much older than you really are."

"All right, then, how old do you think I am?"

"About forty-five, perhaps . . ."

"Come now!" Paulino laughed out loud, and when he laughed his belly shook. "A little bit more than that."

"Fifty?"

"No, fifty-six. So old enough to be your grandfather."

"Well, you don't look it!"

She said this with real sincerity and spontaneity, as Paulino was quick to notice. Lídia stood up. She went over to her lover and tried to lead the conversation back to the real reason for Maria Cláudia's visit.

"Don't forget that Claudinha is more interested in your decision than in your age. It's getting late, and she probably needs to go to bed. Besides . . ." She paused and looked at Paulino with an expressive smile, then said in a soft voice, heavy with implied meanings: "Besides, I need to talk to you alone."

Maria Cláudia gave in at this point. She could not do battle on that terrain. She saw that she was an intruder, that they were both—or at least Lídia was—eager to see the back of her. She felt like crying.

"Of course, yes, you're quite right!" Paulino seemed to remember for the first time that he had a position to maintain, his respectability to safeguard, and that the frivolous nature of the conversation could compromise both. "So you want a job, do you?"

"Oh, I have a job already, Senhor Morais, but my parents don't think I earn enough, and Dona Lídia was kind enough to take an interest and . . ."

"What can you do?"

"I can type."

"Is that all? You don't know shorthand?"

"No, Senhor Morais."

"In the current climate, knowing how to type really isn't enough. How much do you earn?"

"Five hundred escudos."

"Hm, so you don't know shorthand?"

"No, sir . . ."

Maria Cláudia's voice tailed off. Lídia was beaming. Paulino looked thoughtful. An awkward silence ensued.

"But I could always learn," said Claudinha.

"Hm."

Paulino was drawing on his cigarillo and looking at the girl. Lídia chipped in:

"Listen, darling, I'd really like it if you could find Claudinha a job, but if it's just not possible . . . Claudinha's a bright girl. She'll understand."

Maria Cláudia no longer had strength enough to fight back. All she wanted was to be out of there as quickly as possible. She made as if to get up.

"No, wait," said Paulino. "I'm going to give you a chance. My current shorthand-typist is getting married in three months' time and then she's going to leave. You can come and work at my company and, during those three months, I'll pay you the same as you're being paid now, but meanwhile I want you to learn shorthand. Then we'll see. If you do well, I can promise you that your salary will go up by leaps and bounds! Agreed?"

"Oh, yes, Senhor Morais. Thank you so much!" Maria Cláudia's face was like a spring dawn.

"Don't you think you should speak to your parents first?"

"No, there's no need, Senhor Morais. They're sure to say yes."

She said this with such certainty that Paulino eyed her with some curiosity. At the same moment, Lídia remarked:

"And if at the end of those three months you're not satisfied with her or she isn't good enough at shorthand, you'll have to dismiss her, won't you?"

Maria Cláudia fixed Paulino with anxious eyes.

"Well, I don't know if it will come to that . . ."

"Then you'll be the loser . . ."

"I'll learn, Senhor Morais," Maria Cláudia said, breaking in. "And I do very much hope you will be satisfied with me . . ."

"So do I," said Paulino, smiling.

"When should I start?"

"Well, the sooner the better. When can you leave your present job?"

"Now if you want."

Paulino thought for a moment, then said:

"It's the twenty-sixth now. How about the first of the month? Would that be possible?"

"Yes, sir."

"Good. But wait, I won't be in Lisbon that day.

It doesn't matter, though. I'll write you a note to give to the office manager, just in case I forget to warn him beforehand. Not that I will, of course, but . . ."

He took a business card out of his wallet. He looked for his glasses, but failed to find them.

"Where did I leave my glasses?"

"They're in the bedroom," answered Lídia.

"Go and fetch them for me, will you?"

Lídia left the room. Paulino, still holding his wallet, was gazing distractedly at Maria Cláudia. She had been sitting with eyes lowered, but then she raised her head and looked straight at him. There was something in his gaze that she understood at once. Neither of them looked away. Maria Cláudia took a deep breath, making her chest swell. Paulino felt the muscles in his back slowly stretch. From the corridor came the sound of Lídia's returning footsteps.

When she entered the room, Paulino was studiously rummaging around in his wallet, and Maria Cláudia was staring down at the carpet.

21

Lying in bed, his feet resting on a newspaper so as not to dirty the bedspread, Abel was enjoying a cigarette. He had eaten well. Mariana was a good cook and an excellent housewife. You could see this in the way the apartment was furnished, in the small details. His room was further proof. The furniture was poor but clean and had a dignified air about it. There is no doubt that just as pets—well, cats and dogs at least—reflect the temperament and character of their owners, the furniture and even the most insignificant household objects reflect something of the lives of their owners too. They give off coldness or warmth, friendliness or reserve. They are witnesses constantly recounting, in a silent language, what they have seen and what they know. The difficulty lies in finding the best, most private moment, the most propitious light, in which to hear their confession.

Following the seductive movement of the smoke as it rose into the air, Abel was listening to the stories being told to him by the chest of drawers and the table, by the chairs and the mirror, as well as by the curtains. They were not stories with a beginning, a middle and an end, but a gentle flow of images, the language of shapes and colors that leave behind them an impression of peace and serenity.

Doubtless Abel's satisfied stomach had an important part to play in that feeling of plenitude. He had spent many months deprived of simple homey fare, of the particular taste food has when prepared by the hands and palate of a contented housewife. He had grown used to eating whatever insipid dish of the day cheap restaurants served up and the kind of fried fish that, in exchange for a few escudos, gives those with little money the illusion that they have eaten. Perhaps Mariana suspected as much; how else to explain her invitation to join them in a meal when they had only known each other such a short time? Or perhaps Silvestre and Mariana were different, different from all the other people he had met so far. Simpler, more human and more open. What was it that gave to the poverty of his hosts the ring of pure gold? (This, by some obscure association of ideas, was how Abel experienced the atmosphere in their apartment.) "Happiness? That doesn't seem enough. Happiness is like a snail; it withdraws into its shell when you touch it." But if it wasn't happiness, what was it then? "Understanding, perhaps, but understanding is just a word. No one can understand another person unless he is that other person. And no one can be simultaneously himself and someone else."

The smoke continued to drift up from his forgotten cigarette. "Is it simply in the nature of certain people, that capacity to give off some life-transforming energy? Something . . . something that could be everything or almost nothing. But what is it? That's the question. So let's ask that question."

Abel thought and thought again, but only came

up with more questions. He was stuck, at a dead end. "What kind of people are they? What is that capacity of theirs? In what way do they transform life? Are those even the right words to describe it? Does the mere need to use words make it impossible to find an answer? But then how do we find the answer?"

Oblivious to Abel's speculative efforts, his cigarette had burned down as far as the fingers holding it. Taking great care not to drop the long piece of ash, he stubbed the cigarette out in the ashtray. He was about to pick up the thread of his reasoning again when he heard two light taps at the door. He got to his feet:

"Come in."

Mariana appeared, carrying a shirt:

"I'm sorry to bother you, Senhor Abel, but I'm not sure if this shirt can be mended . . ."

Abel took the shirt from her, looked at it and smiled:

"What do you think, Senhora Mariana?"

She smiled too and said:

"I'm not sure. It's certainly seen better days . . ."

"Do what you can, then. You know, sometimes I have more need of an old shirt than I do of a new one. Does that seem odd to you?"

"I'm sure you have your reasons, Senhor Abel."

And she turned the shirt this way and that as if trying to make it clear to him how very decrepit it was. Then she said: "My Silvestre had a shirt a bit

199

like this. I think I still have some scraps, enough at least for the collar . . ."

"That's an awful lot of work, do you think perhaps . . ."

He stopped. He saw in Mariana's eyes how sad it would make her if he did not allow her to mend his shirt:

"Thank you, Senhora Mariana. I'm sure you can save it."

Mariana left the room. She was so fat as to be comical, so kind as to make one weep.

"It's kindness," thought Abel, "but that doesn't seem enough either. There's something here that eludes me. I can see that they're happy. They're very understanding and kind, I can see that too, but there's something I can't put my finger on, possibly the most important thing, which might be the cause of that happiness, understanding and kindness. Or perhaps—yes, that's it—perhaps it's simultaneously the cause and the consequence of that kindness, understanding and happiness."

Abel could not, for the moment, find a way out of this labyrinth. That evening's satisfying, comforting meal may have had a role in dulling his reasoning powers. He thought he might read a little before going to sleep. It was still early, just after half past ten, so he had plenty of time ahead of him. But he didn't really feel like reading either, or going out, even though it was a warm, clear night. He knew what he would see in the

200

street: people idling by or hurrying along, either curious or indifferent. Gloomy houses and brightly lit ones. The egotistical flow of life: greed, fear, longing, hope, hunger, vice, being approached by some woman of the streets—and, of course, the night itself, which removes all masks and shows man's true face.

He made up his mind to go and talk to Silvestre, his friend Silvestre. He knew it wasn't a good time, that the cobbler was busy on an urgent task, but if he couldn't speak to him, at least he could sit near him, watch his skillful hands at work, feel his calm gaze. "Calmness is such a strange thing," he thought.

Seeing him come out onto the enclosed balcony, Silvestre smiled and said:

"No game of checkers tonight, I'm afraid!"

Abel sat down opposite him. The low lamp lit up Silvestre's hands and the child's shoe he was working on.

"Well, that's what happens when you have no fixed working hours."

"I used to, but now that I'm an entrepreneur . . ."

He said this last word in a way that stripped it of all meaning. Mariana, sitting with her back against the sink and mending Abel's shirt, joked:

"Yes, an entrepreneur with no money."

Abel took out a pack of cigarettes.

"Would you like one?"

"Yes, please."

However, Silvestre was too busy with his hands to take the proffered cigarette. So Abel took it from the pack, put it between Silvestre's lips and lit it. All this was done in silence. No one mentioned the word "contentment," but that is what they all felt. Abel's keener sensibility noted the beauty of the moment. A pure beauty. "Virginal," he thought.

His chair was taller than the benches on which Silvestre and Mariana were sitting. He could see their bowed heads, their white hair, Silvestre's lined forehead, Mariana's glossy red cheeks and the familiar light surrounding them. Abel's face lay in shadow, the glow from his cigarette marking the spot where his mouth was.

Mariana was not one for sitting up late. Besides, her eyesight wasn't so good at night. To her despair, her head suddenly drooped. She was definitely more lark than owl.

"You're nodding off," said Silvestre.

"No, I'm not. I was just resting my eyes."

It was no good, though. Five minutes later, Mariana got to her feet and apologized to Senhor Abel, but her eyelids were as heavy as lead.

The two men were left alone.

"I still haven't thanked you for supper," said Abel.

"Oh, it was nothing."

"Well, it meant a lot to me."

"It was just poor folks' food."

"Offered to someone even poorer. It's funny, that's the first time I've ever described myself as poor. I've never thought of myself like that."

Silvestre did not respond. Abel tapped the ash off his cigarette and went on:

"But that isn't why I said it meant a lot to me. It's just that I've never felt so happy as I do today. When I leave, I'm really going to miss you both."

"Why do you have to leave?"

Abel smiled and said:

"Don't you remember what I said the other day? As soon as I feel the octopus of life getting a grip, I cut off the tentacle." After a brief silence that Silvestre made no attempt to interrupt, he added: "I hope you don't think me ungrateful."

"Not at all. If I didn't know you and know about your life, then I might think that."

Abel leaned forward, suddenly filled with curiosity.

"How is it that you're so very perceptive?"

Silvestre looked up, blinking in the light.

"Do you mean that most cobblers aren't?"

"Yes, maybe . . ."

"And yet I've always been a cobbler. You're a clerk of works and have had some education. No one would think . . ."

"But I . . ."

"I know, but you have had an education, haven't you?"

"Yes."

"Well, so have I. I finished primary school, and then I've read quite a lot on my own too. I learned—"

Silvestre stopped abruptly and bowed his head still lower, as if the shoe required all his attention. The lamp lit up his powerful neck and back.

"I'm distracting you from your work," said Abel.

"No, not at all. I could do this with my eyes closed."

He set the shoe aside, picked up three pieces of thread and began waxing them. He did so in long, harmonious movements. Gradually, with each coating of wax, the white thread took on an ever-brighter yellow tone.

"I only do it with my eyes open out of habit," he went on. "And of course if I closed my eyes, it would take much longer."

"Plus it wouldn't be very good," added Abel.

"Exactly. This only goes to show that even when we could close our eyes, we ought to keep them open."

"That sounds rather like a riddle."

"Not really. It's true, isn't it, that I could do the job with my eyes closed?"

"Up to a point. You also agreed that, if you did, you wouldn't do a very good job."

"Which is why I keep them open. But isn't it also true that, at my age, I could easily close my eyes?"

"You mean die?"

Silvestre, who had picked up the awl and was piercing the leather with it in order to begin sewing, stopped what he was doing:

"Die?! What an idea! I'm in no hurry to do that!"

"What do you mean?"

"Closing your eyes just means not being able to see."

"But not being able to see what?"

Silvestre made a sweeping gesture.

"All this . . . life . . . people."

"The riddle continues. I really don't know what you mean."

"How could you? You don't know . . ."

"Now you're intriguing me. Let's see if I can work this out. You said that even when we can close our eyes, we should keep them open, right? You also said that you kept them open so as to see life, people . . ."

"Exactly."

"Well, we all have our eyes open and can see life and people, but you can do that whether you're six or sixty . . ."

"That depends on how you look at things."

"Aha. Now we're getting somewhere. You keep your eyes open so as to see in a certain way. Is that what you mean?"

"That's what I said."

"But see things in what way?"

Silvestre did not answer. He was stretching the threads now, the muscles in his arm tense.

"Look, I'm bothering you," said Abel. "If we carry on talking, you won't have the shoes ready for tomorrow."

"And if we don't carry on talking, you won't sleep all night for thinking about it."

"That's true."

"You're dying to know, aren't you? You're like I was the other day. After twelve years immersed in the stream of life, you've just discovered a very rare bird: a philosophical cobbler! It's like winning the lottery!"

Abel had the feeling Silvestre was making fun of him, but he disguised his displeasure and said in a slightly bittersweet voice:

"Oh, I would certainly like to know, but I've never forced anyone to say anything they didn't want to. Not even people I used to trust . . ."

"Ah, that, I think, was aimed at me! Touché."

The tone in which he said this was so playful and mocking that Abel had to suppress the impulse to give a somewhat sour response, and since that was the only possible response, he preferred to say nothing. Deep down, he wasn't angry with Silvestre at all, and knew that he couldn't be angry with him even if he wanted to be.

"Are you annoyed at me?" asked Silvestre.

"No . . . no . . ."

"That no means yes. I've learned from you to listen to everything that people say to me and how they say it."

"Don't you think I'm right to feel annoyed?"

"Annoyed, yes, and impatient too."

"Impatient? But I just said that I've never forced anyone to tell me anything . . ."

"But if you could?"

"If I could, I would. Now are you satisfied?"

Silvestre laughed out loud:

"Twelve years immersed in the stream of life and you still haven't learned to control your impatience."

"I've learned other things, though."

"You've learned not to trust people."

"How can you say that? I trusted you, didn't I?"

"You did, but what you told me could have been told to anyone. You would simply have to feel the urge to get it off your chest."

"That's true, but you were the one I chose to tell."

"And I'm grateful . . . I'm not joking now. I really am grateful."

"There's no need to be."

Silvestre put down the shoe and the awl and pushed his workbench to one side. He moved the lamp too, so that he could see Abel's face.

"Goodness, you are annoyed."

Abel's face darkened. He was tempted to get up and leave.

"Listen, listen," said Silvestre. "Isn't it true that you distrust everyone, that you're a, oh, what's the word?"

"A skeptic?"

"Yes, that's it, a skeptic."

"Possibly, but given the blows life has dealt me, it would be astonishing if I wasn't. But what made you think I was a skeptic?"

"Everything you told me."

"But at a certain point, what I said moved you."

"That doesn't mean anything. I was moved by what you told me about your life, what you'd been through. I'm equally moved by the terrible things I read in the newspapers."

"That's avoiding the question. Why, in your view, am I a skeptic?"

"All lads your age are. At least nowadays . . ."

"And how many lads do you know who have led the life I've led?"

"Only you. And that's why your life hasn't taught you very much. You want to know life, you said. Why? For your own personal use, for your own benefit, that's all."

"Who told you that?"

"I guessed. I have a gift for it."

"Now you're joking again."

"I'll stop now. Do you remember telling me about the tentacles that try to grab hold of us?"

"I mentioned them again just now."

"That's the heart of the matter! That anxiety of yours about being grabbed and held—"

Abel interrupted him. His frown had vanished; he was interested now, almost excited:

"So would you like to see me stuck in the same job for the rest of my life? Would you like to see me attached to some woman? Would you like to see me living life just as everyone else does?"

"Yes and no. If you really want to know, I just hope that your preoccupation with avoiding imprisonment of any kind doesn't end up with you becoming your own prisoner, the prisoner of your skepticism . . ."

Abel gave a bitter laugh:

"And there I was, thinking I'd been leading an exemplary life . . ."

"You would be if you could take from it what I've taken from mine."

"And may one know what that is?"

Silvestre opened his tobacco pouch, took out a cigarette paper and very slowly rolled himself a cigarette. He took a first puff, then said:

"A certain way of seeing."

"Now we're back where we started. You know what you mean, and I don't, so there's no real possibility of us having a conversation."

"Yes, there is, once I tell you what I know."

"At last! Perhaps if you'd told me that in the first place, we would have got off to a better start."

"I don't think so. Just hear what I have to say first."

"Fine, I'm listening. But woe betide you if you fail to convince me!"

He was wagging his finger at Silvestre, but there was a smile on his face, and Silvestre responded likewise to the threat. Then he leaned his head back and stared up at the ceiling. The tendons in his neck resembled taut ropes. His unbuttoned collar revealed the top of his chest, covered in dark hairs scattered with a few curly silver threads. Slowly, as if he were returning from his abstraction laden with memories, Silvestre looked at Abel. Then he began to talk, in a deep voice that trembled when it uttered certain words and grew firmer and more rigid with others:

"Listen, my friend, when I was sixteen, I was already what I am today: a cobbler. I was working from morning to night in a cramped workshop with four other men. In the winter the damp streamed down the walls, and in the summer we almost died from the heat. You were right when you said that life for me at sixteen wasn't exactly marvelous. You suffered cold and hunger because you wanted to. I did the same, but not out of choice. That makes a big difference. You chose to lead that life, and I don't blame you for that. I didn't have a choice about the life I led. I won't tell you about my childhood either, even though I am, as you put it, old enough to take pleasure in talking about it. It was so wretched that, if I did tell you, it would only upset you. Bad food, not enough clothes and a lot of beatings just about sums it up. So many children have the same experience that people aren't surprised anymore."

Abel was listening intently, his chin resting on one fist. His dark eyes were shining. His slightly feminine mouth had grown harder. He was a picture of concentration.

"That's how I was living when I was sixteen," Silvestre went on. "I was working in Barreiro. Do you know Barreiro? I haven't been there for about two years, and so I've no idea what it's like now, but anyway . . . As I told you, I finished junior school—at night school. I had a teacher who certainly didn't spare the rod. I got beaten along with all the others. I really wanted to learn, but sometimes sleep got the better of me. He must have known what I did during the day, I remember telling him once, but it made no difference. He didn't treat me any better. He's dead now, and may the earth weigh lightly on him. At the time, the monarchy was on its last legs, the very last, as it happens."

"I assume you're a republican," said Abel.

"If being a republican means not liking the monarchy, then yes, I'm a republican. But it seems to me that, in the end, 'monarchy' and 'republic' are just words. That's what I think now. At the time, though, I was a convinced republican, and 'republic' was more than just a word. The republic duly arrived. Nothing to do with me, of course, but I wept as joyfully as if it had all been my work. You, who live in these hard, distrustful times, can't imagine how hopeful we all were then. If everyone felt as happy as I did, then there was a time when there were no unhappy people in the whole of Portugal. I was a child, I know, and I felt and thought like a child. Later on, I realized that my hopes were being stolen from me. The republic was no longer a novelty, and here people only appreciate novelties. We enter like lions and leave like broken old nags. It's in our blood. We were as overflowing with enthusiasm and energy as if a child had been born to us. But there were also plenty of people bent on destroying our ideals. And they didn't care how. Then the worst of it was that a few others turned up wanting, at all costs, to save the Fatherland. As if it needed saving. People no longer knew what they wanted. Men you were friends with yesterday became enemies the next day, without anyone quite knowing why. I listened to both sides and pondered it all. I wanted to do something, but didn't know what. There were times when I would gladly have given my life if necessary. I started talking to my fellow cobblers. One of them was a socialist. He was more intelligent than all of us put together. He knew a lot. He believed in socialism and could explain why. He lent me books. I can see him now. He was older than me and very thin and pale. His eyes flashed when he spoke about certain things. But because of the position he worked in and because he wasn't very strong physically, his back was quite bent and his chest very sunken. He used to say that he liked me because I had it all, brawn and brains!" He paused and relit his cigarette, which had burned out. "He had the same name as you—Abel. That was over forty years ago. He died before the war. One day he didn't turn up for work, and so I went to see him. He lived with his mother. He was in bed with a high fever. He had spat blood. When I went into his room, he smiled. It made a real impression on me, that smile, it was as if he was saying goodbye to me. Two months later, he died. He left me all his books. I still have them . . ."

Silvestre's eyes seemed to withdraw and go back to the distant past. They could see the dying man's shabby room, as shabby as his own, see his long fingers with their purplish nails, his pale face with eyes like burning coals.

"You've never had a friend, have you?" he asked.

"No, never."

"That's a shame. You don't know what it's like to have a friend. You also don't know what it's like to lose one, nor how much you miss him when you think about him. That's one of the things life hasn't taught you."

Abel said nothing, but he nodded. Silvestre's voice and the words he was hearing were reordering his ideas. A dim but insistent light was shining into his mind, illuminating its shadows and dark corners.

"Then came the war," Silvestre said. "I went off to France, not because I wanted to, but because they sent me. I had no choice. There I was, up to my knees in the mud of Flanders. I was at La Couture. When I talk about the war, I can't say much. I imagine what this last one must have been like for those who lived through it, and I say nothing. If that first one was the Great War, what will they call this second war? And the one after that?" Without waiting for a reply, he went on: "When I came back, something was different. Well, after two years away, things are bound to change, but what had changed most was me. I returned to my work as a cobbler, but in another workshop. My new colleagues were family men who, as they said quite openly, didn't want any trouble. And so as soon as they found out who and what I was, they told the boss. I got the sack and was threatened with the police . . ."

Silvestre gave a toothless smile, as if remembering some bitterly comic episode, but soon recovered himself:

"Times had changed. Before I went to France, I could say what I liked to my colleagues and no one would have dreamed of denouncing me to the police or to the boss. Now I had to keep quiet. It was then that I met my Mariana. Seeing her now, you can't possibly imagine what she looked like then. She was lovely as a May morning!"

Almost without thinking, Abel asked:

"Do you love your wife?"

Taken by surprise, Silvestre hesitated. Then, calmly and with deep conviction, he answered:

"Yes, I do, very much."

"It's love," thought Abel, "it's love that gives them this calmness, this peace." And suddenly he was gripped by a violent desire to love, to give himself, to find the red flower of love growing in his arid life. Silvestre continued to speak in his serene voice:

"I thought of my friend Abel, my other friend Abel."

Smiling, Abel nodded his thanks for the compliment.

"I reread the books he'd left me and began to live a double life. By day, I was a cobbler, a silent cobbler who could see no farther than the soles of the shoes he was mending. By night, I was my true self. Don't be surprised if the way I speak is too refined for my profession. I knew a lot of very cultivated people, and although I may not have learned as much as I should, I learned what I could. I sometimes risked my life. I never refused to do anything they asked of me, however dangerous."

Silvestre was speaking more slowly now, as if drawing back from a painful memory or as if, unable to avoid talking about it, he were trying to find a way to do so:

"There was a strike by railway workers. After twenty days they were ordered back to work by the government. In response, the central committee gave orders for the workers to abandon all train stations. I was in touch with the railway workers and had a particular mission to carry out. I was a trusted member, despite my youth. They put me in charge of a group that was supposed to distribute leaflets in an area of Barreiro, at night. In the early hours we got into a fight with some members of the Monarchist Youth Movement . . ."

Silvestre rolled another cigarette. His hands were shaking slightly and he avoided Abel's eyes:

"One of them died. I only caught a glimpse of his face, but he was very young. He was left lying in the road. A very cold, fine drizzle was falling, and the streets were full of mud. The police arrived, and we ran away before they could identify us. We never found out who had killed the lad."

A heavy silence fell, as if the dead man had come and sat down between them. Silvestre kept his head lowered. Abel cleared his throat and asked:

"And then?"

"Well, it went on like that for years. Later, I got

married. Mariana had a pretty tough time on my account, but she always suffered in silence. She thought I was doing the right thing and never criticized me, never tried to divert me from my path. I owe her that. The years passed, and here I am, an old man."

Silvestre went into the apartment and returned shortly afterward bearing the bottle of cherry brandy and two glasses:

"Would you like a drink to warm you up?"

"I would."

With their glasses full, the two men fell silent.

"So," said Abel a few minutes later.

"So what?"

"Where is this 'way of seeing life'?"

"You haven't worked it out for yourself yet?"

"Possibly, but I'd prefer you to tell me."

Silvestre drank his cherry brandy down in one, wiped his mouth with the back of his hand and said:

"If you haven't worked it out for yourself, that means I've failed to tell you what I feel. Nothing surprising about that. There are some things that are very difficult to put into words. We think we've said all there is to say, and it turns out . . ."

"Now don't run away."

"I'm not. I learned to see beyond the soles of these shoes. I learned that behind this wretched life we lead there is a great ideal, a great hope. I learned that each individual life should be guided by that hope and by that ideal. And people who don't feel that must have died before they were born." He smiled and added: "Those aren't my words. It's something I heard someone else say years ago."

"In your view, then, I belong to the group who died before they were born?"

"No, you belong to another group, the ones who haven't yet been born."

"Aren't you forgetting about all *my* experience of life?"

"Not at all, but experience is only worth anything when it's useful to other people, and you're not useful to anyone."

"I agree that I'm not useful, but in what way has your life been useful?"

"I tried to do something, and even if I failed, at least I tried."

"You tried in your own way, yes, but who's to say it was the best way?"

"Almost everyone nowadays would say it was the worst. Is that the group you belong to?"

"To be perfectly honest, I don't know."

"You don't know? At your age and after everything you've seen and been through, you still don't know?"

Abel could not look Silvestre in the eye and lowered his head.

"How can you not know?" Silvestre said again. "Has twelve years of living the way you've been living not shown you how badly people live? The poverty, the hunger, the ignorance, the fear?"

"Yes, but times have changed . . ."

"Yes, times have changed, but people haven't."

"Some have died. Your friend Abel, for example."

"But others have been born. My other friend Abel, for example, Abel Nogueira."

"Now you're contradicting yourself. Just now you were saying I belonged to the group who haven't yet been born."

Silvestre again drew the bench closer to him, picked up the shoe and resumed his work. With a tremor in his voice, he said:

"Perhaps you didn't understand me."

"I understand you better than you think."

"Don't you agree that I'm right, then?"

Abel got to his feet and looked out through the glass panes at the back yard. It was a dark night. He opened the window. All was shadows and silence, but there were stars in the sky. From horizon to horizon the Milky Way unfurled its luminous path. And from the city, rising to the heavens, came a dull volcanic rumble.

22

With the natural vitality of a six-year-old, Henrique made a rapid recovery. And yet, despite the relatively benign nature of the illness, his character seemed to have undergone a radical change. Perhaps the experience of being showered with care and affection had made him more than usually sensitive. At the slightest harsh word, his eyes would well up and he would burst into tears.

The once lively, playful boy had become prudent and sensible. In his father's company he was always serious and silent. He would gaze at him tenderly, in dumb, passionate admiration, even though this sudden interest went unreciprocated and his father was no more affectionate toward him than usual. What attracted Henrique now was exactly what had repelled him before: his father's silence, his few words, his absent air. For reasons unknown to him, and which he would not have understood had he known them, his father had kept vigil at his bedside. His presence there, the anxious yet reserved look on his face, the hostile atmosphere filling the apartment, plus the new receptiveness and keener perception brought on by illness—all these factors, in some obscure way, drove him toward his father. One of the many doors in his small brain, which had until then remained closed, had inched open. Without being conscious of doing so, he had taken a step toward maturity. He began to notice the lack of harmony in the family.

He had, of course, witnessed violent rows between his parents on other occasions, but he had done so as an indifferent spectator, as if he were watching a game that in no way affected him. Not now, though. He was still under the influence of the illness and his weak state, and prior to that he had become, quite against his will, sensitized to the various manifestations of that latent conflict. The prism through which he viewed his parents had shifted very slightly, but enough for him to be able to see them differently. This would inevitably have happened sooner or later, but the illness had sped up the process.

His mother remained undiminished in his eyes, his view of her unchanged, but he saw his father in a different light. Henrique was far too young to realize that the change had taken place inside himself; it must, therefore, have been his father who had changed. In the absence of any real explanation, Henrique had to think back to the care his father had lavished on him during his illness. This then made sense to him. And so Henrique's sudden interest in his father was merely a way of reciprocating his father's interest in him, not now, but then; it was an acknowledgment, a show of gratitude. Each age in life seizes upon the easiest and most immediate explanation available.

This interest manifested itself in both sensible and nonsensical ways. At mealtimes, Henrique's chair was always drawn slightly closer to his father's chair than to his mother's. When, at night, Emílio was sorting through his paperwork—the various orders and invoices he had picked up during the day—his son would stand leaning on the table, watching him. If a piece of paper fell to the floor—and Henrique longed with all his heart for this to happen—he would rush to pick it up, and if his father smiled at him gratefully, Henrique was the happiest of children. There was an even greater happiness, though, one that admitted of no comparison: this was when his father placed a hand on his head. At such moments, Henrique almost fainted.

His son's sudden and apparently inexplicable interest provoked two different and contrary reactions in Emílio. At first he found it very touching. His life was so barren of affection, so removed from love, he felt so isolated, that these small attentions, his son's constant presence at his side, his stubborn devotion to him, touched him deeply. Then he saw how dangerous it was: his son's interest, his own feelings, only made his decision to leave more difficult. He hardened his heart, tried to distance himself from his son, emphasizing the character traits most likely to discourage him. Henrique, however, did not give up. Had Emílio resorted to violence, he might have driven him away, but he couldn't do that. He had never hit him and never would, even if administering such a beating were the price he must pay for his own freedom. He felt almost sick to think that he could attack Henrique with the same hand that had caressed him and which Henrique loved because of that caress.

Emílio thought too much. His brain attached itself to all kinds of things, went over and over the same problems, plunged into them, drowned in them, so that, in the end, his own thoughts became the problem. He forgot what was really important to him and went off in search of motives, reasons. Life was rushing past him and yet he paid it no attention. The matter to be resolved was there, but he could not see it. Even if it could have shouted to him, "Here I am! Over here!," he would not have heard it. Now, instead of looking for a way of distancing himself from his son, he started pondering the reasons for his son's sudden interest in him. And when he could find none, his brain, caught in the web of his subconscious, produced only a superstitious explanation: his son's illness had gotten worse after he announced to him that he was planning to leave, and this was why Henrique, frightened by the prospect of losing him, was showing all this unexpected interest in him. When he emerged from this paralyzing quagmire of thoughts, Emílio realized how irrational this conclusion was: Henrique had barely heard what he had said, he had paid about as much attention to it as to a passing fly, forgotten almost as soon as it was seen. Besides, he had not heard his final, definitive, irrevocable words, because by then he had fallen asleep. Here, though, Emílio's brain set off once more along the tightrope of his subconscious: words spoken, even if not heard, remain hanging in the air, hovering in the atmosphere, and can, so to speak, be inhaled and have as much effect as if they had found in their path ears that could hear them. A foolish, superstitious conclusion, woven out of evil omens and mysteries.

What was happening was further proof to Carmen of her husband's perverse nature. Not content with having denied her any happiness, he was now trying to steal her one remaining possession, the love of her son. She fought against Emílio's dastardly plans. She heaped affection on her son, but Henrique gave more importance to a simple glance from his father than to all his mother's exuberant displays of affection. In despair, Carmen even came to believe that her husband must have bewitched him, given him some potion to drink that had changed his feelings. And once she had this idea lodged in her head, she knew what to do. In secret, she submitted the boy to prayers and incense, terrifying him with threats of beatings if he breathed so much as a word to his father.

Troubled by these weird ceremonies, Henrique became more nervous and excitable. Frightened by her threats, he drew closer to his father.

All Carmen's efforts were in vain: no amount of witchcraft or affection could divert her son from his obstinate obsession. She became aggressive toward him. She began to find reasons to hit him. The smallest misdemeanor was rewarded with a slap. She knew what she was doing was wrong, but couldn't help herself. When, after hitting him, she saw him crying, she would cry too, but alone and out of anger and remorse. She wanted to beat and beat him until she could beat him no more, although she knew that she would regret forever having done such a thing. She had lost all self-control. She felt like committing some monstrous act, smashing everything around her, rampaging through the apartment kicking the furniture and punching the walls, screaming at her husband and shaking and slapping him. Her nerves were constantly on edge, she had lost all sense of prudence, as well as the vague fear that married women have of their husbands.

One night at supper, Henrique moved his stool so close to his father's that Carmen felt a wave of anger rise in her throat. She felt as if her head were about to burst. Everything around her was swaying and dancing, and in order not to fall she instinctively grabbed hold of the edge of the table, knocking over a bottle in the process. This accident, the shattering of glass, was the lit fuse that allowed her rage to explode. Almost screaming, she said:

"*¡Estoy harta*! I've had enough!"

Emílio, who was eating his soup and had not reacted to the bottle falling over, looked up serenely, regarded his wife with his pale, cold eyes and asked:

"Enough of what?"

Before answering, Carmen shot such a furious glance at her son that he shrank back and clung to his father's arm:

"Enough of you! Enough of this apartment! Enough of your son! I've had enough of this life! I've had enough, I tell you!"

"Well, you know what the solution is."

"That's exactly what you'd like, isn't it? For me to leave. *¡Pero no iré*! I won't go!"

"Fine, as you wish."

"And what if I did want to go?"

"Don't worry, I wouldn't come looking for you."

He accompanied these words with a mocking laugh, which to Carmen was worse than a slap in the face. Certain that she would wound her husband deeply, she retorted:

"You might come looking for me . . . because if I leave, I won't leave alone!"

"What do you mean?"

"I'll take my son with me!"

Emílio felt Henrique's hand grip his arm still harder. He glanced down at him, saw his trembling lips and moist eyes, and was filled with a feeling of intense pity and tenderness. He tried to spare his son this degrading spectacle:

"This is a completely stupid conversation. Haven't you noticed that your son is here listening?"

"¡No me importa! I don't care! And don't pretend you don't know what I mean!"

"That's enough!"

"Only when I say so!"

"Carmen!"

She looked at him then. Her strong jaw, grown more pronounced with age, seemed to challenge him:

"I'm not afraid of you, not you or anyone!"

No, Carmen clearly wasn't afraid, but suddenly her voice broke, tears poured down her cheeks and, swept along by uncontrollable emotion, she hurled herself on her son. Kneeling, her voice shaken by sobs, she was murmuring in Spanish, almost moaning:

"Sweetheart, look at me. I'm your mother. I'm your friend. No one loves you as much as I do!"

Henrique was trembling with fear, clinging to his father. Carmen continued her incoherent monologue, ever more aware that her son was slipping away from her and yet incapable of letting him go.

Emílio stood up, tore his son from his wife's arms, then drew her to her feet and sat her down on a stool. Close to fainting, she let him do as he pleased.

"Carmen!"

She was sitting hunched forward, her head in her hands, weeping. On the other side of the table, Henrique seemed to be in a state of shock. He had his mouth open as if he were gasping for air, his eyes as glazed and fixed as if he were blind. Emílio rushed to his side, spoke soothing words to him and carried him out of the kitchen.

With great difficulty, he managed to calm the child down. When they returned, Carmen was wiping her eyes on her dirty apron. Seeing her there, looking suddenly old and tired, her face strained and red, he felt sorry for her:

"Are you feeling better?"

"Yes. What about the child?"

"He's all right."

They sat at the table in silence. In silence they ate. After this stormy scene, the calm of sheer exhaustion imposed that silence on them. Father, mother and son. Three people living under the same roof, in the same light, breathing the same air. A family.

When the meal was over, Emílio went into the dining room, and his son followed. He sat down on an old wicker sofa, as wearily as if he had just been engaged in heavy labor. Henrique came and leaned against his knees.

"How are you feeling?"

"I'm OK, Papa."

Emílio stroked his son's soft hair and felt profoundly affected by the child's small head, almost small enough to fit in his hand. He brushed Henrique's hair out of his eyes, smoothed his fine eyebrows, then followed the shape of his face as far as his chin. Henrique allowed himself to be stroked as if he were a puppy. He was barely breathing, as though afraid that a mere breath would be enough to stop the stroking. His eyes were fixed on his father. Emílio's hand continued to stroke his son's face, unaware now of what it was doing, a mechanical movement in which the conscious mind played no part. Henrique sensed that sudden distancing. He slipped between his father's knees and rested his head on his chest.

Now that Emílio was free from his son's gaze, his eyes wandered from one piece of furniture to another, from object to object. Perched on a column was the clay figure of a boy fishing, his feet in an empty aquarium. Underneath the statuette, a doily, falling in folds from the top of the column, provided evidence of Carmen's domestic talents. A few wine glasses gleamed dully on the sideboard and in the so-called china cupboard, which otherwise contained only a few examples of local ceramics. More doilies were further proof of Carmen's homemaking skills. Everything had a kind of matte finish to it, as if a layer of dust, impossible to remove, were hiding any gloss or color.

Emílio's overriding impression was of ugliness, monotony and banality. The ceiling lamp shed light in such a way that its main function seemed to be to distribute shadows. And it was a modern lamp too. It had three chrome arms, each with its corresponding shade, but for the sake of economy, only one bulb worked.

Carmen continued to make her presence felt from the kitchen, sighing loudly as she pondered her misery and washed the dishes.

With his son pressed to him, Emílio saw the prosaic nature of both his present and past lives. As for the future, he was holding that in his arms, except that it wasn't his future. In a few years' time, the head now resting happily on his chest would be thinking for itself, but thinking what?

Emílio gently lifted his son from where he lay on his chest and looked at him. Henrique's thoughts were still slumbering behind his now serene face. All was hidden.

23

Amélia whispered in her sister's ear:
"The girls have had a falling-out."
"What?"
"A falling-out."
They were in the kitchen. They had finished supper shortly before. In the next room, Adriana and Isaura were busy sewing buttonholes in shirts. The light from there poured out through the open door into the dark passageway. Cândida looked at her sister incredulously.
"Don't you believe me?" asked Amélia.
Cândida shrugged and stuck out her lower lip to indicate her complete ignorance of the situation.
"If you didn't go around with your eyes closed, you would have noticed."
"But what's wrong?"
"That's what I'd like to know."
"It's your imagination . . ."
"Possibly, but you could count on the fingers of one hand the number of words they've said to each other today. And not just today either. Haven't you noticed?"
"No."
"See what I mean? You walk around with your eyes closed. Leave me to tidy the kitchen, and go in there and *observe*."

Taking her usual tiny steps, Cândida walked down the corridor to the room where her daughters were sitting. Absorbed in their work, the two sisters didn't even look up when their mother came in. Donizetti's *Lucia di Lammermoor* was playing softly on the radio; the shrill tones of a soprano were filling the air. More in order to gauge the atmosphere than to make any proper critical comment, Cândida said:

"Goodness, what a voice! She sounds like she's performing somersaults!"

Her daughters smiled, but their smiles seemed as forced and effortful as the singer's vocal acrobatics. Cândida felt concerned. Her sister was quite right. There was something odd going on. She had never seen her daughters like this, reserved and distant, as if they were afraid of each other. She tried to come out with some conciliatory phrase, but her throat, grown suddenly dry, could not produce a single word. Isaura and Adriana carried on with their work. The singer's voice faded out in an ethereal, almost inaudible *smorzando*. The orchestra played three swift chords, and then the tenor's voice rose, strong and compelling.

"How well Gigli sings!" exclaimed Cândida, simply in order to say something.

The two sisters glanced at each other and hesitated, each wanting the other to speak. Both felt they should reply, and in the end it was Adriana who said:

"Yes, he does. He sings really well, but he's getting on a bit now."

Glad, at least for a few minutes, to be able to resume their usual evening banter, Cândida hotly defended Gigli:

"What does that matter? Just listen. There's no other singer like him. And as for being old, well, old people have their value too. Who sings better than Gigli? Tell me that. Some older people are worth a lot more than many younger ones . . ."

As if the shirt she was working on had presented her with some unexpectedly intractable problem, Isaura lowered her head. Although her mother's remark about the relative values of old and young could only remotely have been a reference to her, she turned bright red. Like everyone who has a secret to hide, she saw insinuations and suspicions in every word and glance. Adriana noticed her embarrassment, guessed the reason behind it and tried to bring the conversation to a close.

"Oh, you old people are always complaining about the young!"

"But I wasn't complaining," said Cândida.

"Hm," Adriana responded with a somewhat impatient gesture. She was normally calm, almost indifferent, quite unlike her sister, in whom one sensed a kind of constant tremor beneath the skin, signaling an intense, tumultuous inner life. Now, however, she, too, was agitated. All conversations irritated her, and what irritated her even more was the eternally perplexed and anxious look on her mother's face, as well as the humble tone in which she had spoken.

Cândida noticed the brusque note in Adriana's voice and fell silent. She shrank back into her chair, took up her crochet work and tried to disappear.

Now and then she shot a furtive glance at her daughters. Isaura had not as yet said anything. She was so absorbed in her work that she seemed barely to notice the music. Gigli and Toti Dal Monte warbled a love duet, but all in vain. Isaura was not listening, nor, really, was Adriana. Only Cândida, despite her concerns, allowed herself to be bewitched by the sweet, easy melodies of Donizetti. Taken up with her crocheting and keeping time with the music, she soon forgot about her daughters. Only the sound of her sister's voice calling to her from the kitchen roused her from that abstracted state.

"Well?" asked Amélia when Cândida joined her.

"I didn't notice anything."

"I should have known . . ."

"It's all in your imagination! Once you get an idea in your head . . ."

Amélia rolled her eyes as if she considered her sister's words absurd or, more than that, annoying. Cândida did not dare to finish what she was saying. With a shrug that indicated her displeasure at being interrupted, Amélia declared:

"Leave it with me. I was a fool to think I could count on you."

"But what exactly is it that you suspect?"

"That's my affair."

"No, you must tell me. They're my daughters and I want to know . . ."

"You'll find out in time."

Cândida experienced a flash of anger as unexpected as a furious outburst from a caged canary.

"I think it's all nonsense, another of your foolish obsessions!"

"'Obsession' is a very strong word to use. So my being worried about your daughters is an obsession, is it?"

"But Amélia—"

"Don't 'Amélia' me! I'll do my job and you do yours. You'll thank me one day."

"I could thank you now if you'd tell me what was going on. Is it my fault I'm not as observant as you?!"

Amélia shot her sister a suspicious sideways glance. There was, she felt, a note of mockery in those words. Maybe she was being unreasonable, and she was almost on the point of confessing that she knew nothing. This would reassure her sister, and then, together, they could perhaps find out what lay behind the disagreement between Isaura and Adriana. However, pride stopped her. It was quite simply beyond her capabilities to confess her ignorance after having given Cândida to understand that she knew something. She had grown accustomed to being right, to speaking as if she were the oracle, and she was not in the least inclined to relinquish that oracular role. She murmured:

"Fine, be ironic if you want to. I'll manage on my own."

Cândida rejoined her daughters, feeling more anxious than she had before. Amélia knew something, but didn't want to tell her. But what could it be? Adriana and Isaura were sitting in the same places as before, but Cândida had the feeling now that they were separated by leagues. She sat down on her chair, picked up her crochet work, did a few stitches, but, unable to go on, dropped her work, hesitated for a second, then asked:

"What's wrong with you two?"

Isaura and Adriana both panicked. For a few moments, they didn't know what to say, then they both spoke at once:

"Us? Nothing."

And Adriana added:

"Really, Mama, what a silly idea!"

"Of course," Cândida thought, "of course it's a silly idea." She smiled and looked first at one of her daughters, then at the other, before saying:

"You're right, it's just one of those silly ideas one gets sometimes. Pay no attention."

She picked up her crocheting again and resumed

her work. Shortly afterward, Isaura left the room. Her mother followed her with her eyes. Adriana bent still lower over her shirt. The radio was now a cacophony of voices. It must have been the end of the act, with a lot of people onstage, some with high voices, some with low. It sounded confusing and, above all, noisy. Suddenly, above the clash of brass overwhelming the singers, Cândida called out:

"Adriana!"

"Yes, Mama."

"Go and see what's wrong with your sister. She might be feeling ill . . ."

Cândida noticed Adriana's reluctance to do as she was asked.

"Aren't you going?"

"Yes, of course, why wouldn't I?"

"That's what I'd like to know."

Cândida's eyes had a strange glint in them, as if tears were welling up.

"Whatever are you thinking, Mama?"

"I'm not thinking anything, love, nothing . . ."

"Believe me, there's nothing to think. We're fine."

"Do you give me your word?"

"I do."

"All right, then. Go and see how she is."

Adriana went. Her mother let her crochet work drop into her lap, and the tears she had been holding in finally fell. Just two tears, two tears that had to fall because, having reached her eyes, there was no going back. She did not believe her daughter. She was sure now that Isaura and Adriana had some secret they could not or would not reveal.

Amélia entered the room and cut short her thoughts. Cândida picked up her crochet needle and bowed her head.

"Where are the girls?"

"In their room."

"What are they doing?"

"I don't know. If you're still determined to find out, you can go and spy on them if you like, but you're wasting your time. Adriana gave me her word. There's nothing wrong."

Amélia pushed a chair roughly aside and said in a cutting voice:

"I don't care what you think. And I'll have you know, I've never spied on anyone, but if necessary, I'm willing to start!"

"You're obsessed!"

"Maybe I am, but don't you ever say such a thing to me again!"

"I didn't mean to offend you."

"But you did."

"I'm sorry."

"It's too late now."

Cândida got to her feet. She was slightly shorter than her sister. Involuntarily, she raised herself on tiptoe:

"If you won't accept my apology, that's your loss. Adriana gave me her word."

"I don't believe her."

"But I do, and that's all that matters!"

"Are you saying that I'm of no importance in your lives? I know I'm only your sister and that this isn't my apartment, but I never dreamed you would treat me like this!"

"You're misinterpreting my words. I never said any such thing!"

"A word to the wise—"

"Even the wise make mistakes sometimes!"

"Cândida!"

"You're surprised, aren't you? But I've had enough of your stupid suspicions. Let's not argue anymore. It's dreadful that we should quarrel over something like this."

Without waiting for her sister to answer, Cândida left the room, covering her eyes with her hands. Amélia stayed where she was, not moving, grasping the back of the chair, and her eyes, too, were wet with tears. She again felt an impulse to admit to her sister that she knew nothing, but again pride stopped her.

Yes, pride and the return of her two nieces. They were smiling, but her sharp eyes could see that their smiles were false, that they had applied them to their lips before they came in, like masks. She thought: "They're determined to keep us in the dark." This only made her all the more determined to discover what lay behind those fake smiles.

24

Caetano was pondering how to get his revenge for what Justina had said to him. He cursed himself over and over for his cowardice. He should, as threatened, have beaten her to a pulp. He should have punched her with his big, hairy fists, made her run through the apartment in fear of his anger. He had, however, been quite incapable of doing that; he had lacked the necessary courage, and now he wanted his revenge. He wanted a perfect revenge, though, not just a beating. Something more refined and subtle, not that this need necessarily exclude some physical violence.

Whenever he thought of that humiliating scene, he trembled with rage. He tried to keep himself in that frame of mind, but as soon as he opened the door to the apartment, he felt powerless. He tried to convince himself that it was his wife's frail appearance that held him back, he tried to disguise his own weakness as pity, then flagellated himself mentally because he knew it was nothing but weakness. He thought up ways of heaping more scorn on his wife, but she would merely reciprocate with still more of her own. He tried giving her less money for the housekeeping, then gave up when he was the only one who suffered, because Justina would give him less food. For two whole days (he even dreamed about it) he considered hiding or removing from the apartment their daughter's photo and all reminders of her existence. He knew that this would be the harshest blow he could deal his wife.

Fear stopped him. Not fear of his wife, but of the possible consequences. It seemed to him that such an action bordered on sacrilege. Such a gesture would bring about the worst of misfortunes: tuberculosis, for example, for despite his ninety kilos of flesh and bone and his ridiculously robust health, he feared TB as the worst of all diseases, and just the sight of someone with TB gave him the horrors. The mere mention of the word sent a shudder through him. Even when he was at his Linotype machine, typing in the journalists' copy (a job that involved no brainpower, at least not as regards understanding the text), and the horrible word appeared, he could not help recoiling slightly. This happened so often that he became convinced that the office boss, who knew about this weakness of his, assigned to him every article that the newspaper published on tuberculosis. He was always sent the reports on medical conferences where the illness was discussed. The mysterious words filling such reports—complicated words that sounded terrifyingly like Greek, and that seemed to have been invented for the sole purpose of frightening sensitive people—fixed themselves in his brain like suckers and did not leave him for hours.

Apart from that one impracticable project, any other ideas dreamed up by his anemic imagination would work only if he was on friendlier terms with his wife. He had taken so many things from her—love, friendship, peace of mind and everything else that can make married life bearable and even desirable—that there was nothing left. He almost regretted having, so early on, gotten out of the habit of kissing her hello and goodbye, simply because he could not now abandon that habit too.

Despite all these failures of imagination, he did not give up. He was obsessed with the idea of avenging himself in a way that would force his wife to fall on her knees before him, desperate and begging forgiveness.

One day he thought he had found the way. When he considered his plan properly, he realized it was absurd, but perhaps its very absurdity seduced him. He intended playing a new role in his relations with his wife, that of the jealous husband. Poor, ugly, almost skeletal Justina would not have aroused the jealousy of the fiercest of Othellos. Nevertheless, Caetano's imagination could come up with nothing better.

While he was setting the scene for this plan, he was almost nice to his wife. He went so far as to stroke the cat, much to the cat's surprise. He bought a new frame for their daughter's photograph and said he was thinking of having an enlargement made. All this touched Justina deeply, and she thanked him for the frame and spoke warmly of the idea of having the photograph enlarged. However, she knew her husband well enough to suspect that he had some ulterior motive. She therefore waited, expecting the worst.

Having made his preparations, Caetano struck. One night he went straight home after work. He had in his pocket a letter he had written to himself, disguising his handwriting. He had used different ink from the sort he normally used and an old pen that made his writing more angular and blotted the smaller letters. It was a masterpiece of dissimulation. Not even an expert would spot that it was a fake.

When he put his key in the lock, his heart was pounding. He was at last about to satisfy his desire for revenge and see his wife on her knees, protesting her innocence. He entered the apartment slowly and cautiously. He wanted to take her by surprise. He would rouse her from sleep and place before her the evidence of her guilt. He was smiling to himself as he tiptoed down the corridor, sliding his hand along the wall until he reached the doorframe. With his other hand he groped the empty darkness. The warm air from the bedroom brushed his face. With his left hand, he felt for the switch. He was ready. He affected an angry look and turned on the light.

Justina was not asleep. Caetano had not foreseen this possibility. His anger vanished, all expression drained from his face. His wife looked at him, surprised, but said nothing. Caetano sensed that his whole stratagem would collapse if he did not speak at once. He recovered his composure, frowned angrily and said:

"Hm, lucky you're not asleep. That saves me the trouble of having to wake you up. Read this!"

He threw the letter at her. Justina slowly picked up the envelope. As she did so, she thought it must contain the explanation for her husband's sudden change in behavior. She removed the letter from the envelope and tried to read it; however, the abrupt shift from darkness to light, combined with the bad handwriting, meant that she failed at the first attempt. She changed position, rubbed her eyes and raised herself on one elbow. Caetano found these delays exasperating: nothing was going according to plan.

Justina was now reading the letter. Her husband anxiously followed her every change of expression. The absurd thought came into his head: "What if it were true?" He did not have time to follow this idea through, because Justina fell back on the pillow, roaring with laughter.

"Oh, you're laughing, are you?" bellowed Caetano, but in fact he felt utterly confused.

She could not reply. She was laughing like

mad, a sarcastic laugh; she was laughing at her husband and at herself, but more at herself than at him. She was convulsed with laughter, her body heaving; she was laughing as if she were, at the same time, crying. Her eyes were quite dry, though, and out of her gaping mouth poured forth a hysterical, uninterrupted stream of guffaws.

"Shut up! This is disgraceful!" exclaimed Caetano, walking over to her. Given that it had all begun so badly, he wasn't sure whether or not to continue the performance. His wife's reaction was sabotaging his carefully laid plans.

"Shut up!" he said again, bending over her. "Shut up!"

Now only the occasional tremor of laughter ran through Justina. She was gradually calming down. Caetano tried to pick up the fast disappearing thread of his plot:

"Is that how you respond to such an accusation? It's worse than I thought, then!"

At these words, Justina abruptly sat up in bed. She did this so quickly that Caetano drew back. His wife's eyes glittered:

"This whole thing is a farce, but what you're hoping to gain from it I have no idea."

"A farce, is it? Oh, please! I demand an explanation for what's in that letter!"

"Ask the person who wrote it!"

"It's anonymous."

"I can see that. But I'm not giving you any explanation."

"You dare to say that to me?"

"What do you expect me to say?"

"To tell me whether or not it's true."

Justina looked at him in a way he found unbearable. He averted his gaze and his eyes fell on the photo of their daughter. Matilde was smiling at her parents. His wife followed his gaze, then said softly, slowly:

"You want to know if it's true, do you? You want me to tell you if it's true? You want me to tell you the truth?"

Caetano hesitated. The idea that had occurred to him in his disoriented state of mind resurfaced: "What if it *was* true?" Then Justina said again:

"You want to know the truth, do you?"

She grasped the hem of her nightdress and, in one rapid movement, pulled it up over her head. She stood there before her husband, naked. Caetano opened his mouth to say something, although quite what he had no idea. He could not utter a single word. His wife was speaking again:

"Here it is! Look at me! Here's the truth you wanted. Look at me, go on! Don't look away! Take a good long look!"

As if obeying the orders of a hypnotist, Caetano opened his eyes very wide. He saw the scrawny brown body, made darker by its very thinness, the angular shoulders, the flaccid, pendant breasts, the convex belly, the thin thighs jutting from the torso, the large, misshapen feet.

"Take a good look," Justina repeated in a tense voice that threatened to break at any moment. "Take a good long look. If even *you* don't want me, you who will go with any woman, who else is going to want me? Take a long hard look! Shall I stay like this until you say you've seen enough? Quickly, tell me!"

Justina was trembling. She felt debased, not because she had revealed herself to her husband naked, but for having given in to her indignation, for not having responded to him with silent scorn. It was too late now to show him what she really felt.

She walked over to her husband:

"Nothing to say? Is this why you dreamed up this whole comedy? I should feel ashamed to stand before you in this state. But I don't. That shows you just how much I despise you!"

Caetano turned abruptly and left the room. Justina heard him open the front door and race down the stairs. Then she slumped onto the bed again and, totally drained, began to cry noiselessly. As if ashamed of her nakedness now that she was alone, she pulled the bedclothes up about her.

In the photo, Matilde's smile was unaltered. A happy smile, the smile of a child who has been taken to the photographer's studio, and to whom the photographer has said: "That's it, hold it there! Say 'cheese'! Lovely!" And afterward Matilde went out into the street, hand in hand with her mother, happy because she had been told that she looked lovely.

25

Anselmo was none too pleased at the prospect of another three whole months of receiving only the five hundred escudos that Paulino Morais had agreed to pay his daughter, an amount that would, after tax, come to a mere four hundred and fifty escudos. After those three months were up, what guarantee did they have that he would, as agreed, increase her wages? What if he took against her, decided he didn't want her? After thirty years of working in an office, this was something Anselmo knew all about. He knew that once an employee fell from grace, there was no way back. His own case was proof of that. How many younger men, who had joined the company after him, had been promoted over his head? They were no more competent than he, and yet they had risen up the ladder far more quickly.

"Plus," he said to his wife, "she was used to her old job and might find it hard to adapt. She had a certain seniority there, which always counts for something. Not in my case, it's true, but there are some decent bosses."

"But how do you know Senhor Morais isn't one of them? And you're forgetting that we have an ally in Dona Lídia. Besides, Claudinha's no fool!"

"She's certainly her father's daughter in that respect . . ."

"Exactly."

But Anselmo still did not rest easy. He wanted to free his daughter from a commitment she had taken on without first seeking his advice, and the only reason he refrained from doing so was seeing how much Claudinha was enjoying her new job. She had promised him that she would work hard at learning shorthand and that, in three months' time, her wages would be increased. She had said this with such confidence that Anselmo had refrained from mentioning his own anxieties.

In the evenings, while Rosália darned socks and Anselmo filled up columns with soccer-related names and numbers, Claudinha was becoming initiated into the mysteries of shorthand.

He did not say as much, but Anselmo was filled with admiration for his daughter's abilities. No one knew shorthand at his office, which was an old-fashioned place, with no modern metal furniture and where they had only recently acquired an adding machine. Claudinha's apprenticeship cheered their evenings together at home, and there was general rejoicing when she managed to teach her father to write his name in shorthand. Rosália wanted to learn too, but, being illiterate, she took far longer.

Once he had gotten over the novelty of the situation, Anselmo resumed his interrupted task, that of selecting the national team, his own personal selection. He had worked out a sure and simple method: in goal he would place the player who had let in the fewest balls during the season, and as strikers, logically enough, he quite rightly chose those players who had scored the most goals. The remaining positions he filled with his personal club favorites, deviating from this only when it came to players who were, according to newspaper reports, essential components of any team. This was an ongoing project, because week by week the best scorers would move up and down the ranks. However, since those changes, which he noted on a diagram of his own invention, were not particularly radical, he felt he was very close to choosing the perfect team. Once he had done this, he would await the decision of the official selection committee.

Two weeks into her new job, Maria Cláudia returned home one evening aglow with happiness. Her boss, Paulino Morais, had called her into his office for a long chat, which had lasted more than half an hour. He had told her how pleased he was with her work and that he was sure they would get on famously. He had asked various questions about her family, about her parents and if she got on well with them, if they lived comfortably, and other things that Cláudia had now forgotten.

Rosália saw in all this the beneficent influence of Dona Lídia and said that she would thank her the next time she saw her. Anselmo appreciated the interest Senhor Morais had taken in the family and was flattered when his daughter told him that she had taken the opportunity to praise her father's qualities as an office worker. Anselmo began to savor the seductive possibility of moving to a post in an important company like that of Senhor Morais. That would certainly be one in the eye for his present colleagues. Unfortunately, Claudinha added, there were currently no vacancies, nor any hope of there being any. This fact presented no obstacle to Anselmo: after all, life is full of surprises, and he saw no reason, therefore, to doubt that a cushier future awaited him. It seemed to him that life owed him a great many things and he had the right to expect payment.

That night, there was no darning, no shorthand, no selecting of the national team. After Maria Cláudia's enthusiastic account, her father felt it appropriate to give her some advice:

"You must be very careful, Claudinha. There are envious people everywhere, and I speak from painful experience. If you start getting promoted too quickly, your colleagues will get jealous. So be careful!"

"But everyone there is so nice!"

"They are now, but they won't be later on. You must try to stay on good terms with your colleagues *and* with your boss. If not, they'll start plotting against you and might harm your chances of success. Believe me, I know that world well."

"Yes, but you don't know the people in my office. They're all really decent. And Senhor Morais couldn't be nicer!"

"Maybe, but have you never heard anything bad about him?"

"Nothing of any importance!"

Rosália wanted to join in the conversation:

"Your father has a lot of experience of office life! The only reason he hasn't risen further up the ladder is because they cut the legs from under him!"

This reference to such a violent act did not provoke the surprise one might expect when one considers that Anselmo's lower limbs were still firmly attached to their owner. A foreigner unfamiliar with Portuguese idioms and taking this expression literally would assume he must be in a madhouse when he saw Anselmo nodding gravely and saying earnestly:

"It's true. That's exactly what happened."

"Please, just let me deal with things my own way."

And with these words Claudinha brought the conversation to a close. Her confident smile could only possibly have its source in a thorough knowledge of how to "deal with things," although what those "things" were, no one, possibly not even Maria Cláudia, really knew. She probably thought, as was only natural, that along with being young and pretty, having a ready wit and a ready laugh, would come the solution to all those "things." In any case, the family let the matter drop.

As Maria Cláudia herself discovered, those attributes turned out not to be enough. She was making no headway with her shorthand. Studying from a book was fine for learning the rudiments, but then the subject grew more complicated, and Maria Cláudia's progress came to a halt. Insurmountable difficulties arose on every page. Anselmo tried to help. True, he knew nothing about shorthand, but he had thirty years' experience and practice of office work behind him. He was a past master when it came to writing business letters, and, for heaven's sake, what could possibly be so hard about shorthand? Hard or not, he made a complete and utter mess of it. Claudinha burst into tears, and Rosália, upset to see her husband so defeated, blamed the shorthand.

It was Maria Cláudia who saved the day, which spoke well for her declared ability to deal with things. She announced that what she needed was a teacher who could give her lessons in the evening. Anselmo immediately saw in this yet another expense, but then decided to view it as a capital investment that would, in just over two months, begin to pay dividends. He took it upon himself to find a teacher. Claudinha mentioned various private schools, all of which had imposing names in which the word "Institute" was de rigueur. Her father rejected all these suggestions. First, because they were expensive; second, because he didn't think it would be possible to join a course at that time of year; and third, because he had heard talk of "mixed classes," and he didn't want his daughter going to one of those. After a few days, he found just the right person: a retired teacher, eminently respectable, with whom a nineteen-year-old girl would be perfectly safe. As well as charging very little, he had the inestimable advantage of giving lessons at times that would not involve Claudinha being out on the city's streets late at night. If she left the office at six, she could get the tram to São Pedro de Alcântara where the teacher lived, a thirty-minute journey. The lesson would go on until half past seven, when it was just beginning to grow dark, and it would then take her forty-five minutes to get home. Allowing another quarter of an hour for possible delays, Claudinha should be safely home by half past eight. And, initially, that is precisely what happened. When it was half past eight by Anselmo's watch,

Claudinha would just be coming in through the front door.

She made great strides with her shorthand, and it was this that provided her with an excuse the first time she arrived home late, saying that the teacher, pleased by her keenness to learn, had decided to give her another quarter hour of instruction at no extra cost. Anselmo was pleased by this and believed her, especially when his daughter repeated the teacher's willingness not to charge more for his time. From Anselmo's utilitarian viewpoint, had he been the teacher, he would have milked the situation for all it was worth, but, he reminded himself, there were still some good, honest people in the world, which is just as well, especially when that same goodness and honesty favors those who, not being good or honest themselves, have the necessary nous to use them to their own advantage. Anselmo's nous consisted solely in having found just such a teacher.

However, when his daughter started arriving home at nine o'clock, he began to find that lack of self-interest on the part of her tutor excessive, not to say incomprehensible. He asked questions and received answers: Claudinha had been kept at the office until after half past six, finishing an urgent piece of work for Senhor Morais. Since she was still only on probation, she couldn't possibly have refused or alleged personal reasons for doing so.

Anselmo agreed, but felt suspicious. He asked his boss to let him leave work a little early and waited outside his daughter's office. From six until twenty to seven he was forced to acknowledge that he had been wrong: Claudinha really was leaving work later than usual, doubtless kept behind by some other urgent task.

He considered abandoning his spying mission, but decided instead to follow his daughter, more because he had nothing else to do than in order to dispel any lingering suspicions. He followed her to São Pedro de Alcântara and installed himself in a café opposite the teacher's house. He had barely finished drinking the coffee he had ordered when he saw his daughter coming out again. He hurriedly paid the bill and followed her. A bareheaded young man smoking a cigarette was standing on a corner, and Claudinha went straight over to him. Anselmo froze when he saw her link arms with the young man and walk off down the street with him, chatting. He thought for a moment that he should intervene, but was prevented from doing so by his deep-seated horror of causing a scene. He followed the couple for a while at a distance; then, when he was sure his daughter was heading homeward, he jumped onto a tram in order to arrive before her.

When Rosália opened the door, she was shocked to see the distraught expression on her husband's face.

"Whatever's wrong, Anselmo?"

He went straight into the kitchen without saying a word and slumped down on a bench. Rosália thought that the worst must have happened:

"Oh, no, they haven't given you the sack, have they?"

Anselmo was still too distressed to speak. He shook his head. Then, in a hollow voice, he said:

"Your daughter has been deceiving us! I followed her. She only stayed with the teacher for about a quarter of an hour and then off she went with some good-for-nothing who was waiting for her outside!"

"And what did you do?"

"I didn't do anything. I followed them. Then I came home. She should be here at any moment."

Furious, Rosália blushed to the roots of her hair:

"Well, if I'd been you, I'd have gone over to them . . . and sorted them out good and proper!"

"Think of the scandal, though!"

"What do I care about scandal! I'd have given him a couple of slaps around the face that would have knocked him sideways, and as for her, I'd have dragged her home by the ear!"

Anselmo said nothing, but got up and went to change his clothes. His wife followed him:

"So what are you going to say to her when she arrives?"

There was a hint of insolence in her voice, or so it seemed to Anselmo, who was used to being lord and master of the household. He shot his wife a piercing glance, then, holding her gaze for a few seconds, said:

"That's entirely up to me. And by the way, I am not accustomed to being spoken to in that tone, here or anywhere else!"

Rosália bowed her head:

"But I didn't say anything . . ."

"Well, I didn't like the way you said it."

Relegated to her role as the weaker vessel, Rosália returned to the kitchen from which there came a faint smell of burning. As she struggled to save the supper, the doorbell rang. Anselmo went to open it.

"Evening, Papa," said Claudinha cheerily.

Anselmo did not answer. He let his daughter in and closed the front door. Only then did he speak, ushering her into the dining room:

"In you go."

Surprised, she obeyed. Her father told her to sit down and then, standing before her, fixed her with a fierce, stern gaze.

"What did you do today?"

Maria Cláudia tried to smile and act naturally:

"The usual. Why do you ask?"

"That's my business. Answer me."

"Well, I went to the office. I left just after half past six and . . ."

"And . . ."

"Then I went to my shorthand lesson, and

because I'd arrived late, I left later than usual as well . . ."

"What time did you leave?"

Clearly embarrassed, Claudinha took a while to respond, then:

"Just after eight . . ."

"That is false!"

She shrank back. Anselmo savored the effect of his words. He could have said "That's a lie," but had opted for "That is false" as being more dramatic.

"Oh, Papa . . . ," she stammered.

"I very much regret this present situation," said Anselmo, his voice shaking. "It's unworthy of you. I saw everything. I followed you. I saw you walking along with that . . . that ne'er-do-well."

"He's not a ne'er-do-well," retorted Claudinha resolutely.

"What does he do, then?"

"He's a student."

Anselmo snapped his fingers, intending to express the insignificance of such an occupation. And as if that were not enough, he cried sarcastically:

"Oh, wonderful, a *student!*"

"But he's a really nice boy!"

"Why, then, has he not been to see me?"

"I told him not to come. I know how fussy you are . . ."

Someone knocked lightly on the door.

"Who is it?" asked Anselmo.

This was rather a pointless question given that there was only one other person in the apartment. The answer was equally pointless, but was given nonetheless:

"It's me. Can I come in?"

Anselmo did not bother to give his consent, because while he would have preferred not to be interrupted, he was aware that he could hardly deny his wife access. He chose instead to say nothing, and Rosália joined them:

"So, have you told her off?"

If Anselmo had been in the mood to tell his daughter off, that mood had passed. For some reason even he could not understand, his wife's intervention made him feel that he should take his daughter's side.

"Yes, we've finished now."

Rosália put her hands on her hips and angrily shook her head, saying:

"I can't believe it, Claudinha! How could you? Just when we were feeling so pleased about your new job, you go and do this to us!"

Maria Cláudia sprang to her feet:

"But, Mama, how am I ever going to get married if I don't have a boyfriend?"

Father and mother were dumbstruck. The question was perfectly logical, but hard to answer. Anselmo thought he had found the right riposte:

"But a student . . . I mean, what does a student amount to?"

"He might not amount to much now, but he's studying so that he can become someone!"

Claudinha was regaining her composure. She could see that her parents were wrong and that reason was on her side. She went on:

"Don't you want me to marry? Tell me!"

"It's not that we don't want you to marry, child," said Anselmo. "But we want you to marry well. A girl with your qualities deserves a good husband."

"But you don't even know him!"

"No, I don't, but it doesn't matter. Besides . . ." And here his voice grew stern again: "Look, I don't have to explain myself to you. I forbid you to meet that . . . that student ever again. And so that you don't go trying to pull the wool over my eyes, from now on I'm going to take you to your lesson and bring you back. It means more work for me, but if that's how it has to be . . ."

"But, Papa, I promise . . ."

"I don't believe you."

Maria Cláudia stiffened as if she had been struck. She had frequently lied to her parents, scornfully toyed with them as often as she liked, but now she felt they were treating her unfairly. She was furious. Taking off her coat, she said:

"Do as you please, but I warn you, you'll have to hang around outside the office. Senhor Morais always has jobs to do that require me to stay late."

"That's all right. I don't mind."

Claudinha opened her mouth to speak. From the look on her face, it seemed as if she were about to answer back, but she changed her mind and said nothing, a vague smile playing on her lips.

26

E ver since he had begun to live freely and independently, Abel had sometimes asked himself: "Why?" The answer was always the same comfortable negative: "No reason." But when his thoughts repeated the question, he would say: "No, there is a reason. Otherwise, there would be no point," adding: "I'm just going to let life happen. It's sure to lead somewhere."

He could see perfectly well that "it," his life, was leading nowhere, that he was behaving like a miser who hoards gold simply for the pleasure of looking at it, except that in his case it wasn't gold but experience, which was the one thing he took from life. And yet experience, unless applied to something, is just like that hoard of gold, for it neither produces nor bears fruit and is utterly useless. There is no point in a man accumulating experience the way someone else might collect stamps.

Abel's sparse and ill-assimilated readings in philosophy, gleaned at random from schoolbooks or pamphlets unearthed from amid the dust in the secondhand bookshops on the Calçada do Combro, allowed him to think and to say that he was searching for the hidden meaning of life. But when he was in one of his disenchanted moods, he had to admit that this was a purely utopian desire and that however much experience he accumulated, the veil he was trying to draw aside would only grow thicker. The lack of any real meaning to his life, however, forced him to stand by that desire—which had long since ceased to be one—and to make of it as good or as bad a reason to live as any other. On those grim days when he felt surrounded by the vacuum of absurdity, he always felt particularly weary. He tried to blame his weariness on the daily struggle to earn a living, on the depression brought on by those difficult times when he could barely get by. These were doubtless contributing factors, because hunger and cold do make one weary, but they weren't enough. He had grown inured to everything, and things that had once frightened him he now viewed with indifference. He had hardened body and mind against difficulties and privations. He knew that he could, with relative ease, step free of them. He had learned to do so many jobs in his time that it would have been fairly easy for him to find a permanent position that would give him enough to live on. He had never taken that step, though. He didn't want to be caught, he said, and it was true, but the reason why he didn't want to be caught was that he would then have to admit the pointlessness of his existence so far. What had he gained in taking that long, circuitous route only to end up on the same road being followed by all the people he had tried so resolutely to leave behind? "Do they want me married, futile and taxable?" Fernando Pessoa had asked. "Is that what life wants of everyone?" asked Abel.

The hidden meaning of life . . . "But the hidden meaning of life is that life has no hidden meaning." Abel knew Pessoa's poetry well. He had made of his poems another Bible. He may not have understood them completely and perhaps saw in them things that weren't there, but while he suspected that Pessoa was often mocking his readers and that, while appearing to be sincere, he was, in fact, making fun of them, Abel had grown used to respecting him despite all his contradictions. And while he had no doubts about Pessoa's greatness as a poet, it sometimes seemed to him, especially when he was in his absurd, disenchanted mood, that there was much that was gratuitous in his poetry. "So what?" thought Abel. "Why shouldn't poetry be gratuitous? It can be, of course, and there's nothing wrong with that. But what is the point of gratuitous poetry? Perhaps poetry is like a spring or a mountain stream, which has no point, no reason to exist. Men get thirsty, and that's what gives meaning to the water. Is it the same with poetry? No poet, and no man, whoever he may be, is simple and natural. Pessoa certainly wasn't. No one feeling a thirst for humanity would try to slake that thirst on Fernando Pessoa's verses: it would be like drinking salt water. And yet what wonderful, fascinating poetry! Gratuitous, yes, but what does that matter if, when I plumb my own depths, I find that I, too, am gratuitous and futile? And that's what Silvestre can't stand: the useless life. We should be fully engaged with life, each individual should reach out beyond himself. Being merely present isn't enough. Being a mere witness is tantamount to being dead. That's what he meant to say. It doesn't matter if you stay in one spot, but your life should reach out if it is not to be a mere animal existence, as unconscious as the water flowing from a spring. But how to reach out? And where to? How and where: *there's* a problem that throws up a thousand other problems. It's not enough to say that one's life should reach out, because there are a thousand answers as to the 'how' and the 'where.' Silvestre's is one answer, someone who has a religious belief is another. How many more are there? And, of course, the same answer may be right for various people, just as another may be right for only one person and no one else. Anyway, I got lost along the way. Everything would be all right if I didn't sense that there were many other roads to follow, and if I wasn't so busy removing obstacles from my chosen path. The life I've chosen is a hard and difficult one. I've learned a lot from it. It's in my power to abandon it and start another. So why don't I? Because I like this life? Partly. I find it interesting to choose to lead a life that others would accept only if it was forced on them. But it's not enough, this life isn't enough. What to choose, then? Being 'married, futile and taxable'? Is it possible to be one of those things and not the others? And then what?"

Abel felt confused. Silvestre had accused him of being useless, and that had bothered him. No one likes his weaknesses to be exposed, and his awareness of his own uselessness was Abel's Achilles' heel. His mind was always asking him that awkward question: "Why?" He would avoid it, and then pretend he wasn't by thinking about something else or engaging in vain speculations, but the question wouldn't go away: it stood there stiff, ironic, implacable, waiting for him to return from his meanderings. What he found particularly distressing was that he never saw the same perplexity in other people, some indication that they felt as troubled as he did. Other people's troubles (or so Abel thought) arose from personal misfortune, a lack of money, a case of unrequited love, but not from life itself. Once, this certainty had given him a consoling sense of superiority. Now he found it merely irritating. Such confidence, such sangfroid in the face of those secondary problems, prompted in him a mixture of scorn and envy.

In telling him about his past, Silvestre had only added to his feeling of unease. And yet, for all that, Abel had to say that Silvestre's life had been just as useless as his, since none of the things he had strived for had been achieved. Silvestre was old, doing today what he had always done— mending shoes—but Silvestre himself had said that at least his life had taught him to see beyond the soles of the shoes he was mending, while all life had given Abel was the ability to sense the existence of something hidden, of something capable of giving real meaning to his life. It would be better not to have that ability. He would be able to live peacefully, the peace that comes from dulling one's mind, which was what most people did. " 'Most people,' " he thought, "what a stupid expression! What do I know about 'most people'? I might come across thousands of people in the course of a day, but I only truly see a few dozen. I see them looking serious, happy, slow, harassed, ugly or beautiful, plain or attractive, and I call them 'most people.' I wonder what they think of me. I, too, walk slowly or quickly, am serious or happy. Some will think me ugly, others handsome or plain or attractive. After all, I am 'most people' too. Some would also consider my mind dull. We all receive the daily dose of morphine that dulls our thoughts. Habits, vices, repeated words and hackneyed gestures, boring friends and enemies we don't even really hate, these are all things that dull our minds. A full life! Who can genuinely claim to live a full life? We all wear around our neck the yoke of monotony, we all have hopes, though heaven knows what for! Yes, we all have hopes! Some more obscure than others, but we all have expectations. 'Most people'! Said in that disdainful, superior tone, it's simply idiotic. The morphine of habit, the morphine of monotony. Ah, Silvestre, my good, pure Silvestre, you have no idea what massive doses of morphine you have swallowed! You and your plump wife Mariana, so kind she makes you want to weep!" (As he was thinking these thoughts, Abel was almost weeping himself.) "These thoughts don't even have the merit of being very original. They're like a secondhand suit in a shop full of new clothes, a piece of merchandise left behind after the market, the nausea brought on by indigestion."

Whenever he reached this point, Abel would leave the house. If he was in time and if he had enough money, he would go to the cinema. He found the plots of the films absurd. Men pursuing women, women pursuing men, mental aberrations, cruelties, and stupidity from first frame to last. Stories repeated a thousand times over: a man, a woman and her lover; a woman, a man and his lover; and even worse was the simplistic way they dealt with the battle between good and evil, between purity and depravity, between the mud and the stars. Morphine. A legal drug advertised in all the papers. A way of passing the time, as if we were all going to live forever.

The lights went up, the audience got to their feet with a clatter as the chair seats flipped back into position. Abel sat on for a while. The two-dimensional ghosts occupying the seats had fallen silent. "I am a four-dimensional ghost," he murmured to himself.

Thinking he was asleep, the ushers came to shoo him away. Outside, the last filmgoers were rushing to catch the tram. Newly married couples, arms about each other. Petit-bourgeois couples who had spent years locked in holy matrimony, she walking behind, he in front. Less than half a step separated them, but that half step expressed the insuperable distance that lay between them. The mature, bourgeois couples were the future portrait of the newlyweds whose wedding rings were still shiny and new.

Abel continued along the quiet, almost empty streets where the parallel tram lines gleamed, the proverbial parallel lines that never meet. "They meet in infinity, at least that's what scholars say. We all meet in infinity, in the infinity of stupidity, apathy, stagnation."

"Fancy a good time, dearie?" said a woman's voice in the darkness. Abel smiled sadly.

"What an admirable society this is, providing, as

it does, for everything and everyone, even the poor unhappy bachelors who need an outlet for their sexual urges! Even happily married husbands who like a bit of variety for not much outlay! Ah, Society, you loving mother!"

In the streets of the city's outlying areas, rubbish bins stood outside every door. The dogs look for bones there, the rag-and-bone men for rags and paper. "Nothing is wasted," murmured Abel. "In Nature nothing is created and nothing is lost. Poor dear Lavoisier, I bet you never thought that the proof of your words would be found in a rubbish bin!"

He went into a café: tables, some occupied, others not, yawning waiters, clouds of cigarette smoke, the hum of conversations, the clink of cups—stagnation. And there he was alone. He left, filled with anguish. The warm April night greeted him. The tall buildings were showing him the way. Straight on, always straight on. He turned to left or right only when the street decided for him. The street and the need, sooner or later, to go home. And sooner or later, Abel did go home.

He had taken to speaking very little. And Silvestre and Mariana found this odd. They had grown used to considering him a member of the household, almost one of the family, and they felt hurt, their confidence betrayed. One night Silvestre went into Abel's room on the pretext of showing him some article in the newspaper. Abel was lying on the bed, reading a book and smoking a cigarette. He read the article, which did not interest him in the least, then handed the newspaper back to Silvestre, muttering a few distracted words of thanks. Silvestre stayed where he was, leaning on the foot of the bedstead, looking at Abel. Seen from that angle, Abel looked smaller and, despite the cigarette and his five o'clock shadow, rather childlike.

"Are you feeling trapped?" asked Silvestre.

"Trapped?"

"Yes, you know, the tentacle . . ."

"Ah."

This exclamation was spoken in an indefinable, almost absent tone. Abel sat up, looked hard at Silvestre and added slowly:

"No, perhaps I'm feeling the lack of a tentacle. The conversations we've had have made me think about things I thought had long since been safely filed away."

"I don't think they could have been filed away, or only very haphazardly. If you really were the kind of person you try so hard to appear to be, I would never have told you about my life."

"You should be pleased, then."

"Pleased? On the contrary. I think you're in the grip of tedium. You're tired of life, you think you've learned all there is to learn, and everything you see around you only increases your sense of tedium. Why, then, should I feel pleased? It isn't always easy to cut off a tentacle. You can always leave a boring job and, even more easily, a boring woman, but tedium, how do you cut yourself off from that?"

"You've said all this before, you're surely not going to repeat—"

"I'm obviously annoying you."

"No, not at all!"

Abel leapt to his feet and reached out one arm to Silvestre, who, having made as if to leave the room, now remained where he was. Abel sat down on the edge of the bed, half turned toward Silvestre. They were looking at each other, unsmiling, as if waiting for something important to happen. Then Abel said:

"You do know, don't you, that I'm your friend?"

"I do," answered Silvestre. "And I'm your friend too, but we seem to have had a falling-out."

"That's my fault."

"Perhaps it's mine. You need someone who can help you, and I don't seem to be that person."

Abel got up, put on his shoes and went over to a trunk in one corner of the room. He opened it and, pointing to the books almost filling it, said:

"Even in my worst moments it never once occurred to me to sell them. These are all the books I brought from home, plus others I've bought over the past twelve years. I've read and reread them all. I've learned a lot from them. Half of what I learned I've forgotten, and the other half

272

might be quite wrong, but right or wrong, the truth is that they have only contributed to making my own uselessness more obvious."

"But you were quite right to read them. Think of all the people who live their entire lives without ever realizing how useless they are. In order for someone to be truly useful, he must, at some point, feel his own uselessness. At least then he's less likely to go back to being useless . . ."

"Be useful, that's all you ever say to me. But how can I be useful?"

"That's something you have to discover for yourself, like everything else in life. No one can give you advice about that. I'd really like to—if I thought it would do any good."

"And I'd like to know what you really mean."

Silvestre smiled:

"Don't worry. All I mean is that we won't become what we are meant to be in life by listening to other people's words or advice. We have to feel in our own flesh the wound that will make us into proper men. Then it's up to us to act . . ."

Abel closed the trunk. He turned to Silvestre and said in a dreamy tone:

"To act . . . If everyone acted as we have done, there would be no proper men . . ."

"My time is past," said Silvestre.

"That's why it's so easy for you to criticize me. Listen, how about a game of checkers?"

27

That night, Paulino had arrived late, at around eleven o'clock. He gave Lídia a peck on the cheek, then went over to his favorite sofa, where he sat smoking his usual cigarillo.

As it happened, Lídia was not wearing the obligatory negligee, which may have contributed to Paulino's unspoken irritation. Even the way he gripped his cigarillo between his teeth and drummed his fingers on the arm of the sofa were signs of his displeasure. Sitting at his feet on a low stool, Lídia was doing her best to amuse him by recounting the minutiae of her day. She had begun to notice a change in her lover some nights before. He no longer "devoured" her with his eyes, and while this could be attributed to long familiarity, it could also mean that he was losing interest in her for some other reason. Lídia's permanent feeling of insecurity meant that she always feared the worst. Apparently insignificant details, a certain degree of inattentiveness and brusqueness on his part, a slightly abstracted air, only added to her anxiety.

Paulino was doing nothing to keep the conversation going. There were long pauses during which neither of them knew what to say, or, rather, during which Lídia didn't know what to say, for it seemed Paulino preferred to remain silent. She racked her brain for ways to keep the conversation alive, but he responded only distractedly. And the conversation, for lack of substance, was burning out like a lamp with no oil in it. That evening, Lídia's clothes seemed a further motive for his distant behavior. Paulino kept blowing out great clouds of smoke with a long, impatient sigh. Abandoning her attempt to find a subject that might interest him, Lídia said, almost casually:

"You seem a bit preoccupied."

"Hm."

Such a vague response could mean anything. He appeared to be waiting for Lídia to decide what he meant. Gripped by the vague fear of the unknown that lurks both in dark houses and in imprudent words whose consequences one can never predict, Lídia added:

"You've been behaving differently for a few days now. You always used to tell me your problems. I don't wish to be indiscreet, of course, but it might help you to talk about them."

Paulino stared at her in amusement. He even smiled. Lídia found both look and smile terrifying. She regretted having spoken. Seeing her shrink back, and not wishing to miss the opportunity she was offering him, Paulino said only:

"Problems at work . . ."

"You always used to say that when you were with me, you forgot all about work."

"I know, but it's different now."

His smile was full of malice. His eyes had the implacable concentration of someone carefully noting imperfections and blemishes. Lídia felt herself blush. She had a feeling something bad was about to happen. When she still said nothing, Paulino added:

"No, now I can't forget about work. Not that I no longer feel at ease with you, not at all, but some problems are so complicated we can't help but think about them all the time regardless of the company we're in."

Lídia had not the slightest desire to know what those problems were. She sensed that it would only hurt her to hear about them, and at that precise moment she longed for the phone to ring, for example, or for some other interruption that would bring the conversation to a close. The phone, however, did not ring, and Paulino was clearly in no mood now to be silenced.

"You women don't understand men. Just because we really like a woman doesn't mean we never think of anyone else."

"Of course. It's the same with us women."

Some mischievous demon had prompted Lídia to say these words. The same demon was whispering still more daring things to her, and she had to bite her tongue so as not to say them out loud. Her sharp eyes were now trained on Paulino's ugly features. And he, slightly piqued by what she had said, answered:

"Naturally. It wouldn't do to be thinking about the same person all the time."

There was a hint of spite in his voice. They eyed each other mistrustfully, almost like enemies. Paulino was trying to find out just how much Lídia knew. She, for her part, was turning his words this way and that in her effort to discover what lay behind them. Suddenly an intuitive flash lit up her brain:

"Changing the subject entirely, I forgot to mention that my upstairs neighbor, the young girl's mother, asked me to thank you for your interest . . ."

The change that came over Paulino's face proved to her that she had been right. She knew now whom she was up against. At the same time, she felt a shiver of fear run through her. The little demon had hidden himself away somewhere, and she was alone and helpless.

Paulino knocked the ash off the end of his cigarillo and shifted uncomfortably in his seat. He looked like a boy who has been caught eating jam while his mother wasn't looking.

"Yes, she's a bright young thing."

"Are you thinking of increasing her wages?"

"Yes, possibly. I said I'd do so after three months, but her family's pretty badly off, or so you told me. And Claudinha gets on really well with the other staff . . ."

"So it's Claudinha, is it?"

"Yes, Maria Cláudia."

Paulino was absorbed in watching the ash dulling the glow of his cigarillo. With an ironic smile, Lídia asked:

"And how's her shorthand coming along?"

"Oh, really well. She's a quick learner."

"I'm sure she is."

The demon had returned. Lídia was now confident that as long as she kept her cool, she would win in the end. She must, above all, avoid offending Paulino, but without revealing to him her own secret fears. She would be lost if he so much as suspected how insecure she was feeling.

"Her mother talks to me a lot, you know, and from what she's told me, it seems that Claudinha has been a naughty girl recently."

"A naughty girl?"

Paulino's evident curiosity would have been enough to convince Lídia, if she hadn't been convinced already.

"I don't know *what* you're thinking," she said insinuatingly. Then, as if the idea had only just occurred to her, she exclaimed: "Oh, good heavens, it's nothing like that. If it were, do you think her mother would have told me? Don't be so silly, sweetheart!"

Perhaps Paulino was being silly, but the fact is he seemed disappointed. He managed to splutter out:

"I wasn't thinking anything . . ."

"It's quite simple, really. Her father was getting concerned because she started arriving home late each evening. Her excuse was that you had kept her at the office, finishing some urgent work . . ."

Paulino realized that he should fill in the pause: "Well, it wasn't quite like that. It happened a few times, but—"

"Oh, no, that's all perfectly understandable, no, that wasn't the problem. Her father followed her one evening and caught her with her boyfriend!"

The little demon was so overjoyed now that he was performing somersaults and rolling around laughing. Paulino had grown somber. He gritted his teeth and muttered:

"You can't trust these modern girls . . ."

"Now you're being unfair, sweetheart. What's she supposed to do? You're forgetting that she's only nineteen, and what's a girl of nineteen supposed to do? Her Prince Charming is bound to be some handsome, elegant boy her own age who tells her the sweetest things. Don't forget, you were nineteen once."

"When I was nineteen . . ."

But he said no more and sat there chewing on his cigarillo, muttering incomprehensibly. He was greatly put out, not to say furious. He had spent valuable time courting the young typist only to learn that she had been stringing him along all the while. He had never gone beyond smiling and being attentive and talking to her—when they were alone in his office, of course, after six o'clock—but nothing more than that. She was very young and there were her parents to consider . . . In time, perhaps . . . but his intentions were, of course, entirely honorable. He simply wanted to help the young woman and her struggling family . . . Then he said:

"And do you think it's true?"

"You see how silly and naive you are? People don't invent things like that. When they happen, one's first instinct is usually to cover them up. And the fact that I know about it means that Claudinha's mother trusts me—" She broke off and added anxiously: "I hope you're not too upset. It would be a shame if you were to turn against the girl. I know how scrupulous you are about such matters, but please don't take it out on her!"

"I won't, don't worry."

Lídia got up. It was best to drop the subject now. She had sown the seed of doubt in Paulino's pleasant little flirtation, and this, she believed, would be quite enough to put a stop to his fantasy. She prepared his coffee, taking care to make her every gesture elegant. She then served Paulino herself. She sat on his lap, put her arm about him and gave him the coffee to sip as if he were a baby. The subject of Maria Cláudia had been safely dealt with. Paulino drank his coffee, smiling at the way Lídia was stroking the back of his neck. Suddenly Lídia expressed unusual interest in his hair:

"What are you using on your hair these days?"

"It's a new lotion I bought."

"Yes, it smells different. Hang on, though . . ."

She looked hard at his bald pate and said, beaming:

"Sweetie, you've got more hair!"

"Really?"

"Yes, I mean it."

"Let me look in the mirror."

Lídia slid off his lap and ran to the dressing table to get the mirror.

"Here you are!"

Squinting around in order to see his own image, Paulino said softly:

"Yes, you're right . . ."

"Look, here and here! See those little hairs. That's new hair growing!"

Paulino handed the mirror back to her, smiling:

"It's good stuff. I was told it was. It contains vitamins, you know."

"Oh, I see."

Paulino then went into elaborate detail as to the precise composition of the lotion he was using and the mode of application. In this way, the evening, having begun badly, ended very well. It did not go on for as long as usual. It was Lídia's "time of the month," and so Paulino left before midnight. Although not in so many words, they both expressed their regret at this imposed abstinence, but made up for it with kisses and tender words.

When he had left, Lídia went back into the bedroom. She was just starting to tidy up when she heard the sharp click of heels crossing the floor above her. The sound came and went, disappeared, then returned. While she listened, Lídia stood perfectly still, fists clenched, head slightly raised. Then came two louder thumps (the shoes being taken off) and silence.

28

Carmen added yet another letter to a long correspondence that consisted largely of complaints and lamentations. In her faraway hometown of Vigo, her parents would be left terrified and tearful when they read the ever-growing catalog of woes sent by their daughter, who continued to live in bondage to that foreigner.

Condemned in her everyday life to speak a foreign tongue, she could only fully express herself in her letters. She told her parents everything that had happened since her previous letter, lingering over her son's illness and describing the terrible scene in the kitchen—although she took pains to show herself in a more dignified light. For, once she had calmed down, she had to admit that her behavior had been most *un*dignified. Kneeling in the presence of her husband was, she felt, the worst of ignominies. As for her son, well, he was still only a child and would doubtless forget, but her husband would not, and that was what pained her most.

After some hesitation, she also wrote to her cousin Manolo. In doing so, she felt a vague sense of betrayal and had to acknowledge that writing to him was hardly appropriate. She had received no correspondence from him apart from a brief note each year on her birthday and at Christmas and Easter. However, she knew all about his life. Her parents kept her up to date on happenings in the family clan, and her cousin Manolo, along with his brush factory, always provided plenty to write about. Business had boomed, but he was, alas, still a bachelor, which meant that, when he died, there would be so many heirs to his wealth that each of them would inherit very little. Unless, of course, he were to favor one of those heirs over all the others. He was free to dispose of his goods and chattels as he wished, and so anything could happen. These concerns were set out at great length in the letters she received from Vigo. Manolo was still young, only six years older than Carmen, but he needed to be reminded of Henriquinho's existence. Carmen had never given much importance to these suggestions, nor was there any easy way to make him more aware of her son. Manolo barely knew him. The only time he had seen him was when Henriquinho was a baby, on a trip Manolo had made to Lisbon with Carmen's parents. Carmen knew (from her mother) that Manolo had declared his dislike of Emílio. At the time, being only recently married, she had ignored this comment, but now she could see that Manolo had been right. The Portuguese say, "From Spain expect only cold winds and cold wives," but some similar saying could equally be applied to Portugal regarding husbands, except that, although she knew all there was to know about the evils that proliferated this side of the Spanish–Portuguese frontier, she lacked the necessary poetic imagination to come up with a nice alliterative pairing for "husbands."

Once she had written the letters, she felt relieved. Replies to them would not be long in coming, bringing with them consolation and sympathy, which was all Carmen wanted. Manolo's sadness regarding her situation would make up for this minor act of disloyalty toward her husband. She could imagine her cousin in his office at the factory, which she could still vaguely remember. A pile of letters, orders and invoices stood on the desk, and her letter was on the very top of the pile. Manolo would open it, then read and reread it intently. Then he would put it down on the desk before him and, once he had sat for a few moments, with the look of someone recalling pleasant past events, he would push all the other documents to one side, take a clean sheet of paper (with the name of the factory at the top in block capitals) and begin to write.

As she pondered this scene, homesickness and nostalgia began to gnaw away at Carmen's heart. Nostalgia for everything she had left behind: her town, her parents' house, the factory gates, the soft Galician way of speaking that the Portuguese could never imitate. Remembering all these things, she began to cry. True, she had long been troubled by such feelings, but they vanished as quickly as they came, crushed beneath the ever-growing weight of time. Everything was disappearing, she could barely dredge up the faded images from her past, but now she could see it all there before her, as clear as day. That's why she was crying. She was crying for all that she had lost and would never see again. In Vigo, she would be among her own people, a friend among friends. No one would snigger behind her back at the way she spoke, no one would call her *galega*—or Galician—in the scornful way they did here; she would be a *galega* in the land of the *galegos*, where *galego* was not a synonym for "errand boy" or "coalman."

"¡*Ah, desgraciada, desgraciada!*"

Her son was staring at her in amazement. With instinctive obstinacy, he had resisted all his mother's attempts to win him back, just as he had resisted the beatings and the witchcraft. Every beating and every prayer had driven him closer to his father. His father was calm and serene, while his mother was excessive in everything she did, whether in love or in hate. Now, though, she was crying, and Henrique, like all children, could not bear to see another person cry, much less his mother. He went over to her and consoled her as best he could, wordlessly. He kissed her, pressed his face to her face wet with tears, and soon they were both crying. Then Carmen told him long stories about Galicia, speaking, without realizing it, in Galician rather than in Portuguese.

"I don't understand, Mama!"

She realized then what she was doing and translated the stories into that other hateful language, Portuguese, and the stories, once stripped of their native tongue, lost all their beauty and savor. Then she showed him photographs of Grandpa Filipe and Grandma Mercedes, and another in which cousin Manolo appeared, along with other relatives. Henrique had seen all these pictures before, but his mother insisted on making him look at them again. Showing him a picture of part of her parents' garden, she said:

"I often used to play here with cousin Manolo . . ."

The memory of Manolo had become an obsession. Her thoughts always led her to him along hidden paths, and Carmen felt quite troubled when she realized that she had been thinking about him for a long time now. After all these years, it was mere folly. She was old, though

286

she was only thirty-three. And she was married. She had a home, a husband, a son. No one in her situation had the right to harbor such thoughts.

She put the photos away and immersed herself in housework, but however hard she tried to drown out those thoughts, they refused to go away: memories of her hometown, her parents and, only belatedly, of Manolo, as if his face and voice, grown too remote, took a long while to arrive.

At night, lying in bed beside her husband, she was unable to sleep. Her longing for her past life had become suddenly urgent, as if demanding immediate action from her. Immersed in these distant memories, she grew calmer. Her fiery temperament softened, a sweet serenity filled her heart. Emílio was bewildered by this trans-formation, but made no comment. He suspected that it was simply a change of tactic intended to recapture her son's love, and when he noticed that Henrique now divided his favors equally between him and his mother, he assumed he must be right. It was almost as if Henrique were trying to bring them back together. Ingenuously and possibly unwittingly, he did his best to interest both of them in his needs and interests. The results were not encouraging. His father and mother, so ready to speak to him when he addressed them individually, pretended not to notice when he tried to include them both in the conversation.

Henrique could not understand this. He had not been fond of his father before, but had discovered that he was capable of loving him unreservedly; for a while, he had felt afraid of his mother, but seeing her crying had made him realize that he had, in fact, never stopped loving her. He loved them both and yet he could see them growing ever more distant one from the other. Why did they not speak? Why did they look at each other sometimes as if they didn't know each other or knew each other all too well? Why those silent evenings in which his childish voice seemed to wander, lost, as if in a vast, dark forest that muffled all sounds and from which all the birds had vanished? Yes, all the lovebirds had flown far away, and without the life that only love can engender, the forest had turned to stone.

The days passed slowly. The postal service had dispatched Carmen's letters across the country and across the border. The replies were perhaps setting off along the same route on their return journey (perhaps, who knows, carried by the same hands). Each hour and each day brought them closer. Carmen did not even know what she was hoping for. Compassion? Kind words? Yes, that was what she needed. She would feel less alone when she read those words, as if she were once again surrounded by her own family. She could see their compassionate faces bent over her, instilling her with courage. That was all she could hope for, but perhaps because she had also written to Manolo, she was hoping for something more. The days passed. Her own intense need made her forget that her mother was never quick to answer letters, and that often weeks went by without her receiving a response. She feared she had been forgotten.

Tied to his routine as a salesman and seeing the day of his liberation moving ever further off, Emílio allowed the time to pass. He had announced that he would be leaving, but had taken not one step in that direction. His courage was failing him. As he stood poised on the threshold ready to leave and never come back, something held him there. Love had vanished from his home. He did not hate his wife, but he was weary of being unhappy. Everyone has his limits: he could bear a certain degree of unhappiness, but no more than that. And yet still he did not leave. His wife had stopped making those terrible scenes and had grown meek and quiet. She never raised her voice or complained about her wretched life. When he considered this, Emílio felt afraid that she might perhaps be trying to rebuild their home life. He already felt too trapped to want such a thing. On the other hand, he realized, Carmen spoke to him only when absolutely necessary, so there were little grounds for thinking she wanted a reconciliation. It was clear that she had managed to regain her son's trust, but that was a very long way from wanting to win back her husband as well; no, that was a distance she seemed unwilling to travel. The transformation intrigued him, though. Henrique had resumed his close relationship with her, so why no more of those stormy scenes? When he asked himself this question and received no answer, Emílio would shrug his shoulders and surrender himself to time, as if time would give him the courage he lacked.

Then a letter arrived. Emílio was out, and Henrique had gone off on an errand. When she received the letter from the postman and recognized her mother's handwriting, Carmen felt a kind of shudder run through her and asked:

"Are there no other letters for me?"

The postman looked through the bundle of letters he was holding and said:

"No, only that one."

Only that one! Carmen felt like crying. She realized then that what she had been hoping for was a letter from Manolo. And that letter had not come. With a slowness that intrigued the postman, she closed the door. How foolish she had been! What *had* she been thinking! Had she been completely out of her mind when she wrote to her cousin? So deeply immersed was she in these thoughts that she quite forgot about her mother's letter, until suddenly she became aware of the touch of paper on fingertips. She murmured in Galician:

"*Miña nai* . . . Mother . . ."

She tore open the envelope. Two large sheets of paper, filled from top to bottom in the small, dense handwriting she knew so well. It was too dark in the corridor for her to read. She ran to the bedroom, turned on the light and sat down on the edge of the bed, and she did all this as urgently as if she were afraid the letter might dissolve in her hands. Her eyes were too filled with tears for her to be able to make out the words. She nervously wiped them away, blew her nose, and only then could she read what her mother had written.

She said exactly what Carmen had expected her to say. How much she regretted her situation, but that it was no fault of hers, because right from the start she had warned her against marrying that man. Carmen knew all this perfectly well, and had read the same words in other letters, but was that all her mother had to say? Nothing more? What else could she say? But wait, what was this?

There it was. Her mother was inviting her to leave Lisbon and spend some time with them. Two months, possibly three. She could bring Henrique with her. They would pay both their fares. It would be . . . well, Carmen didn't know what it would be like. Her eyes again filled with tears and she could read no more. It would, of course, be a great source of happiness. Two months, perhaps three, far from this apartment, with her family, and with her son beside her.

She dried her eyes and read on: news about the house, the family, the birth of a nephew and, at the end, love and best wishes. In the margin, in smaller writing, was a postscript. The doorbell rang. Carmen didn't hear it. It rang again. Carmen had now read those lines, but still heard nothing. The postscript explained everything: Manolo had asked her mother to say that he wouldn't write now because he was looking forward to seeing her in Vigo. Once more the doorbell rang out: strident, impatient, urgent. As if she were returning from the end of time itself, Carmen finally heard the bell. She went to open the door. It was her son. Henrique was bewildered to find his mother crying and laughing at the same time. He found himself clasped in her arms, felt her kisses and heard her say:

"We're going to see Grandpa Filipe and Grandma Mercedes, sweetheart, we're going to spend some time with Grandpa and Grandma!"

When Emílio arrived that night, Carmen showed him the letter. He had never taken any interest in his wife's correspondence and had the good taste not to go reading it when she wasn't looking. Suspecting that the letters would be full of complaints and that he doubtless appeared in them in the role of tyrant, he had no desire to read them. And though Carmen wouldn't have minded her husband knowing what her family said about him, she showed him only the part of the letter in which her mother mentioned the possibility of a visit: she needed his permission, and if he read the rest of the letter he might, out of pure spite, refuse. Emílio noticed that one margin had been cut off with scissors. He did not ask why. He handed back the letter and said nothing.

"So?" asked Carmen.

He did not reply at once. He saw stretching ahead of him two, possibly three months of solitude. He saw himself free and alone in the empty apartment. He could go out when he wanted, come back when he wanted, could choose to sleep where he wanted, on the floor or in the bed. He could see himself doing all the things he longed to do, so many that he could not, just then, think of a single one. His lips opened in a smile. From that moment, he began to feel free, felt the chains that bound him fall away. A large, full life awaited him, a life in which there would be room for all his dreams and all his hopes. It might only be three months, but what did that matter? Perhaps by then he would have screwed up enough courage to—

"So?" his wife asked again, sensing a refusal in his silence.

"Fine. Why not."

Just three words. For the first time in many years, there were three contented people in that apartment. Henrique was excited at the prospect of a holiday, at riding on the clickety-clack train, excited, as any child would be, by the whole marvelous idea of a journey. For Emílio and for Carmen, it meant being liberated from the nightmare that bound them to each other.

Supper passed peacefully. There were smiles and friendly words. Henrique was happy. Even his parents seemed happy. The light in the kitchen seemed somehow brighter. Everything was brighter and purer.

29

Nothing was said about the night when Justina had revealed herself naked to her husband for the first time. Caetano kept quiet out of cowardice, and Justina out of pride. All that remained was a still-greater coldness between them. After leaving work, Caetano spent the rest of the night and the following morning in someone else's bed. He returned home only at lunchtime, after which he slept all afternoon. They kept the bare essentials of communication as brief and monosyllabic as possible. Their mutual dislike of each other had never been so complete. Caetano avoided all contact with his wife, as if he feared she might suddenly appear before him again stark naked. Justina, on the other hand, eyed him with scorn, almost insolence. He felt the weight of that look and seethed with impotent rage. He knew that many men beat their wives, and that some husbands and wives found this natural. He knew that, for many men, this was considered a proof of their virility, just as some believed that catching a venereal disease was a sign of manliness. However, although he could boast of having been afflicted by various forms of the French disease, he could not pride himself on ever having beaten his wife, not as a matter of principle, as he would like to have claimed, but, again, out of cowardice. He was intimidated by Justina's serenity, whose calm surface he had seen crack only on that one occasion and in a way that filled him with shame. The vision returned to him over and over of that scrawny, naked figure and that strange sobbing laughter. The sheer unexpectedness of his wife's reaction had only increased his feeling of inferiority in relation to her, which is why he avoided her, spent as little time as possible at home and shrank from lying beside her in bed. There was another reason too. He knew that if he lay down with her in the same bed, he would feel impelled to have sex with her. When he first became aware of this impulse, he felt frightened. He tried to suppress it, called himself an idiot, listed all the reasons that should make such a feeling impossible: her graceless body, the many times she had rejected him, her scorn. But however many reasons he added to the list, his desire only grew in intensity. He tried to quench that desire elsewhere, but never succeeded. He would arrive home drained, unsteady and hollow-eyed, but he just had to smell the peculiar smell of Justina's body for a wave of desire to wash over his innermost being. It was as if he had emerged from a long period of sexual abstinence only to find a woman lying within arm's reach. When he went to bed after lunch, even the warmth of the sheets was a torment to him. His eyes would be drawn to some item of clothing his wife had left draped over a chair. In his mind's eye, he endowed that empty dress, that folded stocking, with the shape and motion of a living body, of a tense, vibrant leg. His imagination constructed perfect forms that bore no relation to reality. And if, at that moment, Justina came into the room, he had to draw on every ounce of willpower not to leap out of bed and drag her onto it. He was filled with a base sensuality. He had the kind of erotic dreams that had besieged him as an adolescent. He exhausted his various temporary lovers and heaped insults on them because they could not assuage his longings. Desire, like a bothersome fly, constantly buzzed about him. Just as a moth, with one side of its body paralyzed by the light, flies in ever-diminishing circles until it's burned by the flame, so he circled about his wife, attracted by her smell, by her gaunt, unlovely shape.

Justina had no clue as to the effect her presence

had on her husband. She noticed that he was unusually nervous and excitable, but attributed this to her redoubled scorn. Like someone toying with a dangerous animal and perfectly aware of the risks she is running, but too consumed with curiosity to flee, Justina wanted to see just how much her husband could take. She wanted to gauge the depth and breadth of his cowardice. She shifted from silent disdain to becoming almost talkative, so that she might have more opportunities to reveal her disdain. In every word, in every inflection of her voice, she was showing her husband how unworthy she considered him. Caetano reacted in a way she could not have foreseen. He had become a masochist. All her insults, all her blows to his pride as a man and a husband, provoked in him new paroxysms of desire. Justina, all unwitting, was playing with fire.

One night, unable to resist any longer, Caetano raced home after leaving work. He completely forgot that he had arranged to meet someone else, not that the woman expecting him could possibly have satisfied him. Like a madman who could still remember the place where reason would be restored to him, he hurried home. He hailed a passing taxi and promised the driver a fat tip if he got him to his destination quickly. The taxi bounded along the deserted streets and covered the short distance in no time at all. The tip was generous, even extravagant. As he entered the apartment, Caetano suddenly remembered the humiliation he had suffered the last time he had come home at that hour. In a brief moment of lucidity, he understood what he was going to do and feared the consequences. Then he heard Justina's regular breathing, felt the warmth of the room, touched the body lying stretched out on the bed, and a sexual frenzy rose in him like a wave out of the depths of the sea.

The room lay in darkness. Justina recognized her husband instantly. Still half immersed in sleep, she tried frantically to defend herself, but he was stronger than she and held her pinned to the mattress. She lay there motionless, detached, unable to react, as if caught up in one of those nightmares in which some monstrous Thing, strange and horrible, falls upon us. She finally managed to free one arm and groped in the darkness for the bedside lamp. When she turned it on, she saw her husband. His face terrified her: the bulging eyes, the more than usually pendulous lower lip, the red, perspiring face, the animal grimace. The only reason Justina did not cry out was that her throat was so tight with terror she could not utter a single sound. Suddenly Caetano's mask-like visage contracted in such a way as to become unrecognizable. It was the face of an utterly alien creature, that of a man plucked from a prehistoric animality, a wild beast in human form.

Then, eyes glinting coldly, Justina spat in his face. Stunned and still trembling, Caetano looked at her. He could not quite understand what had happened. He ran his hand over his face and looked at the still-warm saliva stuck to his fingers. He spread his fingers wide and saw how the saliva formed shining threads between them, threads that grew thinner and thinner until they broke. Then Caetano understood, finally understood. It was like the whiplash too far that causes the tame tiger to rise up on its back legs, claws extended, teeth bared. Justina closed her eyes and waited. Her husband still did not move. Fearfully, she half opened her eyes and immediately felt him begin thrusting away at her again. She tried to slide out from under him, but his body had hers in its grip. She tried to remain cold, as she had the first time, but that coldness had been quite natural, not an act of will. Now willpower alone could maintain that coldness, but her will had begun to weaken. Powerful forces that had lain dormant until then were stirring inside her, breaking over her like fast-running waves. A kind of bright light flickered on and off inside her head. She gave an inarticulate groan. Her will was drowning in the deep well of instinct. For a moment it managed to keep its head above water, before flailing helplessly about and vanishing. Like a thing possessed, Justina responded to her husband's embrace. Her thin body was barely visible beneath his. She trembled and writhed, as mad with desire as he, subject to the same blind instinct. A simultaneous loud moan emerged from both and their bodies rolled about on the bed, entwined, pulsating.

Then, propelled apart by a mutual feeling of repugnance, they separated and lay in silence on their respective sides of the bed. Caetano's heavy breathing drowned out Justina's, whose breathing now came in the form of a few final shudders.

A void opened up in Justina's mind. Her limbs felt limp and painful. The stink of her husband's body had impregnated her skin. Sweat dripped from her armpits, and a profound lassitude prevented her from moving. She seemed still to feel the weight of her husband on top of her. She tentatively reached out an arm and switched off the bedside lamp. Caetano's breathing gradually grew more regular. Sated, he slipped into sleep. Justina was left alone. The shuddering stopped, her tiredness diminished. Only her mind remained empty of thoughts. Very slowly, small scraps of ideas began to appear. They followed one on the other, fragmentary, inconclusive, with no connecting thread. Justina tried to think about what had happened, tried to grab hold of one of those fleeting ideas, which appeared and disappeared like beans in a boiling pot of water that rise to the surface only to vanish at once. It was still too soon for coherent thought; instead, she was suddenly gripped by horror. What had happened only minutes before seemed to her so absurd she thought she must have dreamed it. However, her bruised body and a strange sense of indefinable plenitude in certain parts of her anatomy gave the lie to that. It was then, and only then, that she was struck, or allowed herself to be struck, by the full horror of it all.

She did not sleep for what remained of the night. She stared into the darkness, disoriented, unable to think. She had a vague sense that her relationship with her husband had undergone a change. It was as if she had passed from the shadows into the blinding glare of day, preventing her from seeing the surrounding objects except as blurred, indeterminate shapes. She heard the clock strike each and every hour. She observed the withdrawal of night and the approach of morning. Bluish reflections began to seep into the room. The door that opened onto the corridor glowed opalescent in the dim light. With the coming of morning the building filled with vague sounds. Caetano was sleeping, lying on his back, one leg uncovered as far as the groin, a soft, white leg, like the belly of a fish.

Rebelling against the torpor in her limbs, Justina sat up and remained sitting, back bent, head hanging. Her whole body hurt. She slid out of bed very cautiously so as not to wake her husband, put on her dressing gown and left the room. She still could not string two ideas together, but her involuntary thought processes, the ones that evolve and develop independent of the will, were nevertheless beginning to work.

It took only a matter of seconds for Justina to reach the bathroom and another moment for her to look at herself in the mirror. She looked and did not recognize her own image. The face before her either did not belong to her or had remained hidden until then. The dark shadows encircling her eyes made them seem still duller. Her cheeks were hollow. Her unruly hair was a reminder of the night's agitation. None of this, however, was new to her: whenever her diabetes worsened, the mirror showed her just that face. What was different was the expression. She should be indignant and yet she was calm, she should feel offended and yet she felt as if she had pardoned an insult.

She sat down on a bench in the enclosed balcony. The sun was already slanting in through the topmost panes, striping the wall with a sliver of pink light that gradually grew longer and brighter. In the fresh morning air she could hear the twitter of passing swallows. On an impulse she went back into the bedroom. Her husband had not moved. He was sleeping, his mouth open, his teeth very white in his beard-blackened face. She crept slowly toward the bed and bent over him. Those inert features bore only a remote resemblance to the contorted face she had seen earlier. She remembered that she had spat in that face, and she felt afraid, a fear that made her draw back. Caetano stirred slightly. The sheet covering him slipped from his bent leg and left his penis exposed to view. A wave of nausea rose from Justina's stomach. She fled the room. Only then did the last knot binding up her thoughts come undone. As if trying to make up for lost time, her brain whirred furiously into action until it fixed on one obsessive thought: "What am I going to do? What am I going to do?"

She felt neither scorn nor indifference now, only hatred. She hated her husband and she hated herself. She knew that she had given herself to him with the same uninhibited frenzy with which he had possessed her. She took a few indecisive steps about the kitchen, as if lost in a labyrinth. Wherever she turned she met with closed doors and dead ends. Had she been able to remain indifferent, she could have seen herself as the victim of brute force. She knew that, as a married woman, she had no right to refuse, but pure passivity would have been a way of refusing. She could have allowed herself to be possessed without surrendering herself, but she had surrendered herself, and her husband had seen that she had; he would consider this a victory and would behave like a victor. He would impose what laws he liked and laugh in her face when she tried to rebel. A moment's madness, and the work of years had been destroyed. A moment's blindness, and strength had become weakness.

She must think about what she should do, and think quickly before he woke up. Think before it was too late. Think while her hatred was still raw and bleeding. She had given in once and did not want to give in again. However, the memory of what she had felt that night began to trouble her. Until then, she had never scaled the highest peak of pleasure. Even when she used to have normal sexual relations with her husband, she had never experienced the kind of intensity of sensation that makes one both fear and desire madness. She had never been thrown, as then, into the maelstrom of pleasure, with all ties broken, all frontiers crossed. What for other women was an ascent into the heavens was, for her, a fall.

The sound of the doorbell interrupted her thoughts. She ran on tiptoe to the door. She paid the milkman and returned to the kitchen. Her husband had still not woken up.

The situation was clear to her now. It was a choice between pleasure and power. If she kept silent, she would be accepting defeat in exchange for other such moments, always assuming her husband was prepared to grant them to her. If she spoke, she ran the risk of having him throw her impassioned response back in her face. It was easy enough to set out those two alternatives, but rather harder to choose between them. Shortly before, she had felt nausea and disgust, but now those moments of sexual ecstasy roared inside her like the sea inside a shell. Speaking out would mean that last night's experience would never be repeated. Saying nothing would mean subjecting herself to whatever conditions her husband chose to impose on her. Justina moved between those two poles—newly awoken desire and the desire to be in control. One excluded the other. Which to choose? And what scope did she have to make such a choice? If she chose control, how could she resist desire now that she had experienced it? If she chose submission, how could she bear submitting to a man she despised?

The Sunday-morning sun flooded in through the window like a river of light. From where she was sitting, Justina could see the small, raggedy white clouds chasing across the blue sky. Good weather. Bright skies. Spring.

From the bedroom came a mumbling sound. The bed creaked. Justina shuddered and felt her face flush scarlet. The line of thought she had been carefully drawing snapped. She sat paralyzed, waiting. The creaking continued. She went to the bedroom and peered around the door: her husband was sitting there, eyes open. He saw her. There was no going back. She entered in silence. Caetano looked at her in silence. Justina didn't know what to say. All her powers of reasoning had abandoned her. Her husband smiled. She did not have time to find out what that smile meant. Almost without realizing she was speaking, she said:

"Just pretend that nothing happened last night, and I'll do the same."

The smile vanished from Caetano's lips. A deep frown line appeared between his eyebrows.

"Perhaps that won't be possible," he answered.

"You know plenty of other women. You can amuse yourself with them."

"And what if I demand my conjugal rights?"

"I couldn't refuse you, but you'd soon grow weary of that."

"I see—at least I think I do. How do you explain your behavior last night, then?"

"If you had an ounce of dignity, you wouldn't ask such a question! Have you forgotten that I spat in your face?"

The expression on Caetano's face hardened. His hands, resting on the mattress, clenched. He seemed about to stand up, but stayed where he was. In a slow, sarcastic voice, he said:

"Ah, yes, I'd forgotten about that. I remember now, though, but I also remember that you only spat in my face *once* . . ."

Justina saw what he was driving at and said nothing.

"Come on, answer!"

"No, I feel ashamed for you and for me."

"What about me? I've had to suffer years of being despised by you."

"You deserve it."

"Who are you to despise me?"

"No one, but I do."

"Why?"

"I began to despise you as soon as I knew you, and I only really knew you once we were married. You're depraved, you are."

Caetano shrugged impatiently:

"You're just jealous."

"Jealous? Me? Don't make me laugh! You can only feel jealous of someone you love, and I don't love you. I may have once, but it didn't last. When my daughter was ill, did you care? You spent all your time with your fancy women!"

"Now you're talking nonsense!"

"If that's what you think, fine. I just want you to know that what happened last night won't happen again."

"We'll see about that."

"What do you mean?"

"You called me depraved. Maybe I am, but what if, for some reason, I should start taking an interest in you again?"

"Don't bother. Besides, it's been years since you thought of me as a woman."

"You sound almost sorry."

Justina did not respond. Her husband was eyeing her malevolently:

"Are you sorry?"

"No! If I was, I'd be sinking as low as all those other women you know!"

"Going with them, of course, is less convenient. With you, I just have to reach out and grab you. I am your husband after all."

"Unfortunately for me."

"Now you're being nasty. Just because I didn't react when you spat at me doesn't mean I'm prepared to put up with all your back talk."

"You don't frighten me. You threatened to beat me to a pulp once, and I didn't so much as turn a hair."

"Don't provoke me."

"Like I said, you don't frighten me!"

"Justina!"

She had moved closer as she spoke. She was standing by the bed, looking down at her husband. He reached out his right arm and caught her by the wrist. He didn't pull her toward him, but held her firm. Justina felt a tremor run through her whole body. Her knees were shaking as if they were about to buckle beneath her. Caetano said in a hoarse voice:

"You're right . . . I am depraved. I know you don't love me, but ever since I saw you naked the other night, I've been mad for you, do you hear, mad. If I hadn't come home last night, I would have died!"

It wasn't so much his words as the tone in which

he said them that troubled Justina. Feeling her husband drawing her toward him, she desperately tried to free herself from his grip:

"Let me go!"

What little strength she had was ebbing away. She could feel herself being drawn downward, feel her own pulse pounding in her ears. Then her eyes fell on the photograph of her daughter and her stubbornly sweet smile. She pushed hard against the edge of the bed, resisting his efforts to pull her down, and when she saw that he was about to grab her with his other hand, she squirmed around and bit the fingers gripping her. Caetano let out a scream and released his grip.

She ran into the kitchen. She understood now, understood why he had acted as he did. If she hadn't given in to that impulse to reveal herself naked to her husband, none of this would have happened. The Justina she was today would be the same Justina she had been yesterday. She had spoken out, but what had she gained? Only the certain knowledge that everything had changed. It was pure chance that she hadn't given in this time. The photo of her daughter would have been of little help if the conversation with her husband earlier hadn't given her the strength to resist; that, of course, and what had happened only a few hours before . . . "Which means that if, instead of trying to have sex with me so soon afterward, he'd allowed a day or two to pass and then tried again, I probably wouldn't have resisted . . ."

Justina was busy making lunch, her thoughts elsewhere. And what she was thinking was this: "He's depraved, a lecher, which is why I've always despised him. He's still depraved, which is why I still despise him. And yet, even though I despise him, I gave in to him, and I know that, given the opportunity, I'd do the same again. Is that a marriage? Must I conclude, then, that after all these years I am just as depraved as he? If I loved him, I wouldn't use a word like 'depraved.' I would find it all perfectly natural and would always give myself to him as I did last night. But is it possible not to love a man and still feel what I felt? I don't love him and yet he drove me mad with pleasure. Is it the same for other people? Do they feel nothing but loathing and pleasure? And what about love? Can pure animal lust give you the kind of pleasure you should only get from love? Or is love just lust in disguise?"

"Justina! I'm getting up. Where are my pajamas?"

Getting up? Already? Was he planning to spend all morning with her? Perhaps he was going out . . . She went into the bedroom, opened the wardrobe and handed him his pajamas. He took them from her without a word. Justina didn't even look at him. Deep down, she still despised him, despised him more and more, but she lacked the courage to look him in the face. She was trembling when she returned to the kitchen. "I'm afraid, afraid of *him!* Me! If someone had told me yesterday that one day I would feel afraid of him, I would have laughed."

Hands in his pockets, slippers flapping, Caetano slouched through the kitchen on his way to the bathroom. His wife breathed again: she had feared he might speak to her and she was not prepared for that.

In the bathroom, Caetano was whistling a tuneful *fado*. He stood in front of the mirror and interrupted his whistling in order to run his hand over his rough beard. Then, while he was preparing his razor, he began again. He lathered up his face and again stopped whistling to concentrate on his shaving. He had nearly finished when he heard his wife's voice outside the closed door:

"Your coffee's ready."

"All right, coming."

Caetano didn't care two hoots about the conversation he'd had with his wife. He knew he had won. A bit of resistance on her part would just make things all the more interesting. Dona Justina was going to have to pay, however reluctantly, for the shabby way she'd treated him. He had caught her out. Why had it never occurred to him before that sex would be the best way to humiliate her? Her scorn and pride lay shattered and broken! And the slut had enjoyed it too! True, she'd spat in his face, but he'd make her pay for that as well. He'd do the same to her one day, possibly more than once. Yes, next time she began moaning and writhing around, he'd give her a taste of her own medicine—take that! How would she react, he wondered. She might get angry . . . but only afterward.

Caetano felt very pleased with himself. Even the pimples on his neck didn't burst when he ran the razor over them. He was feeling calmer now. She may have had him under her thumb before, but now he had her in the palm of his hand. Even if his old feelings of repugnance returned, as they were bound to, he would not deny her his services as a husband.

The word "services" made him smile: "Services, eh? What a joke!"

He washed, using a lavish amount of soap and water. While he was combing his hair, he was thinking: "What a fool I've been. Anyone could have seen that the anonymous letter wasn't going to work . . ."

He stopped, slowly opened the window and peered out. It came as no surprise to him to see Lídia; in fact, that's why he'd stopped what he was doing. Lídia was looking down at something and smiling. Caetano followed her gaze, and in the yard belonging to the ground-floor apartment where the cobbler and his wife lived, he saw their lodger chasing after a chicken while Silvestre, leaning against the wall with a cigarette in his mouth, was slapping his thighs and laughing:

"If you don't catch her, Abel, it means no soup for lunch!"

Lídia laughed too. Abel looked up and smiled:

"Oh, sorry, I didn't see you there. Would you like to give me a hand?"

"No, I'd only make matters worse."

"Well, it's not very kind of you to laugh at my misfortunes!"

"I'm not laughing at you. I'm laughing at the chicken—" She broke off to greet both men. "Good morning, Senhor Silvestre! Good morning, Senhor . . ."

"Abel," said the young man. "No need to bother with surnames, you're too far away for formal introductions."

Safe in a corner, the chicken was ruffling its feathers and clucking.

"She's making fun of you," said Silvestre.

"Really? Well, I'm going to make her give that lady up there another good laugh."

Caetano preferred not to hear any more. He closed the window. The chicken resumed its agitated clucking. Smiling, Caetano sat down on the toilet seat while he put his thoughts in order: "That first letter may not have worked, but this one will . . ." He wagged his finger at the window in Lídia's direction and murmured:

"I'm going to have my revenge on you too, or my name's not Caetano."

30

All of Amélia's endeavors bumped up against her nieces' obstinate defenses. She tried to make the girls confess outright, reminding them of the harmony and perfect understanding that had once reigned in the family. Isaura and Adriana responded with laughter. They tried to demonstrate, in every way possible, that they were not angry with each other, that it was only because Amélia was used to seeing them constantly happy that she had now started imagining things that simply did not exist.

"We all get annoyed sometimes," Adriana would say.

"I know, I'm the same, but don't think you can deceive me. *You* still talk and smile, but Isaura doesn't. You'd have to be blind not to see it."

She gave up trying to coax from them the reason behind the coldness between them. She could see they had made a kind of pact to delude both her and her sister. However, while Cândida might be taken in by appearances, Amélia would only be satisfied with hard facts. She began, quite openly, to observe her nieces. She forced them into a state of tension verging on panic. They only had to make some slightly obscure comment for Amélia to come out with an insinuating riposte. Adriana made light of the matter, and Isaura took refuge in silence, as if afraid her aunt might draw unwarranted conclusions from even the most innocent of words.

"Cat got your tongue, Isaura?" Amélia would ask.

"No, I simply have nothing to say."

"We all used to get on so well here. Everyone talked and everyone had something to say. We've gotten to the point where we don't even listen to the radio anymore!"

"That's because you don't want to, Auntie."

"What's the point when our minds are all on something else!"

If it hadn't been for Isaura's behavior, she might have abandoned her idea, but her niece still seemed cowed and tormented by some hidden thought. Amélia decided not to bother with Adriana and to focus all her efforts on Isaura. Whenever Isaura went out, Amélia would follow her. She would return disappointed. Isaura spoke to no one and never once diverged from the path that led her to the shop she worked for, and she neither wrote letters nor received them. She no longer went to the library from which she used to borrow books:

"You've stopped reading, Isaura."

"I don't have time."

"You have just as much time as you had before. Was someone at the library unpleasant to you?"

"Of course not!"

When her aunt asked Isaura about her sudden indifference to books, Isaura blushed. She bowed her head and avoided her aunt's eyes. Amélia noticed her embarrassment and thought that therein lay the root of the problem. She went to the library on the pretext of inquiring about its opening hours, but what she really wanted was to see who worked there. She left no wiser than she had entered, for the staff consisted of two bald, toothless old gentlemen and a young woman. Her suspicions vanished into the air like smoke. Feeling all doors closing on her, she turned to her sister, but Cândida pretended not to understand.

"There you go again, you and your ideas!"

"Yes, and I won't give up either. I know you're acting as a cover for your daughters. When you're with them, you're all sweetness and light, but you don't fool me. I've heard you sighing at night."

"I'm thinking about other things, old things."

"The time for sighing over those 'old things' is long gone. You have the same griefs as me, but I put them away, as did you. Now you're sighing over new things, over the girls . . ."

"You're obsessed, woman! You and I have fallen out time and again and made up time and again too! Why, only the other day—"

"Exactly. We fell out with each other and we made up. They haven't fallen out, you're right, but you won't convince me that there isn't something wrong."

"I'm not trying to convince you of anything. If you enjoy making a complete idiot of yourself, then go on, but you're ruining our lives. We were all getting along so nicely . . ."

"It's not my fault everything's gone wrong. I'm doing my best to make everything go right again, but"—she blew her nose hard to disguise her emotion—"what I can't bear is to see the girls like this!"

"Adriana seems cheerful enough. Why, only the other day, when she was telling us about how her boss tripped on the carpet—"

"Pure pretense. Would you say Isaura was cheerful too?"

"We all have our off days . . ."

"Yes, but she has an awful lot of them. You've come to some agreement, haven't you? You know what's going on!"

"Me?!"

"Yes, you. If you didn't, you would be just as worried as I am."

"But only a moment ago you said you'd heard me sighing at night."

"Aha, caught you!"

"Oh, very clever. But you're quite wrong if you think I know anything. You and your silly ideas."

Amélia was indignant. Silly ideas indeed! When the bomb went off, then she'd see how silly—

or not—they were. She changed tactics. She stopped tormenting her nieces with questions and insinuations. She pretended to have lost interest, to have forgotten about the whole business. She noticed at once that the tensions eased. Even Isaura began to smile at her sister's tall tales of the office, but Isaura's attitude only convinced Amélia that there was still some hidden mystery. Free from the pressure of suspicion and persecution, Isaura was able to relax a little; she seemed to want to help her aunt to forget. But Amélia did not forget. She merely took a few steps back in order to be able to jump still farther.

While maintaining her pose of indifference, she listened out for every word, but without reacting to them, however strange they were. She believed that, bit by bit, she would untangle the whole sorry plot. She began to rummage around in the past for anything that might help her. She tried to remember when "it" had all begun. Her memory had grown weak and vague, but helped by the calendar, she battled on until she found the source. "It" had begun on the night when she'd heard her nieces talking and Isaura crying. Just a bad dream, Adriana had said. So the bad dream must have been Isaura's. What could they have said to each other? She knew that girls tell each other everything, at least that's how it was in her day. There were two possibilities: either Isaura was crying about something Adriana had told her, in which case the problem lay with Adriana, or she was crying about something she herself had said, which would explain why Adriana had tried to cover it all up. And if it was Adriana's problem, how had she managed to stay so cool and collected?

These thoughts caused her to turn her attention back to Adriana, whose cheerfulness had always rung false to her, had seemed merely a brave front. Isaura kept silent, and Adriana disguised her feelings, unless that disguise was intended to act as a cover for Isaura. Trapped in this blind alley, Amélia despaired.

Then it occurred to her that Adriana was gone almost all day, out of sight, but Amélia couldn't simply drop in at the office as she had at the library. Perhaps the office held the key to the mystery. But if so, why had the problem only arisen after two years of working there? This thought, of course, made no sense: sometimes things do just happen, and the fact that they didn't happen yesterday doesn't mean they won't happen today or tomorrow. She decided then that the "problem" lay with Adriana and had to do with the office. If it turned out she was wrong, then she would try another tack. Provisionally, she put Isaura to one side. Except that she still couldn't understand Isaura's tears. Something grave must have happened for her to cry as she had on that night and for her to remain so sad and silent ever since. Something extremely grave . . . Amélia could not or preferred not to think what it could have been. Adriana was a girl, a young woman, and the only grave thing in a woman's life, the only one that could make that woman's sister cry, was . . . But no, the idea was absurd and she tried to drive it from her mind. Now, however, everything was conspiring to make that idea seem more probable. First: Adriana spent all day away from the apartment; second: she occasionally worked late; third: every night she shut herself up in the bathroom . . . In a flash of insight Amélia recalled that, since that night, Adriana had stopped doing that. She always used to be the last to bed and always took her time. Now, while she wasn't always the first, she was rarely the last to use the bathroom, and when she was, thought Amélia, she didn't spend much time in there. Everyone knew that Adriana kept a diary, a childish whim of no importance, and that she wrote her diary while in the bathroom. Was the explanation for this whole muddle to be found in that diary? And how could she go about getting the key to the drawer in which Adriana kept it?

Each of the four women had a drawer that was for her use alone. All the others were left unlocked. Living as they did, using the same bed linen and the same towels, it would be absurd to lock those drawers, but each of them had her own particular drawer in which to keep her private

320

mementos. For Amelia and Cândida these were old letters, the ribbons from their wedding bouquets, a few yellowing photographs, the odd dried flower, perhaps a lock of hair. When they were alone and the past called to them, those private drawers became a kind of sanctuary where each could go to pay homage to her memories. Amélia and Cândida, knowing what their own mementos were, could each have said, with a fair degree of accuracy, what the other's drawer contained too, but neither of them had any idea what Adriana and Isaura kept in theirs. Adriana kept her diary in hers, that much was certain, and Amélia was sure she would find the explanation she was looking for in there. Even before she considered how she would gain access to the diary, what weighed on her was the thought of committing such an act of violation. She wondered how she would feel if someone were to discover her own rather pathetic secrets, which were, besides, only the remnants of facts the others all knew about anyway. It would, she thought, be a terrible abuse. On the other hand, having promised to uncover her nieces' secret and being only a step away from honoring that promise, she could not now draw back. Whatever the consequences might be, she had to know. It would not be easy. Quite apart from Amélia's deep conviction that their respective secrets should be inviolable and that none of them would dare to open any drawer other than their own, a further problem was that Adriana always had the keys to her drawer with her. When she was at home, she kept them in her purse and it would be impossible to get hold of them, open the drawer and read whatever there was to read without Adriana knowing. And it was highly unlikely that Adriana would forget her keys. Unless Amélia stole them from her and managed to persuade Adriana that she had lost them. That would be the easiest way, but Adriana might get suspicious and try to block the keyhole with something. There was only one solution: to get another key made, but to do that she would have to make a copy, and that would involve taking the key to the locksmith. Was there no other way? A tracing might work, but how to get hold of the key?

Amélia racked her brain. It was a matter of finding the right opportunity, the few minutes necessary for her to make a drawing of the keys. She tried several times, but at the last moment someone always came into the room. All these obstacles only increased her desire to know. The locked drawer made her tremble with impatience. She had lost all scruples now. Regardless of the consequences, she had to know. If Adriana had committed some shameful act, it would be best to find out before it was too late. It was that "too late" that frightened Amélia.

Her persistence soon paid off. The cousins from

Campolide came to visit them, a return visit for the one made sometime before by Cândida and Amélia. It was a Sunday. They spent all afternoon there, drinking tea and chatting. The usual memories were trotted out, always the same ones, which they all knew by heart, but to which they listened politely as if hearing them for the first time. Adriana had never been so lively and her sister had never made such an effort to appear to be contented. Cândida, deceived by her daughters' gaiety, forgot all about the "situation." Only Amélia did not. At an opportune moment, she got up and went to her nieces' room. Heart pounding and hands shaking, she opened Adriana's purse and took out the keys. There were five. She recognized two of them, one for the street door and the other for the door to their apartment. There were two other medium-sized keys and a smaller one. She hesitated. She didn't know which of them was the key to the drawer, although she felt it must be one of the medium-sized keys. The drawer was only a few steps away. She could try one of the keys in the lock, but was afraid that any noise might attract her nieces' attention. She decided to make a drawing of all three, which she did, although not without some difficulty. The pencil slithered from her fingers and refused to follow the exact shape of the keys. She had sharpened it to a long, sharp point to make the drawing more faithful, but her hands were shaking so much she almost gave up. From the next room came the sound of Adriana's giggles: the story about her boss tripping on the carpet, which the cousins had not heard before. They all laughed uproariously and their laughter drowned out the tiny click of the purse closing.

That night after supper, while the radio was murmuring a Chopin nocturne—the radio having been turned on in the warm afterglow of that jolly afternoon—Amélia said how pleased she was to see her nieces getting on so well together.

"You see, it was all in your imagination," said Cândida, smiling.

"Yes," said Amélia, "it must have been."

31

With her monthly allowance safely stowed away in her handbag, the notes neatly folded up inside her greasy purse, Lídia's mother was drinking a cup of tea. She had placed on the bed the knitting with which she occupied her evenings. She always visited twice a month, once to collect her money and again in order to show a friendly interest in her daughter's life. Familiar with Paulino Morais's habits, she appeared only on Tuesdays, Thursdays or Saturdays. She knew she wasn't wanted, on those days or any others, but she turned up nonetheless. In order to "live decently" she needed that monthly subsidy. Given her daughter's good financial position, it would seem wrong simply to abandon her. And because she was sure that Lídia would not, of her own volition, go out of her way to help, she felt it wise to remind her regularly of her existence. And so that Lídia would not think that she had purely venal reasons for coming to see her, she would call again about two weeks after receiving her allowance to inquire after Lídia's health. Of the two visits, the first was the more bearable because it had a real objective. The second, despite that display of affectionate interest, was tedious for both mother and daughter.

Lídia was sitting on the sofa, a book open on her lap. Having interrupted her reading to pour herself a coffee, she had not yet gone back to it. She was staring at her mother without a glimmer of affection in her eyes, as coldly as she might look at a complete stranger. Her mother did not notice or was so inured to her daughter's icy gaze that it had no effect. She was sipping her coffee with the cool, composed air she always adopted when in her daughter's apartment. The only less-than-delicate gesture she allowed herself—one demanded by her sweet tooth—was using her spoon to scrape up the sugar from the bottom of the cup.

Lídia looked down again at her book as if she could no longer bear the disagreeable sight of her mother, whom she disliked intensely. She felt exploited, but that wasn't the reason for her enmity. She didn't like her because she knew she did not love her as a daughter. On several occasions she had considered sending her packing. The only reason she hadn't was because she feared some terrible scene. The price she had to pay for keeping the peace was fairly high, but hardly excessive. She had grown accustomed to those twice-monthly visits. Flies are a nuisance too, but you just have to put up with them.

Her mother stood up, placed her empty cup on the dressing table, then returned to her chair and resumed her knitting. The wool was distinctly grubby and her work advanced at a snail's pace. Indeed, so slowly did the work progress that Lídia had not as yet been able to ascertain what the finished garment would be. She suspected that her mother only brought out her knitting on those visits to her apartment.

She tried to immerse herself in her reading, having first glanced at her watch to calculate how much longer her mother would stay. She had decided not to utter a word until it was time to say goodbye. She felt irritable. Paulino had grown distracted again, however hard she tried to please him. She would kiss him ardently, something she did only when absolutely necessary. The same pair of lips can kiss in many ways, and Lídia knew them all. The passionate kiss, the kiss that involves not just lips but tongue and teeth as well, was reserved for important occasions. Lately, seeing Paulino growing ever more remote, or so it seemed, she had made liberal use of such kisses.

"What's wrong, dear?" asked her mother. "You've been staring at that page for ages now and you still haven't finished it!"

She spoke in the mellifluous, ingratiating tones of an employee thanking the boss for his Christmas bonus. Lídia shrugged and said nothing.

"You seem worried. Have you quarreled with Senhor Morais?"

Lídia looked up and asked ironically:

"What if I have?"

"That would be most unwise, dear. Men can be very odd. They get annoyed over the slightest thing. There's no talking to them sometimes . . ."

"You speak as if you'd had a lot of experience of men."

"I lived with your late father for twenty-two years, what more experience do I need?"

"If you lived with my father for twenty-two years and never knew any other man, how can you speak of experience?"

"Men are all the same, dear. If you've known one, you've known them all."

"Yes, but how?"

"You just have to open your eyes and look."

"You must have very good eyesight, then."

"Oh, I do. I don't wish to boast, but I just have to look at a man to know him!"

"Well, you know more than I do, then. And what do you make of Senhor Morais?"

Her mother put down her knitting and said warmly:

"Ah, you really landed on your feet when you met him. However nice you are to him, you could never repay him for what he's done for you. Just look at this apartment! Not to mention the jewelry and the clothes! Has anyone else ever treated you like this? When I think what I suffered . . ."

"Oh, I know all about your suffering."

"You say that as if you didn't believe me. All mothers suffer. And what mother wouldn't be pleased to see her children doing well?"

"Yes, what mother wouldn't be pleased?" echoed Lídia mockingly.

Her mother took up her knitting again and said nothing. She completed two rows, very slowly, as if her thoughts were elsewhere. Then she resumed the conversation:

"It sounds to me like you've quarreled. Well, you be careful!"

"What's it got to do with you? If we have or haven't quarreled, that's my business."

"Well, I think you're wrong, even if . . ."

"Go on . . . even if what?"

The woolen thread had become so coiled and tangled it appeared to be full of knots, or, rather,

her mother was bending so low over her work at this point, it was as if the Gordian knot itself had been resuscitated.

"Go on, spit it out."

"What I meant to say was . . . even if you'd found a better position!"

Lídia snapped the book shut. Startled, her mother dropped a whole row of stitches.

"The only thing that would prevent me from kicking you out right now is my respect for you as my mother. Except, of course, that I don't respect you, not one bit, and yet, for some unfathomable reason, I still can't bring myself to kick you out!"

"Goodness, whatever did I say for you to get so hot under the collar?"

"How can you ask? Put yourself in my place!"

"Oh, what a fuss about nothing! What did I say that was so wrong? I'm just concerned about you."

"Please, just shut up, will you?"

"But—"

"Like I said, please, shut up!"

Her mother whimpered:

"How can you treat me like this? Me, your own mother, the one who brought you up and loved you? Is this all the thanks a mother gets?"

"If I was a normal daughter and you were a normal mother, you'd be justified in complaining."

"And what about all the sacrifices I made, what about them?"

"You've been richly rewarded, if, that is, you ever made any sacrifices. You're in an apartment paid for by Senhor Morais, you're sitting on a chair bought by him, you've just drunk the same coffee he drinks, the money in your purse is money he gave to me. Isn't that enough?"

Her mother continued to whimper:

"How can you say such things? I feel positively ashamed . . ."

"Oh, yes, I can see that. You only feel ashamed when things are spelled out for you. If you just *think* them, though, then you're not ashamed."

Her mother quickly dried her eyes and said:

"I wasn't the one who forced you into this way of life. It was your choice!"

"Thank you very much. I fear that, given the turn the conversation is taking, this will be the last time you set foot in my apartment!"

"Which isn't yours anyway!"

"Thank you again. But regardless of whether it's mine or not, I'm the one who gives the orders here. And if I say get out, you will."

"You might need me one day."

"Don't worry, I won't come knocking at your door! I'd rather starve to death than ask you for so much as one cêntimo back of what I've given you."

"Which wasn't yours either!"

"But which I earned, right? I actually earned that money. I earned it with my body. There has to be some point in having a nice body, even if it's only to feed *you!*"

"I don't know why I don't just leave!"

"Shall I tell you why? It's fear, fear of losing the goose who lays the golden eggs. I'm the goose, the eggs are there in your purse, the nest is this bed and the gander, well, you know who he is, don't you?"

"Don't be so coarse!"

"I feel like being coarse today, and sometimes the truth can be very coarse indeed. Everything's all fine and dandy until we start being coarse, until we start telling the truth!"

"That's it, I'm leaving!"

"Please do. And don't come back either, because you might still find me in the mood to tell you a few home truths!"

Her mother rolled and unrolled her knitting, delaying having to get up. Still playing for time, she said:

"Look, you're not yourself today, dear. It's your nerves. I didn't mean to upset you, but you went too far. You two have probably had a bit of a tiff, which is why you're all on edge, but it'll pass, you'll see . . ."

"You know, it's like you're made of rubber. However hard you're punched, you always bounce back. Can't you see that I want you to leave?"

"Yes, yes, but I'll ring you tomorrow to find out how you are. It'll pass."

331

"You'll be wasting your time."

"Look, dear . . ."

"I've said what I have to say. Now please leave."

Her mother gathered her things together, picked up her handbag and prepared to go. Given the way in which the conversation was ending, she had little hope of ever coming back. She tried to soften her daughter's heart with tears:

"You can't imagine how upsetting this is for me . . ."

"Oh, yes I can. What's upsetting you is the thought of your little allowance being docked. Isn't that right? Well, all good things come to an end . . ."

She broke off when she heard the front door open. She got up and went out into the corridor:

"Who is it? Oh, it's you, Paulino! I wasn't expecting you today . . ."

Paulino came in. He was wearing a raincoat and didn't bother to remove his hat. When he saw Lídia's mother, he cried:

"What are you doing here?"

"I'm—"

"Get out!"

He almost shouted these words. Lídia intervened:

"Whatever's gotten into you, Paulino? You're not yourself. What's wrong?"

Paulino glared at her:

"What do you think?" He turned around again

332

and bawled: "Are you still here? Didn't I tell you to leave? No, wait, now you'll find out what a sweet little thing your daughter is. Sit down!"

Lídia's mother fell back onto her chair.

"And you can sit down too!" Paulino said to Lídia.

"I'm not used to being spoken to in that tone. I don't want to sit down."

"Do as you please, then."

He removed his hat and coat and threw them on the bed. Then he turned to Lídia's mother and said:

"You're a witness to the way I've always treated your daughter . . ."

"Yes, Senhor Morais."

Lídia broke in:

"So is this a matter for me or for my mother?"

Paulino wheeled around as if he'd been bitten by something. He took two steps toward Lídia, expecting her to draw back, but she didn't. Paulino took a letter from his pocket and held it out to her:

"Here's the proof that you've been cheating on me!"

"You're mad!"

Paulino clutched his head:

"Mad? Mad? You have the nerve to call me mad? Read it, read what it says!"

Lídia opened the letter and read it in silence. Her face remained utterly impassive. When she reached the end, she asked:

"And you believe what it says in this letter, do you?"

"Do I believe it? Of course I do!"

"So what are you waiting for?"

Paulino stared at her, uncomprehending. He found Lídia's coolness disconcerting. Mechanically, he folded the letter and put it away. Lídia was looking him straight in the eye. Embarrassed, he turned to her mother, who was watching, mouth wide in amazement:

"Your daughter has been unfaithful to me with a neighbor, the young man who lodges with the cobbler and his wife, a mere boy!"

"Oh, Lídia, how could you?" exclaimed her mother, horrified.

Lídia sat down on the sofa, crossed her legs, took out a cigarette and put it between her lips. Out of sheer habit, Paulino offered her a light.

"Thank you," she said, exhaling a cloud of smoke. "I don't know what you're both waiting for. Paulino, you say you believe what's in that letter, and you, my mother, find me accused of having an affair with a young man who, I imagine, hasn't a cêntimo to his name. So why don't you both just leave?"

Paulino went over to her and spoke more calmly:

"Tell me if it's true or not."

"I have nothing further to add."

"It's true, then, it must be! If it wasn't, you would protest your innocence and—"

"If you really want to know what I think, I'll tell you. That letter is just an excuse."

"An excuse for what?"

"You know as well as I do."

"Are you suggesting that *I* wrote it?"

"Some people will do anything to get what they want . . ."

"That's an out-and-out lie!" roared Paulino. "I would never do such a thing!"

"Possibly . . ."

"Don't push me too far!"

Lídia stubbed out her cigarette in the ashtray and got to her feet, trembling with rage:

"You burst in here like some kind of savage, make some ridiculous accusation and expect me not to react?"

"So it's *not* true, then?"

"Do you honestly expect me to answer that? It's up to you whether you choose to believe what the letter says rather than believe me, but you've already said that you believe the letter, so what are you waiting for?" She gave a sudden laugh and added: "Men who think they've been deceived usually either kill the woman or leave. Or pretend they know nothing. What are you going to do?"

Paulino slumped down on the sofa, defeated:

"Just tell me it's a lie . . ."

"I've said what I had to say. I only hope you don't take too long to come to a decision."

"You're making things very awkward for me . . ."
Lídia turned her back on him and went to the
window. Her mother followed her and whispered:
"Why don't you tell him it's a lie? He'd feel
better then . . ."

"Leave me alone!"

Her mother sat down again, gazing at Paulino
with a commiserating look on her face. Paulino,
still sitting hunched on the sofa, was beating his
head with his fists, unable to find a way out of the
labyrinth into which he had been plunged. He had
received the letter after lunch and almost had a
heart attack when he read it. The letter was
unsigned. It gave no indication of where the illicit
meetings took place—which meant he had no
chance of catching Lídia in flagrante—but it did
go into long, detailed descriptions and urged
Paulino to be a man. When he reread it (shut up in
his office so as not to be disturbed), it occurred to
him that the letter had its good side. He was still
intoxicated by Maria Cláudia's freshness and
youth. He was always finding pretexts to call her
into the office, and this was already setting
tongues wagging among the other employees.
Like any self-respecting employer, he had a
trusted employee who kept him informed of
everything that was said and done in the company.
Paulino, however, had gone on to provoke still
more gossip by redoubling his attentions to Maria
Cláudia. The letter could not have come at a better

time. A violent scene, a few insults, and goodbye, I'm off to pastures new! There were, of course, obstacles in his path: Maria Cláudia's age, her parents . . . He had considered keeping both irons in the fire, so to speak: continuing his relationship with Lídia, who was, after all, a very tasty morsel, and wooing Claudinha, who promised to be an even more tasty morsel. But that was before he had received the letter. It was a formal accusation and called upon him to be a man and take a stand. The worst thing was that he wasn't entirely sure about Claudinha and feared losing Lídia. He had neither the time nor the inclination to find another mistress. But what to do about the letter? Lídia was cheating on him with some poor wretch obliged to live in rented rooms: that was the worst possible insult, a slur on his manhood. Young woman, old man, young lover. He could not possibly let such an insult pass. He called Claudinha into his office and spent the whole afternoon talking to her, without, of course, mentioning the letter. He very carefully tested the waters and was quite pleased with the result. When she left, he reread the letter and decided to take whatever radical steps the case demanded. Hence the present scene.

Lídia, however, had reacted in a completely unforeseen way. He had explained the dilemma to her as coolly as possible: to stay or to leave, reserving for himself the right to proceed as he saw fit should he decide on the former option. But why had she not answered his question? Why would she not just say yes or no?

"Lídia, why can't you just give me a yes or a no?"

She eyed him haughtily:

"Are you still harping on about that? I thought the matter was settled."

"This is ridiculous. We've always been such good friends . . ."

Lídia gave a sad, ironic smile.

"How can you smile at a time like this? Answer my question!"

"If I tell you it's true, what will you do?"

"Well, I don't know . . . leave you, I suppose!"

"Fine. And I assume you've already considered that if I tell you it's not true, you're liable to receive more such letters? How long do you think you could stand that? Do you expect me to wait here at your beck and call until the time comes when you stop believing me?"

Her mother said:

"Surely you can see it's a lie, Senhor Morais. You just have to look at her."

"Shut up, Mother!"

Paulino shook his head, perplexed. Lídia was right. When the person who had written the letter saw that nothing had come of it, he would write more letters, giving more details, more infor-mation. He might become still more insolent, calling him the worst names a man can be called. How long would he be able to stand that? And what guarantee was there that Claudinha would be prepared to play second fiddle? He sprang to his feet.

"Right, that's it! I'm leaving. Now."

Lídia turned pale. Despite all she had said, she had not expected her lover to leave her. She had been totally honest with him, but, she realized, she had also been imprudent. Feigning serenity, she answered:

"Fine, if that's the way you want it."

Paulino put on his raincoat and picked up his hat. He wanted to end the matter honorably, as befitted his dignity as a man.

"You shouldn't have done what you did. I didn't deserve to be treated like that. I hope things work out well for you."

He headed for the door, but Lídia stopped him:

"Hang on. The things in this apartment that belong to you, which is just about everything, are yours for the taking. You can send for them whenever you choose."

"I don't want anything. You can keep them. I have money enough to set up another woman in her own apartment. Good night."

"Good night, Senhor Morais," said Lídia's mother. "I still think—"

"Shut up, Mother!"

Lídia went to the door that gave onto the

corridor and said to Paulino as he was about to turn the handle and leave:

"I wish you every happiness with your new mistress. Take care they don't make you marry her!"

Paulino left without answering. Lídia turned around and sat down on the sofa. She lit another cigarette. She looked scornfully at her mother and said:

"What are you waiting for? There'll be no more money, so go! Wasn't I just saying that all good things come to an end?"

Wearing an expression of wounded dignity, her mother went over to her. She opened her handbag, took the money from her purse and placed it on the bed:

"Here you are. You might need it yourself."

Lídia did not move:

"Keep the money! I can always earn more the same way I earned that. Now go!"

Her mother took the money and left, as if this had been her intention all along. She was not very pleased with herself. Her daughter's last words reminded her that she could have continued to count on that financial support had she been less aggressive, had she taken her daughter's side and been more affectionate . . . But then the filial bond is a strong one . . . and so she left, hoping that, sooner or later, she might still be able to come back.

The noise of the door slamming shut startled Lídia. She was alone. Her cigarette was slowly burning out between her fingers. Yes, she was alone again, as she had been three years ago when she had first met Paulino Morais. It was over. She had to start again. Start again. Start again.

Two slow tears welled up in her eyes. They trembled for a moment on her lower lid, then fell. Just two tears. That's all life is worth.

32

Not being the most persistent of men, Anselmo soon wearied of keeping watch over his daughter. What got him down most was not just having to hang around from six o'clock on for Maria Cláudia to leave the office, but then having a further wait while she was at her shorthand class. On the first day, he had the pleasure of seeing her student boyfriend flee as soon as he saw him. On the second, he enjoyed that same pleasure again. But when the boy did not reappear, Anselmo grew bored with his role as guardian angel. His daughter, possibly out of resentment, said nothing during the tram journey, and that troubled him too. He tried to talk to her, asked questions, but received such terse replies that he gave up. Besides which, accustomed as he was to being domestic royalty, the mission he

341

had set himself seemed rather undignified. And while there can be no possible comparison—and with all due respect—it was as if the President of the Republic were to be found standing in the street directing traffic. Anselmo just needed an excuse to bring his guardianship to an end: for example, a promise from his daughter to behave like a respectable young woman. Or some other excuse.

The excuse duly turned up, albeit not in the form of that hoped-for promise. At the end of the month, Claudinha handed him about seven hundred and fifty escudos, which meant that her boss had increased her wages to eight hundred escudos. This unexpected rise in salary cheered the whole family, especially Anselmo, who, given that Claudinha had proved her worth, felt a "moral obligation" to be magnanimous. And since his precarious economic situation only allowed him to be morally rather than financially magnanimous, he announced to his daughter that he would no longer accompany her from work to her shorthand lessons and home again. Claudinha's response was only lukewarm, and thinking that she had not fully understood, he repeated what he had said. Her response remained lukewarm. Despite her ingratitude, however, Anselmo kept his word, although, just to make sure that his daughter did not abuse the freedom granted to her, he did follow her for a few days more, at a distance. There was not a sign of the boyfriend.

Reassured, Anselmo returned to his beloved daily routine. By the time Claudinha came home, he would already be poring over his tables of sports statistics. He had also begun to create an album of photographs of soccer stars, to which end he bought a weekly adventure magazine for boys, which, in order to bump up sales, always included a full-color insert bearing the face of some celebrated player. When he bought the magazine, he always made a point of saying that he was buying it for his son, and carried it home wrapped in a sheet of paper so that the neighbors would not discover his weakness. He went so far as to buy back numbers too, which meant that, in one fell swoop, he became the owner of some dozens of photographs. Claudinha's raise could not have come at a more opportune moment, for Rosália had boldly protested the expense and waste involved in buying the magazine, but Anselmo, once more enthroned in power, was immediately able to silence her.

At last they were all contented. Claudinha was free, Anselmo busy and Rosália her usual self. The family machinery resumed its normal rhythm, only to be disturbed one evening when Rosália commented:

"I think there's been some change in Dona Lídia's situation."

Father and daughter glanced at each other.

"Do you know anything, Claudinha?" asked her mother.

"Me? No, I don't know anything."

"Or do you just not want to tell us . . ."

"I've already told you: I don't know anything!"

Rosália slipped the darning egg into the sock she was working on. She did this very slowly, as if hoping to fan the curiosity of husband and daughter. Then she said:

"Haven't you noticed that more than a week has gone by since Senhor Morais visited her?"

Anselmo hadn't noticed and said so at once. Claudinha had, but said nothing. Then:

"Senhor Morais hasn't been well. He told me so himself."

Somewhat disappointed, Rosália thought that not feeling well was hardly reason enough.

"You might be able to find out, Claudinha . . ."

"Find out what?"

"Well, if they've had a falling-out, because that's what I think must have happened."

Claudinha gave a bored shrug:

"I'm hardly going to ask that, am I?"

"Why not? You owe Dona Lídia a big favor, so it's only natural you should take an interest."

"What favor do I owe Dona Lídia? If I owe anyone anything, it's Senhor Morais."

"Be fair now, dear," said Anselmo. "If it hadn't been for Dona Lídia, you wouldn't have gotten this job . . ."

Claudinha did not answer. She turned to the radio and started twiddling the dial in search of a station broadcasting the kind of music she liked. She found a commercial station. A singer with a "romantic" voice was lamenting his amorous misfortunes in music and words that were equally banal. Once the singer had finished, and seduced perhaps by that silly song, Claudinha said:

"All right. If you like, I can try to find out. Besides," she added after a long pause, "if I ask him, Senhor Morais is sure to tell me."

Claudinha was right. When she got home the next evening, she knew the whole story. They hadn't expected her so early. It was just after half past seven. Having greeted her parents, she announced:

"OK, I know everything."

Before allowing her to continue, however, Anselmo wanted to know what she was doing home at that hour.

"I didn't go to my lesson," she said.

"So you're late, then."

"I stayed behind so that Senhor Morais could tell me all about it."

"So?" asked Rosália eagerly.

Claudinha sat down. She seemed somewhat nervous. Her bottom lip was trembling slightly, her breast heaving, although this could have been the result of the brisk walk home from the office.

"Come on, dear, we're dying to hear."

"They've split up. Senhor Morais received an anonymous letter saying . . ."

"Saying what?" asked husband and wife, impatient with the delay.

"Saying that Dona Lídia was deceiving him."

Rosália clapped her hands to her thighs:

"I thought as much."

"There's worse to come," Claudinha went on.

"Worse?"

"The letter said she was deceiving him with Senhor Silvestre's lodger."

Anselmo and Rosália were duly horrified.

"That's disgraceful!" exclaimed Rosália. "But I can't believe Dona Lídia would do such a thing!"

Anselmo disagreed:

"It seems perfectly possible to me. What else can you expect from someone living the kind of life she lives?" And more quietly, so that his daughter would not hear, he added his favorite phrase: "Well, you know what I always say: birds of a feather . . ."

Claudinha heard the muttered comment and blinked rapidly, pretending that she hadn't. Rosália said:

"It just doesn't seem possible."

An awkward silence ensued, broken by Claudinha:

"Senhor Morais showed me the letter. He said he had no idea who had sent it."

Anselmo thought it proper to condemn all anonymous letters, describing them as "vile," but

Rosália leapt in with all the holy indignation of someone defending a just cause:

"If it wasn't for anonymous letters, a lot of things would remain hidden. You wouldn't want poor Senhor Morais playing the cuckold, would you?"

They were heading toward the decision that the events cried out for. Anselmo agreed:

"Naturally, if I was in the same situation, I'd certainly want to know . . ."

Scandalized at such a hypothesis, his wife broke in:

"So that's what you think of me, is it? Our daughter is here listening, you know!"

Claudinha got up and went to her room. Still bristling, Rosália commented:

"Honestly, the things you come out with! How could you?"

"All right, all right. Isn't it about time we ate?"

The decision was postponed for the time being. Claudinha returned from her room and, shortly afterward, they were seated at the supper table. During the meal, husband and wife talked of nothing else, while Claudinha remained silent throughout, as if this were too scabrous a conversation for her to take any part in. Rosália and Anselmo examined the matter from all angles, except one, the one that would require them to make a decision. They both knew it was necessary, but tacitly put it off until later.

Rosália declared that she had never liked Senhor Silvestre's lodger and reminded her husband that the very first time she'd clapped eyes on the man, she had commented on his shabby appearance.

"What I don't understand," said Anselmo, "is why Dona Lídia would get involved with some vagrant who has to live in rented rooms. Whatever can have possessed her?"

"It's obvious, isn't it? As you yourself said just now: what can you expect of someone living the life she lives?"

"Yes, you're right."

When supper was over, Claudinha said she had a headache and was going to bed. Feeling able at last to talk more freely, husband and wife looked at each other, shook their heads and simultaneously opened their mouths to speak, then promptly closed them again, each waiting for the other to begin. In the end, it was Anselmo who spoke:

"Well, what can you expect of a whore?"

"Shameless hussy!"

"I don't blame him, of course. He's a man, after all, and simply took what was offered. But her, when she's so well set up at home!"

"Nice dresses, lovely furs, beautiful jewelry . . ."

"That's what I mean, but once you've stumbled, it's easy enough to stumble again. It's in the blood. People like her are only happy when they're thinking shameless thoughts."

"If only they were just thoughts!"

"And with Senhor Silvestre's lodger too, right under Senhor Morais's nose!"

"The woman has no shame at all!"

All these things had to be said, because the decision could only be made when blame had been duly allotted. Anselmo picked up his knife and, using the blade, began carefully shepherding the crumbs on the table into a neat pile. His wife observed him intently, as if the very foundations of the building depended on the successful outcome of this task.

"Well, in the circumstances," said Anselmo, once all the crumbs were safely gathered in, "we have to take a stand."

"Indeed."

"We have to act."

"I agree."

"Claudinha must have nothing more to do with her. She's a bad influence."

"I wouldn't let Claudinha near her. In fact, it's been on my mind for a while now."

Anselmo picked up his plate to reveal more crumbs, which he added to the others, declaring:

"And as for us, we will never again speak to that woman, not even to say good morning or good afternoon. We'll just pretend she doesn't exist."

They were in complete agreement. Rosália began clearing the table and Anselmo took his photo album out of a drawer in the sideboard.

They did not linger long after supper, though. High emotion is always draining. Husband and wife went to their bedroom, where they continued their harsh assessment of Lídia's behavior. Their conclusion was this: some women—women whose mere existence is a blot on the lives of honest folk—simply deserve to be wiped from the face of the earth.

Claudinha could not sleep, but it wasn't the alleged and very real headache that prevented her from sleeping. She kept thinking about her conversation with Senhor Morais, which had not been quite as straightforward as she had given her parents to understand. She'd had no difficulty finding out what had happened between him and Lídia, but what had followed was less easy to describe. Nothing very terrible had occurred, nothing that could not or should not be told, but it was complicated. Not everything is as it seems, and not everything that seems is. Between being and seeming there is always a point of agreement, as if being and seeming were two inclined planes that converge and become one. There is a slope and the possibility of sliding down that slope, and when that happens, one reaches a point at which being and seeming meet.

Claudinha had asked her question and been given an answer, but not immediately, because Paulino had a lot of work to do and could not give her the desired explanation there and then. She had to wait for six o'clock. Her colleagues left, and she stayed. Paulino called her into his office and told her to sit in the armchair reserved for the company's more important clients. The armchair was a well-padded affair and rather low-slung. Claudinha had not given in to the latest fashion for long skirts, and so when she sat down, her skirt rode up above her knees. The soft upholstery held her there as if she were seated on a warm lap. Paulino paced up and down the office, then perched on one corner of his desk. He was wearing a light gray suit and yellow tie, which made him look more youthful. He lit a cigarillo, and the already stuffy atmosphere grew still heavier. It would soon become suffocating. Long minutes passed before Paulino spoke. Maria Cláudia found the silence, broken only by the tick-tock of the solemn grandfather clock, increasingly awkward. Paulino, on the other hand, seemed perfectly at ease. He had already smoked half his cigarillo when he said:

"So you want to know what's going on, do you?"

"I realize, Senhor Morais"—that is how Maria Cláudia had responded—"I realize that I probably have no right to ask, but given my friendship with Dona Lídia . . ."

That is what she said, as if she knew already that a quarrel was the only possible explanation for Paulino's absence. She may have been under the influence of her mother, who could think of no other motive. Her response would have appeared foolish in the extreme if it turned out that there had been no such quarrel.

"And does your friendship with me not count?" asked Paulino. "If your only reason for coming to talk to me about the matter is your friendship for her, I'm not sure I should . . ."

"It was wrong of me to ask. Your personal life is none of my business. Please forgive me . . ."

This show of disinterest could have provided Paulino with an excuse not to explain what had happened, but Paulino had been expecting Maria Cláudia to ask and had even considered how he might respond.

"You haven't answered my question. Is it just your friendship for her that makes you ask that question? Does the friendship you feel for me not count at all? Are you not my friend as well?"

"You've always been very kind to me, Senhor Morais . . ."

"I'm kind to the other employees too, and yet I'm not about to reveal details of my private life to them, nor do I invite them to sit in that armchair."

Maria Cláudia said nothing. She found his remark embarrassing and bowed her head, blushing. Paulino pretended not to notice. He drew up a chair and sat down opposite Claudinha. Then he told her what had happened: the letter, the conversation with Lídia, the breakup. He omitted any episodes that might show him in an unfavorable light and presented himself with a dignity that would have been fatally compromised had he included them. When he faltered in his account of events, Maria Cláudia sensed that this was because he might well have emerged from the encounter as the less dignified of the two. However, as to the crux of the matter, there was no room for doubt once she had read the letter that Paulino showed to her:

"I'm really sorry I asked you, Senhor Morais. I realize now that I had no right to."

"You had more right than you might think. We're good friends, and there can be no secrets between friends."

"But . . ."

"Naturally I'm not going to ask you to tell me yours. We men confide much more in women than they do in us, which is why I told you the whole story. I trust you, trust you completely." He leaned forward, smiling. "So now we share a secret, and secrets bring people closer, don't they?"

Maria Cláudia merely smiled, as all women do when they don't know what to say. The person at whom the smile is directed can interpret it as he or she wishes.

"It's good to see you smile. At my age, it's always good to see young people smile. And you're very young indeed."

Another smile from Maria Cláudia. Encouraged, Paulino went on:

"And not just young, but pretty too."

"Thank you, Senhor Morais."

This time the smile did not come unaccompanied, and her voice quavered slightly.

"There's no need to blush, Claudinha. I'm only saying what's true. I don't know anyone as pretty as you."

In order to say something, since a smile was no longer enough, Claudinha said what she should not have said:

"Dona Lídia was much prettier than me!"

Yes, "was"! As if Lídia had died, as if she were no longer relevant to the conversation except as a point of comparison.

"Not at all. I'm speaking as a man now, and you're quite different. You're young and pretty and there's something about you that I find really . . . touching."

Paulino was very polite, so polite that he even said "May I?" before reaching out a hand to remove a stray hair that had fallen onto Claudinha's shoulder. However, the hand did not follow the same trajectory on the way back. It brushed Claudinha's face, so slowly it resembled a caress, so lingeringly it appeared not to want to move away. Claudinha sprang to her feet. Paulino's voice, grown suddenly husky, said:

"What's wrong, Claudinha?"

"Nothing, Senhor Morais. I have to go. It's late."

"But it's not even seven o'clock yet."

"Yes, but I have to go."

She made as if to leave, but Paulino blocked the way. She looked at him, tremulous and frightened. He reassured her. He touched her cheek as an affectionate grandfather might do and murmured:

"Don't be silly. I wouldn't hurt you. I only want what's best for you."

Exactly what her parents used to say to her: "We only want what's best for you."

"Did you hear? I only want what's best for you."

"I have to go, Senhor Morais."

"But you do believe what I just said, don't you?"

"Of course I do, Senhor Morais."

"And we're friends?"

"Yes, Senhor Morais."

"And we always will be?"

"I hope so, Senhor Morais."

"Excellent!"

He stroked her cheek again, saying:

"What I told you is strictly between you and me. It's a secret. You can tell your parents if you like, but if you do, be sure to say that I only left that woman because she proved unworthy of me. I could never leave someone I truly cared about, not without some pressing reason. It's true that, for some time now, I haven't felt entirely comfortable with her. I think my feelings for her were already beginning to fade. There's someone else, someone

I've only known for a few weeks. And I've found it very hard having that other person so close to me and not being able to talk to her. Do you understand, Claudinha? It was you I was thinking of!"

Arms outstretched, he approached Claudinha and gripped her shoulders. Claudinha felt his lips brush her face in search of her lips. She smelled his cigar breath, felt his greedy mouth devouring hers. She didn't have the strength to push him away. When he released her, she sat down on the armchair, exhausted. Then, without looking at him, she murmured:

"Please let me go now, Senhor Morais."

Paulino took a deep breath, as if he could at last breathe freely, his lungs unconstricted. He said:

"I'm going to make you very happy, Claudinha!"

Then he opened his office door and summoned the office boy, telling him to fetch Claudinha's coat. The office boy was his trusted inside man, so trusted that he did not appear to notice Maria Cláudia's agitated state or express surprise when the boss helped her on with her coat.

And that was it. That was what Maria Cláudia did not tell her parents. Her head still throbbing, sleep continued to elude her. She lay on her back, hands behind her head, thinking. It was impossible not to understand what Paulino wanted. Impossible to close her eyes to the evidence. She was still on the slippery slope of "seeming," but as close to "being" as one hour is to the next. She knew she had not reacted as she should have, not just during that last conversation, but since the very first day, from the moment when, left alone with Paulino in Lídia's apartment, she had felt his insatiable eyes undressing her. She had not written that letter, but she knew nonetheless that she had been responsible for his breakup with Lídia. She knew that she had reached this point not because of what she had done, but because of what she had not done. She knew all this. The only thing she did not know was whether she wanted to take Lídia's place, because that was what it came down to now, wanting or not wanting. If she had told her parents everything, she would not be going back to the office in the morning. But she preferred not to tell them. Why? Was it a desire to deal with things in her own way? But "her own way" had gotten her into this situation. Was it the reserved silence of someone who wants to be independent? But at what price?

A few seconds before, Maria Cláudia had heard the click-clack of high heels in the apartment below. She took no notice at first, but the sound continued and finally penetrated her thoughts. She was intrigued. Then she heard the door of the downstairs apartment opening, the key turning in the lock and, after a brief silence, someone going down the stairs. It was Lídia. Maria Cláudia glanced at the luminous face of the clock on her bedside table. A quarter to eleven. What was Lídia doing out and about at that hour? Barely had she formulated this question than she found the answer. She gave a wry smile, but realized at once how monstrous that smile was. She felt a sudden impulse to weep. She drew the bedclothes up over her head to muffle her sobs. And there, almost suffocating from the lack of air and from her tears, she determined that the next day she would tell her parents everything.

33

When, after much bureaucratic toing and froing and at vast expense, Emílio finally came home bearing all the documents that his wife and son needed in order to leave, Carmen almost jumped up and down with delight. The days of waiting had seemed to her like years. She had feared that some obstacle would force her to postpone the journey for longer than her impatience could bear. Now, though, there was nothing to fear. She kept leafing through her passport with childlike curiosity. She read it from cover to cover. Everything was in order, she just had to decide on a date and forewarn her parents. Had it been up to her, she would have left the very next day and sent a telegram, but there were still the suitcases to be packed. Emílio helped her, and the evenings taken up with this task were some of the happiest they had spent together as a family. Henrique, quite unwittingly, cast a pall over the general mood of contentment when he expressed his regret that his father would not be coming with them. However, once Carmen and Emílio's combined efforts and combined goodwill had convinced him that this was a matter of no importance, he soon forgot about that minor cloud. If his parents were happy, then he should be too. If his parents did not weep as they apportioned clothes and other personal items, it would be absurd for him to cry. After just three of these evening sessions, everything was ready. The suitcases already bore the wooden labels with Carmen's name and destination on them. Emílio bought the tickets and told his wife that they would sort out these matters on her return, for, since her parents had promised to pay for the tickets and Emílio had been obliged to borrow money in order to buy them, there would have to be a settling of accounts. Carmen assured him that she would send him the money as soon as she arrived, so that he would not get into any financial difficulties. Both husband and wife took great pains to be as considerate to each other as possible, and so Henrique had the joy of spending those last few hours with his parents reconciled and more communicative than he had ever seen them before.

Carmen learned what had happened to Dona Lídia only the day before her departure. On the pretext of wishing Carmen a safe journey, Rosália spent a large part of the morning telling her about Paulino's justifiable anger. She explained the reasons and, entirely on her own initiative, suggested that this was not the first time Lídia had abused Senhor Morais's good faith. She was prodigal in her praise of her daughter's employer and the delicate, noble way in which he had dealt with the whole affair. And she was quick to mention, too, that after only one month in her new post, Claudinha had already received a wage increase.

At the time, Carmen merely expressed the natural dismay of anyone hearing such a sorry tale. She shared Rosália's outrage, bemoaned the immoral behavior of certain women and, like her neighbor, rejoiced privately that she was not like them. When Rosália left, she realized that she was still thinking about the affair, which would be fine if she wasn't about to leave the next day and if it didn't distract her from other concerns. What did it matter that Dona Lídia, about whom she personally had no complaints (on the contrary, Dona Lídia had been very kind to her and always gave Henriquinho ten tostões for running errands for her), what did it matter to her that she had committed such a vile act?

The act in itself did not matter, but the

consequences did. After what had happened, Paulino would never be able to return to Lídia's apartment: it would be too shameful. And somehow or other Carmen felt that she was in the same situation as Paulino, or almost. No public scandal separated her and her husband, but they shared a whole past life, a difficult, disagreeable life, full of resentments and enmities, violent scenes and painful reconciliations. Paulino had left, doubtless for good. She was leaving too, but would be back in three months. But what if she didn't come back? What if she stayed in her hometown with her son and her family?

When she admitted this as a possibility, when she thought that she might never come back, she felt quite dizzy. What could be simpler? She would say nothing now, but would set off with her son and, when she arrived in Spain, write a letter to her husband, telling him of her decision. And then? She would start all over again from the beginning, as if she had just been born. Portugal, Emílio and their marriage would merely be a nightmare that had dragged on for years. And perhaps later she could . . . although they would have to divorce, of course . . . yes, perhaps later . . . It was then that Carmen remembered that, as the law stood, she could not stay abroad without her husband's consent. She was leaving with his authorization, and she could only stay on with his authorization.

These thoughts clouded her happiness. She

would, of course, leave anyway, but the temptation not to come back made her happiness almost painful. Would it not be the worst of punishments to have to return to Lisbon after three months of freedom? To condemn herself to spending the rest of her life putting up with the presence and the words, the voice and the shadow, of her husband, would that not be like going down into hell again after having regained paradise? She would have to fight constantly to keep her son's love. And when her son (Carmen's imagination vaulted over the years)—and when her son married, it would be even worse because she would have to live alone with her husband. Everything would be resolved if he would agree to a divorce. But what if, on a whim or out of sheer malice, he forced her to return?

All day she was tormented by these thoughts. She had forgotten the good times in their marriage, of which there had been a few. She could think only of Emílio's cold, ironic gaze, his censorious silence, his permanent look of a man who has failed and doesn't care who knows it, who makes of his failure a placard that everyone can read.

Night fell without her having moved a step closer to finding answers to the questions that kept surfacing in her mind. She was so silent that her husband asked if something was worrying her. No, nothing, she said. She was just excited about their imminent departure. Emílio understood and did not insist. He felt excited too. In a few hours' time he would be free. Three whole months of solitude, freedom and an unencumbered life . . .

They left the next day. All the neighbors knew they were leaving and almost all came to the windows to watch. Carmen said goodbye to those neighbors with whom she was on good terms and got into the car with her husband and son. They reached the station shortly before the train was due to leave. They just had time to put the luggage on board, take their seats and say their farewells. Henrique barely had time to cry. The train vanished into the mouth of the tunnel, leaving behind it a cloud of white smoke that dissolved into the air, like a white handkerchief swallowed up by the distance.

It was his first day of freedom. Emílio wandered the city for hours. He discovered places he had never known existed, had lunch in a cheap restaurant in Alcântara and looked so happy that the owner charged him double for the meal. Emílio uttered not a word of protest and even left a tip. He caught a cab back to the Baixa, bought some foreign cigarettes and, when he walked past an expensive restaurant, cursed himself for having had lunch at that other, cheaper place. He went to the movies and, during intermission, drank a coffee and struck up a conversation with a stranger who, on the subject of coffee, discoursed at length on his terrible stomach problems.

When the film ended, he followed a woman out into the street, but soon lost sight of her, not that he cared. He stood on the pavement, smiling up at the tall monument in Praça dos Restauradores. In one leap, he thought, he could reach the very top, but he didn't make that leap. He spent more than ten minutes watching the traffic policeman and listening to his whistle. He found everything amusing and looked at people and things as if seeing them for the first time, as if he had recovered his sight after years of blindness. Approached by a young man trying to persuade passersby to have their photo taken, he promptly agreed. He took up his position and, at a signal from the photographer, walked straight ahead, with a determined step and a smile on his face.

He had dinner that night at the expensive restaurant. The food was good, so was the wine. He had very little money left after all these extravagances, but he didn't regret it. He didn't regret anything. He had done nothing that merited any feelings of regret. He was free, not as free as the birds, who have no obligations or duties, but as free as he could hope to be. When he left the restaurant, all the neon signs in the Rossio were blazing out. He looked at them, one by one, as if they were the stars of the Annunciation. There was the sewing machine, the two watches, the glass of port wine that emptied of its own accord, the carriage that never went anywhere, with its two horses, one blue, one white. And down below were the two fountains with their fishtailed ladies holding cornucopias so parsimonious that only water poured forth from them. And there were the statue of Emperor Maximilian of Mexico and the columns of the Teatro Nacional, and the cars trundling over the tarmac roads, and the cries of the newspaper vendors and the pure air of freedom.

He returned home late, feeling slightly weary. The few glum streetlamps cast only the dimmest of lights. All the windows were closed and dark. As were his.

When he opened the door, he was immediately aware of the uncanny silence. He walked from room to room, leaving the lights on behind him and the doors open, like a child. Not that he was afraid, of course, but the stillness, the absence of familiar voices, the vaguely expectant atmosphere, made him feel uneasy. He sat down on the bed of which he would be the sole occupant for the months of May, June, July and possibly part of August. What better time to savor freedom! Sun, heat, fresh air. He would go to the beach every Sunday and lie in the sun like a lizard just woken from its winter sleep. He would stare up at the cloudless blue sky. He would take long walks in the countryside. The woods of Sintra, the Castelo dos Mouros, the beaches on the opposite shore. He would do all these things alone. All that and more, things he could not even imagine now, because he had lost the habit of imagining. He was like a bird who, on seeing the cage door open, hesitates before making the leap that will carry it beyond the bars.

The silence in the apartment closed about him like a hand. All his plans, whatever they might be, would have to be paid for. He had to work very hard and that would eat up his time. But he would work more enthusiastically, and if he had to cut back on anything it would be food. He now regretted the expensive supper and the foreign cigarettes, but it was, after all, only the first day, and it was natural that he should get carried away. Others, in his place, might have done much worse.

He got up and went to turn out the lights before returning to bed. He felt bewildered, like someone who has won the lottery and doesn't know what to do with the money. He discovered that, having achieved his longed-for freedom, he now had no idea how to enjoy it. The plans he had made earlier seemed paltry and frivolous. He would simply be doing alone what he had done with his family. He would be visiting the same places, sitting under the same trees, lying on the same sand. That wasn't good enough. He had to do something more important than that, something he could look back on when his wife and son returned. But what? Orgies? Drunken sprees? Love affairs? He had experienced those things when he was single, and had no desire to revisit them. He knew that such excesses always leave a bitter, melancholy aftertaste of regret. To repeat them would be to sully his freedom. However, apart from going on a few outings and indulging his baser instincts, he couldn't see how else to fill the months that lay before him. He wanted something loftier, more dignified, but didn't know what that might be.

He lit another cigarette, then got undressed and lay down on the bed. There was only one pillow: it was as if he were a widower or a bachelor or divorced. And he thought: "What am I going to do tomorrow? Well, I have to go to the shop. In the morning I'll do a round of my customers. I need to get some really substantial orders in. And in the afternoon? The movies perhaps? No, that's a sheer waste of time. There are no films worth watching. But if I don't go to the movies, where will I go? For a walk, I suppose, somewhere or other. But where? Lisbon is a city where you can only really live if you've got plenty of money. If you don't, then you have to work to fill up the time and earn enough to eat. And I don't earn that much. And at night? What will I do at night? The movies again? Great! It looks like I'm going to spend my days watching films, as if there were nothing else to see or do! And what about money? Just because I'm on my own doesn't mean I can stop eating and paying the rent. I'm free, yes, but what's the use of freedom if I don't have the means to make the most of it? If I continue in this vein, I'll end up wishing they were back . . ."

He sat up in bed, feeling anxious: "I've so longed for this day, and I enjoyed it thoroughly until I came home, but the moment I got here, my head started filling up with these idiotic thoughts. Have I become like one of those battered wives who, despite the beatings, can't live without their husbands? That would be stupid, absurd. It would be positively comical to have spent all these years longing for my freedom and, after only one day, feel like running back to the very person who had deprived me of it." He took a long drag on his cigarette and murmured:

"It's all a question of habit. Smoking's bad for the health too, but do I give that up? No. And yet I could if the doctor said to me: 'Smoking is killing you.' Man is a creature of habit, and all this indecision is just one of the consequences of habit. I simply haven't gotten used yet to being free."

Reassured by this conclusion, he lay down again. He aimed his cigarette end at the ashtray and missed. It rolled across the marble top of the bedside table and onto the floor. To prove himself that he was a free man, he made no attempt to pick it up. The cigarette gradually burned down, scorching the wooden floor. The smoke rose slowly, and the lighted end disappeared into ash. Emílio pulled the bedclothes up around his ears and turned out the light. The apartment grew still more silent. "It's a new habit . . . the habit of freedom. A starving man would die if you gave him too much food at once. His stomach would have to get used to it first . . ." Then sleep abruptly overwhelmed him.

It was late morning when he woke. He rubbed his eyes and felt a pang of hunger. He was about to open his mouth and call out to his wife when he remembered that she had left and he was alone. He leaped out of bed. Barefoot, he ran through all the rooms. No one. He was alone, just as he had wanted to be. But he didn't think, as he had when he went to bed, that he didn't know how to enjoy his freedom. He thought only that he was free. And he laughed. He washed, shaved, got dressed, picked up his sample case and went out into the street, and he did all these things as if he were dreaming.

It was a bright morning of clear skies and warm sun. The buildings were ugly and so were the people walking past. The buildings were tethered to the earth and all the passersby looked like condemned men and women. Emílio laughed again. He was free. With money or without, he was free. Even if all he could do was take the same steps he had taken before and see what he had seen before, he was free.

He pushed back his hat as if bothered by the shadow it cast. And then he set off down the street, with a new light in his eye and a bird singing in his heart.

34

At last the day had come when all secrets would be revealed. After performing veritable miracles of diplomacy, Amélia had finally persuaded her sister to accompany Isaura to the shop for which Isaura made shirts, declaring that it was a lovely day and a bit of sunshine and fresh air would do her good, that it was a crime to stay indoors when, outside, the spring seemed quite mad with joy. She waxed positively lyrical in her praise of spring, so eloquent, in fact, that her sister and her niece made gentle fun of her. Since she was so inspired, they said, why didn't she come too? She declined, however, saying that she had supper to prepare, and, with that, propelled them toward the front door. Fearing that one of them might come back for something, she watched from the window. Cândida had grown forgetful and almost always left something behind.

She was now alone in the apartment: her sister and niece would be gone for a good two hours, and Adriana wouldn't be home until later on. She went to fetch the keys she had hidden away and returned to her nieces' bedroom. The dresser had three small drawers; the one in the middle belonged to Adriana.

As she approached the drawer, Amélia felt a sudden wave of shame. She knew that what she was about to do was wrong. It might help her find out what it was that her nieces were so carefully concealing from her, but if forced to confess, how could she admit that she had shown such a lack of respect? Once they knew, they would all fear further raids on their privacy, and they would hate her for that. Discovering their secret by chance or by some more dignified means would not, of course, have damaged her moral authority, but using a fraudulently acquired key and tricking those people—who might get in her way—into leaving the house, well, one really couldn't sink much lower.

With the keys in her hand, Amélia wrestled with her desire to know and the undignified nature of what she was about to do. And what guarantee was there that she wouldn't find something she would prefer not to know at all? Isaura seemed fine now, Adriana was as cheerful as ever, and Cândida, as always, had total confidence in her daughters, regardless of what might be going on in their heads. The lives of all four seemed set to return to calm, tranquil, serene ways. Would violating Adriana's secrets make such a return impossible? Once those secrets were unveiled, would there be no going back? Would they all turn against her? And even if her niece had committed some grave fault, would Amélia's good intentions be enough to justify her infringing the right we all have to keep our secrets secret?

These same scruples had troubled Amélia before and been successfully repelled. However, now that it would require just one small movement to open the drawer, they returned in force, like the last, desperate burst of energy from a dying man. She looked at the keys in her open hand. And while she was thinking, she noticed, unconsciously, that the smaller key would not fit. The opening in the lock was too wide.

Scruples continued to rush in upon her, each trying to appear more urgent and more convincing than the others, and yet already they were growing less forceful, less confident. Amélia took one of the larger keys and put it in the lock. The clink of metal, the creak as the key turned, banished all scruples. It was the wrong key. Forgetting that she had one more key to try, she persisted and was alarmed when it seemed to stick. Tiny beads of sweat appeared on her brow. In the grip of an irrational panic, she tugged hard at the key, then tugged harder still and finally managed to pull it out. The other key was clearly the right one. But after that physical effort, Amélia felt so weak and tired she had to sit down on the edge of her nieces' bed, her legs shaking. After a few minutes, feeling calmer, she got up. She tried the other key, and slowly turned it in the lock. Her heart began to pound so loudly that her head throbbed. The key worked. There was no going back.

The first thing she noticed when she opened the drawer was the intense smell of lavender soap. Before moving any of the objects in the drawer, she made a point of noting their various positions. At the front were two monogrammed handkerchiefs, which she recognized at once as having belonged to her brother-in-law, Adriana's father. To the left, a bundle of old photographs, bound together with an elastic band. To the right, a black box embossed in silver, but with no lock. Inside were some loose beads from a necklace, a brooch with two stones missing, a sprig of orange blossom (a souvenir from a friend's wedding) and little else. At the back was a larger box, this time with a lock. She ignored the photographs: they were too old to be of any interest. Carefully, so as not to displace any of the other objects, she removed the larger box. She opened it with the smallest key and found what she was looking for: the diary, as well as a bundle of letters tied up with a faded green ribbon. She did not bother to untie the knot: she already knew about those letters, which dated from between 1941 and 1942. They were all that remained of a failed romance,

Adriana's first and only one. It seemed ridiculous to Amélia to hang on to those letters ten years after the breakup.

She thought all this while she was removing the diary from the box. From the outside, it looked utterly banal and prosaic. It was an ordinary school exercise book. On the cover, in her best handwriting, Adriana had obediently written her name in the space provided, along with the word DIARY in capital letters that had a slightly Gothic look to them, at once childish and earnest. She must have been really concentrating when she wrote that word, her tongue between her teeth, like someone marshaling all her calligraphic skills. The first page was dated January 10, 1950, more than two years ago.

Amélia began to read, but soon realized that there was nothing of interest. She jumped over dozens of pages, all written in the same upright, angular writing, and stopped at the final entry. When she read the first few lines, she thought perhaps she had found the source of the problem. Adriana was writing about some man. She didn't give his name, referring to him only as *he* or *him*. He was a colleague at work, that much was clear, but nothing led Amélia to suspect the grave fault she had feared. She read the preceding pages. Complaints about his indifference, disdainful outbursts about how foolish it was to love someone who proved unworthy of that love, all mixed up with minor domestic events, comments about the music she had heard on the radio—in short, nothing definitive, nothing that might justify Amélia's suspicions. Until she came to the entry where Adriana talked about the visit her mother and aunt had made on March 23 to the cousins in Campolide. Amélia read the passage attentively: the tedium of the day . . . the embroidered sheet . . . the acknowledgment of her own ugliness . . . her pride . . . the comparison with Beethoven, who was also ugly and unloved . . . *If I'd been alive in his day, I would have kissed his feet, and I bet none of those pretty women would have done that.* (Poor Adriana! Yes, she would have loved Beethoven, and she would have kissed his feet as if he were a god!) The book Isaura was reading . . . Isaura's face, at once happy and as if contorted in pain . . . the pain that caused pleasure and the pleasure that caused pain . . .

Amélia read and reread. She had a vague feeling that the answer to the mystery lay somewhere there. She no longer suspected Adriana of having committed any grave fault. Adriana obviously liked that man, but he didn't love her. *Why would he want to make me jealous when he doesn't even know I like him?* Even if Adriana had spoken of her love to her sister, she couldn't have said any more than she'd written in the diary. And even if she was afraid of being indiscreet and hadn't confided to her diary everything that had happened, she wouldn't have written that *he* didn't love her! However insincere she was when writing the diary, she wouldn't conceal the whole truth. If she did, what then would be the point of keeping a diary? A diary is made for unburdening oneself. The only thing she had to unburden herself about was the pain of an unrequited, indeed totally unsuspected love. So why were the two sisters so cold and distant with each other?

Amélia continued to read, going back in time. Always the same complaints, problems at work, some mistake she had made adding up a column of figures, music, the names of musicians, her mother's and her aunt's occasional tantrums, her own tantrum over the matter of her wages . . . She blushed when she read what her niece had to say about her: *Aunt Amélia is very grumpy today.* But immediately after that, she was touched to read: *I love my aunt. I love my mother. I love Isaura.* Then back to Beethoven again, the mask of Beethoven, Adriana's god. And always that ever-futile *he.* She went further back in time: days, weeks, months. The complaints vanished. Now it was love newborn and full of uncertainty, but still at too early a stage to doubt *him.* Before the page on which *he* appeared for the first time, there were only banalities.

Sitting with the notebook open on her lap, Amélia felt cheated and, at the same time, pleased. There was nothing terrible, only a secret love turned in upon itself, a failed love like the one recorded in that bundle of letters tied up with green ribbon. So where was the secret? Where was the reason behind Isaura's tears and Adriana's pretended good humor?

She leafed through the diary again to find the entry for March 23: Isaura's eyes were red . . . as if she had been crying . . . she was in a nervous state . . . the book . . . the pleasurable pain or the painful pleasure . . .

Was that the explanation? She put the diary back in the box. She locked it. She locked the drawer. She could get no further information from it. Adriana, it seemed, had no secrets, and yet there clearly was a secret, but where?

All paths were blocked. There was that book, of course . . . Now what was the last book Isaura had read? Amélia's memory resisted and closed all doors. Then suddenly it opened them again to reveal the names of authors and the titles of novels, although not the one she was looking for. Her memory kept one door shut, a door to which she could not find the key. Amélia could remember it all. The small package on the table next to the radio. Isaura had told her what it was and the name of the author. Then (she remembered this clearly) they had listened to Honegger's *The Dance of the Dead.* And she recalled the ragtime music coming from the neighbors' apartment and the argument with her sister.

Perhaps Adriana had written about that in her diary. She opened the drawer again and looked for Adriana's entry for that day. Honegger and *him* were there, but that was all.

Having closed the drawer again, she looked at the keys in the palm of her hand. She felt ashamed. *She* was certainly guilty of having committed a grave fault. She knew something she was not supposed to know: Adriana's thwarted love.

She left the room, crossed the kitchen and opened the window of the enclosed balcony. The sun was still high and bright. The sky and the river were bright too. Far off, the hills on the other side were blue with distance. Her throat tightened with sadness. That was what life, her life, was like— sad and dull. Now she, too, had a secret to keep. She clutched the keys more tightly in her hand. The buildings opposite were not as tall as theirs. On one of the rooftops, two cats were lazing in the sun. With a sure, determined hand, she threw the keys down at them one by one.

The cats scattered beneath this unexpected onslaught. The keys rolled down the roof and into the gutter. And that was that. And it was then that it occurred to Amélia that one other possibility remained: she could open Isaura's drawer. But no, what would be the point? Isaura didn't keep a diary, and even if she did . . . Amélia felt suddenly weary. She went back into the kitchen, sat down on a bench and wept. She had been defeated. She had tried and she had lost. Just as well. She hadn't discovered her nieces' secret and now she didn't want to. Even if she could remember the title of that book, she wouldn't go to the library to find it. She would make every effort to forget, and if that closed door in her memory should ever open, she would lock it again with every key she could find, apart from the "stolen" ones she had just thrown out of the window. Stolen keys . . . violated secrets . . . No more! She was too ashamed ever to repeat what she had done.

She dried her eyes and stood up. She had to get the supper ready. Isaura and her mother would soon be back and would wonder what had delayed her. She went into the dining room to fetch a utensil she needed. There was a copy of *Rádio-Nacional* on the radio set. It had been such a long time since she had listened properly to any music. She picked up the magazine, opened it and looked for that day's program. News, talks, music . . . then her eyes were drawn irresistibly to one particular line. She read and reread the three words. Just three words—a whole world. She slowly put the magazine down again. Her eyes remained fixed on some point in space. She appeared to be waiting for a revelation. And the revelation duly came.

She quickly untied her apron and put on her shoes and coat. She opened her own private drawer, took out a small piece of jewelry: an old gold brooch in the form of a fleur-de-lis. She scribbled a note on a scrap of paper: *Had to go out. Make your own supper. Don't worry, it's nothing grave. Amélia.*

It was almost dark by the time she returned, and she was so tired she could barely walk. With her she had brought a parcel, which she took to her room. She refused to say why she had gone out.

"But you're exhausted!" cried Cândida.

"I certainly am."

"Has something happened?"

"It's a secret—for now anyway."

Sitting down, she looked at her sister and smiled. Then she looked at Isaura and Adriana and continued to smile. And her gaze was so gentle, her smile so affectionate, that her nieces were touched. They asked more questions, but she silently shook her head, still maintaining that same gaze and that same smile.

They ate supper, then settled down for the evening. Trifling tasks filled the long, slow minutes. A woodworm could be heard gnawing away somewhere. The radio was silent.

At around ten o'clock, Amélia suddenly got up.

"Are you going to bed?" asked her sister.

Without responding, Amélia turned on the radio. The apartment filled with sounds as an inexhaustible torrent of chords burst forth from an organ. Cândida and her daughters looked up, surprised. The expression on Amélia's face intrigued them. The same smile, the same gaze. Then, after one last phrase of baroque eloquence, the organ fell silent, like a cathedral collapsing in on itself. The silence lasted only a few seconds, then the presenter announced the next piece of music.

"Beethoven's Ninth! Oh, how wonderful, Auntie!" exclaimed Adriana, clapping her hands like a child.

They all settled back in their chairs. Amélia left the room and returned a moment later, when the first movement had already begun. She had brought the parcel with her and placed it on the table. Her sister shot her an inquiring look. Amélia took down from the wall two of the portraits decorating it. Slowly, as if performing a special ritual, she unwrapped the package. Relegated to the background, the music continued to play. The rustle of paper drowned it out. Then the paper slipped to the floor and the mask of Beethoven appeared.

It was like the end of the final act of a play, except that the curtain did not fall. Amélia looked at Adriana and said, as she fixed the mask to the wall:

"Ages ago, I remember hearing you say that you'd like to have a mask of his face. I wanted to surprise you!"

"Oh, Auntie, that's so sweet of you!"

"But how could you afford it?" asked Cândida.

"That doesn't matter," said her sister. "It's a secret."

When they heard that word, Adriana and Isaura glanced furtively at their aunt, but there was not a hint of suspicion in her eyes. There was only great tenderness, a tenderness that shone through what would have resembled tears—if Aunt Amélia had been the crying type.

35

"Abel's taking a long time. Do you want to start your supper?"

"No, wait a bit longer."

Mariana sighed:

"He might not come. I'm not sure that two people should wait for one . . ."

"If he wasn't going to be here for supper, he'd have said. If you don't want to wait, go ahead. I'm not that hungry."

"No, nor am I."

Hearing the front door open, they both jumped. When Abel appeared, Silvestre asked:

"So what happened?"

"Nothing."

"You mean you didn't get anywhere?"

Abel drew up a bench and sat down:

"I went to the office. I told the office boy I was

a client and wanted to speak to Senhor Morais. I was ushered into a room and, shortly afterward, Senhor Morais joined me. As soon as I told him why I'd come, though, he immediately rang the bell for the office boy and told him to throw me out. I tried to explain, but he just turned on his heel and left. In the corridor I passed the young girl from the upstairs apartment, and she looked at me contemptuously. Anyway, the long and the short of it is, they put me out in the street."

Silvestre thumped the table:

"Bastard!"

"That's what he called me a little while ago when I phoned him at home. He called me a bastard and hung up."

"So now what?"

"Well, if he wasn't an old man, I'd go around and punch him in the face. As it is, I can't even do that."

Silvestre got to his feet and paced angrily up and down the kitchen:

"Life's nothing but a dung heap, really, a great steaming pile of dung. So there's nothing to be done, then?"

"I'm afraid not. I'll just have to do what I have to do—"

Silvestre broke in:

"*Have* to do? I don't understand."

"It's quite simple. I obviously can't stay here. All the neighbors know what happened. It would seem arrogant of me to stay. Besides, she's not going to feel comfortable knowing I'm still here and knowing what the neighbors are saying."

"You mean you want to leave?"

Abel gave a slightly weary smile:

"No, I don't want to leave, but I must. I've found another room already. I'll move my things out tomorrow. Please, don't look at me like that!"

Mariana was crying. Silvestre went over to Abel, placed his hands on his shoulders and tried to speak, but failed.

"It's all right," said Abel.

Silvestre attempted a smile:

"If I was a woman, I'd be crying too. But since I'm not . . ."

He turned abruptly toward the wall, as if he didn't want Abel to see his face. Abel got up and made him turn around:

"Come on now, you don't want us all crying, do you? We can't have that."

"I'm just so sorry to see you go!" sobbed Mariana. "We're used to having you here now. You're like one of the family."

Abel listened, greatly moved. He looked from one to the other and asked very slowly:

"Do you really think I should stay?"

Silvestre hesitated for a moment, then said:

"No."

"Oh, Silvestre," exclaimed his wife, "why not say yes? Then he might stay!"

"Don't be silly. Abel's right. It'll be very hard for us, but there's nothing we can do."

Mariana dried her eyes and blew her nose loudly. Making an attempt at a smile, she said:

"But you will come and see us now and then, won't you, Senhor Abel?"

"Only if you promise me one thing."

"What? I'll promise anything!"

"That you'll stop calling me Senhor Abel and call me just plain Abel. Is that a deal?"

"It's a deal."

They felt happy and sad at the same time: happy because they loved each other, sad because they had to part. It was their last supper together. There would be others, of course, when things had calmed down and Abel could safely come back, but those suppers would be different. They would no longer be a gathering of three people living under the same roof and sharing their griefs and joys as if they were bread and wine. Their one compensation was the love they felt for each other—not the obligatory love one has for relatives, which is often a burden imposed by convention, but a spontaneous, self-sustaining love.

When supper was over and while Mariana was washing the dishes, Abel went off with Silvestre to pack his suitcases. They made short work of it, and with a sigh Abel lay down on the bed.

"Fed up?" asked Silvestre.

"What do you think? As if it wasn't hard enough to deal with the bad things we do knowingly. As you see, just existing can be a bad thing too."

"Or a good thing."

"Not in this case. If I'd never come to live here, this might never have happened."

"Possibly. But if the person who wrote the letter was determined to write it, he or she would have found some other way. It could just as easily have been someone else."

"You're right. But it happened to be me!"

"Yes, you of all people, when you've always been so careful to cut off all tentacles!"

"Don't joke."

"I'm not joking. Cutting off tentacles isn't enough. You'll be leaving tomorrow. You'll disappear and cut off the tentacle, but the tentacle will still be here, in my friendship for you, in the change in Dona Lídia's life."

"That's what I meant when I said that the mere fact of existing can be a bad thing."

"Well, for me it was a good thing. I met you and we became friends."

"And what did you gain from that?"

"A friendship. Or don't you think friendship is that important?"

"Of course I do."

Silvestre said nothing. He drew a chair closer to the bed and sat down. He took his tobacco pouch and cigarette papers out of his vest pocket and rolled himself a cigarette. He looked at Abel through the ensuing cloud of smoke and said softly, as if he were joking:

"Your problem, Abel, is that you have no love."

"I'm your friend, aren't I, and friendship is a form of love."

"Agreed."

There was another silence, during which Silvestre did not take his eyes off Abel.

"What are you thinking?" asked Abel.

"About our old arguments."

"I don't see the connection."

"Everything connects with everything else. When I said your problem was that you had no love, you assumed I was referring to love for a woman, didn't you?"

"Yes, I did. I've fancied lots of women, but never loved one. I must be dead inside."

Silvestre smiled:

"What, at twenty-eight? Don't make me laugh! Wait till you're my age."

"All right. Anyway, were you or were you not referring to love for a woman?"

"No."

"So?"

"I meant a different kind of love. When you're walking down the street, have you never felt a sudden desire to embrace the people around you?"

"If I was trying to be funny, I'd say yes, but only the women, and not all of them either. But wait,

387

don't get annoyed. No, I've never felt such a desire."

"Well, that's the love I'm talking about."

Intrigued, Abel propped himself up on his elbows and looked at Silvestre:

"You'd make an excellent apostle, you know."

"I don't believe in God, if that's what you mean. Maybe you think I'm an old sentimentalist . . ."

"Not at all!"

"Maybe you think it's just old age speaking. Well, in that case, I've always been old. I've always thought and felt the same. And if there's one thing I do believe in, it's love, that kind of love."

"It's wonderful to hear you say that, but it's pure utopianism. And contradictory too. Didn't you say earlier on that life was a dung heap, a steaming dung heap?"

"It is, but life is like that because certain people wanted it to be, people who had, and still have, their disciples."

Abel sat up on the bed. The conversation was beginning to interest him:

"Would you want to embrace them too?"

"I'm not as sentimental as that. How could I love the very people who are responsible for the lack of love between others?"

These words, so laden with meaning, reminded Abel of someone else's words:

"*Pas de liberté pour les ennemis de la liberté.*"

"I didn't understand. It sounds like French, but I didn't understand . . ."

"It's something Saint-Just said, one of the leaders of the French Revolution. It means, more or less, that there should be no freedom for the enemies of freedom. Applying it to our conversation, you could translate it as: we should hate the enemies of love."

"He was quite right, that Monsieur . . ."

"Saint-Just."

"Yes, him. Don't you agree?"

"About what Saint-Just said or about everything else?"

"Both."

Abel seemed to retreat into thought. Then he said:

"I agree with Saint-Just, but as for the rest, no, I've never met anyone I could love like that. And I've met a lot of people. They're all as bad as each other. I may have found an exception in you, not because of what you've just been telling me, but because of what I know about you and your life. I understand that you can feel that kind of love, but I can't. I've taken a lot of knocks in life, I've suffered. I certainly wouldn't do what that other fellow did, and turn the other cheek . . ."

Silvestre said vehemently:

"Neither would I. I'd cut off the hand of anyone who hit me."

"If everyone did that, there'd be no two-handed

people left in the world. If someone takes a beating, they're sure to beat up someone else one day, if they haven't done so already. It's all a question of opportunity."

"That way of thinking is called pessimism, and people who think like that are only helping those who want to spread a lack of love among ordinary people."

"Forgive me, but like I said, what you're proposing is pure utopianism. Life is a fight to the death, always and everywhere. It's a case of every man for himself. Love is the cry of the weak, hatred is the weapon of the strong. Hatred for their rivals and competitors, for those contending for the same piece of bread or land or the same oil well. Love is either just a joke or something that gives the strong a chance to make fun of the weakness of the weak. For them, the existence of the weak is useful as a pastime, an escape valve."

Silvestre appeared not to think much of the comparison. He looked at Abel very seriously, then smiled and asked:

"And are you one of the strong or one of the weak?"

Abel felt he had been caught out:

"Me? That's hardly a fair question."

"I'll help you. If you're one of the strong, why don't you do as they do? If you're one of the weak, why don't you do as I do?"

"Don't look so pleased with yourself. Like I said, it's not a fair question."

"Well, answer it anyway!"

"I can't. Perhaps there's some halfway house. On the one side, the strong, on the other, the weak, and in the middle, me and all the others."

Silvestre stopped smiling. He looked hard at Abel and said slowly, counting off each statement on his fingers:

"All right, I'll answer for you. You don't know what you want, you don't know where you're going, and you don't know what you have."

"In short, I know nothing."

"Don't make a joke of it. What I'm saying is very important. When, some time ago, I said that you needed to—"

"I know, to be useful," broke in Abel impatiently.

"When I said that, I had no idea you would be leaving us so soon. I also said that I couldn't give you any advice, and I say the same now. But you're leaving tomorrow and we might never see each other again. I decided that, even if I can't advise you, I can at least tell you that a life without love, a life like the one you described just now, isn't life at all, it's a dung heap, a sewer."

Abel stood up impulsively:

"Indeed it is, but what are we going to do about it?"

"Change it!" answered Silvestre, also springing to his feet.

"How? By loving each other?"

Abel's smile vanished when he saw Silvestre's grave expression:

"Yes, but loving each other with a lucid, active love, a love that can overcome hatred!"

"But man . . ."

"Listen, Abel, when you say the word 'man,' think 'men.' Man, with a capital M, as I sometimes read in the newspapers, is a lie, a lie that serves as a cover for all kinds of villainy. Everyone wants to save Man, but no one wants to know about men."

Abel gave a resigned shrug. He could see the truth of what Silvestre was saying. He himself had often thought the same, but he lacked Silvestre's faith. He asked:

"And what can we do? What can you or I do?"

"Live among men and help them."

"And how do *you* help them?"

"I mend their shoes, because that's all I know how to do. You're young, intelligent, you have a good head on your shoulders. Open your eyes and look, and if you still haven't understood, then lock yourself in your room and don't come out, and wait for the world to fall in on you!"

Silvestre was speaking more loudly now. His lips were trembling with barely suppressed emotion. The two men stood looking at each other. There was a flow of understanding between them, a silent exchange of thoughts far more eloquent than words. Abel said:

"That's a rather subversive idea, isn't it?"

"Do you think so? I don't. If it is subversive, then everything else is too, even breathing. I feel and think as naturally and necessarily as I breathe. If men hate each other, then there's no hope. We will all be the victims of that hate. We will slaughter each other in wars we don't want and for which we're not responsible. They'll put a flag in front of us and fill our ears with words. And why? To plant the seeds for a new war, to create more hatred, to create new flags and new words. Is that why we're here? To have children and hurl them into the fiery furnace? To build cities and then raze them to the ground? To long for peace and have war instead?"

"And would love solve everything?" asked Abel with a sad, slightly ironic smile.

"I don't know. It's the only thing we haven't tried so far . . ."

"And will we be in time?"

"Possibly. If those who suffer can be convinced that it's true, then yes, we might be in time . . ." He paused, as if assailed by a sudden thought. "But don't forget, Abel, you must love with a love that is lucid and active! And make sure that the active side never forgets about the lucid side, and that the active side never commits the same kinds of villainous deeds as those who want men to hate each other. Active, but lucid. And above all, lucid!"

Like a spring that breaks under too much tension, Silvestre's enthusiasm sagged and he said, smiling:

"The cobbler has spoken. If anyone else was listening, they'd say: 'He speaks far too well for a cobbler. Perhaps he's a professor in disguise.'"

Abel laughed and asked:

"Are you a professor in disguise?"

"No, I'm just a man who thinks."

Abel paced the room for a moment, saying nothing. Then he sat down on the trunk where he kept his books and looked at Silvestre, who, somewhat embarrassed, had started rolling himself another cigarette.

"A man who thinks," murmured Abel.

Silvestre looked up, curious to know what Abel would say next.

"We all think," Abel said. "But we think wrongly most of the time, or there's a great gulf between what we think and what we do . . . or did."

"What do you mean?" asked Silvestre.

"It's easy enough. When you told me about your life, I had an acute, painful sense of my own uselessness. I feel slightly better about it now, because you, my friend, have fallen into an attitude as negative as mine or perhaps even more so. You're no more useful than I am."

"I don't think you can have understood me, Abel."

"Oh, but I did. Your way of thinking serves only to convince yourself that you're better than the others."

"I don't think I'm better than anyone!"

"You don't *think* so, no."

"I give you my word."

"Fine. I believe you. But that isn't the point. The point is that when you were able to act, you didn't think like this, and your beliefs were quite different. Now that age and circumstances force you to be silent, you're trying to deceive yourself with this almost evangelical love. Pity the man who has to substitute words for actions! You'll end up being able to hear only your own voice! The word 'act' on your lips, my friend, is a mere memory, an empty word!"

"Are you saying you doubt my sincerity, Abel?"

"Not at all, but you've lost touch with life, with your roots, you think you're still fully engaged in the battle, but the truth is you don't even have the shadow of a sword in your hand and you're surrounded by nothing but shadows . . ."

"How long have you thought this about me?"

"Since five minutes ago. After all you've been through, your last resort is love!"

Silvestre did not answer. Hands trembling, he finished rolling his cigarette and lit it, then, screwing up his eyes against the exhaled smoke, he waited.

"You called me a pessimist," Abel went on, "and said my pessimism helped those who want to sow discord among men. I won't deny that. But your entirely passive attitude helps them too, because those same people also use the language of love. The same words, yours and theirs, declare or conceal different objectives. I would even say that your words *only* serve their objectives, because I don't think you have any real objective yourself. You say, 'I love all men,' and that's it, quite forgetting that your past demands something more from you than a mere affirmation. Tell me, please, of what interest are those words to the world, even if spoken by millions of men, if those millions of men lack all the necessary means to do anything more with them than give expression to an emotional impulse?"

"I don't really know what you mean, Abel. Are you forgetting that I talked about a love that was both active and lucid?"

"Another empty phrase. In what sense are you active? In what sense are the people who think like you active, I mean the ones who don't have the excuse of old age for their inactivity? Who are they?"

"Now it's your turn to give me advice . . ."

"That's not what I intended. Advice is useless, isn't that what you said? One thing I do believe is that the great ideal, the great hope you spoke of, will never be anything more than words if we rely on love alone to make that ideal and that hope real."

Silvestre retreated to a corner of the room and from there asked abruptly:

"So what are you going to do?"

Abel did not reply at once. In the silence that followed Silvestre's words, he heard, coming from who knows where, a whole chorus of voices.

"I don't know," he said at last. "At the moment, I am, as you said, quite useless, but I prefer that temporary uselessness to your imaginary usefulness."

"We've swapped roles. Now it's your turn to criticize me."

"I'm not criticizing you. What you said about love is really very fine, but of no use to me."

"I was forgetting that there's a forty-year age difference between us. How could you possibly understand me?"

"The Silvestre you were forty years ago wouldn't understand you either, my friend."

"So are you saying that it's just my age that makes me think like this?"

"Possibly," said Abel, smiling. "Age can do a lot of things. It brings experience, of course, but it also brings with it a certain tiredness."

"To hear you talk, no one would say that, up until now, you've lived entirely for yourself."

"That's true, but why criticize me for that? Perhaps my apprenticeship will be a slow one, perhaps I'll have to receive many more wounds before I become a real man. Meanwhile, I'm someone who, when described as useless, says nothing in response because he knows it to be true. But I won't always be useless . . ."

"What do you think you'll do, Abel?"

Abel walked slowly over to Silvestre and said:

"Something very simple: I'm going to live. I will leave your home feeling much more confident than when I entered it. Not because the path you showed me was the right one for me, but because you made me realize that I need to find my own path. It will take time, though . . ."

"Yours will always be the path of pessimism."

"Probably, but I want my pessimism to keep me safe from facile, comforting illusions—like love."

Silvestre gripped him by the shoulders and shook him:

"But Abel, anything that isn't built on love will only generate hate!"

"You're right, my friend, but perhaps that's how it will have to be for a long time yet. The day when we can build on love has still not arrived."

Translator's Acknowledgments

I would like to thank my fellow Saramago translator Maartje de Kort for her helpful insights and the students who attended translation workshops at University College Cork, University College Dublin and Glasgow University for the fruitful discussions we had about two short extracts from the novel. And my thanks, as always, to my husband, Ben Sherriff.

Center Point Large Print
600 Brooks Road / PO Box 1
Thorndike, ME 04986-0001 USA

(207) 568-3717

US & Canada:
1 800 929-9108
www.centerpointlargeprint.com